Misty Lake

Margaret Standafer

MISTY LAKE

By Margaret Standafer

ISBN-13: 978-1511752930

For Phil, who always knew I could do this.

1

Sam stood at her kitchen sink, sipping her coffee and looking out the window at the early morning mist swirling on the surface of the lake. It was cool with the window open but she knew the temperature would rise quickly. It had been a warm spring and the forecast was for a hot, dry summer. That suited Sam fine. Hot and dry, cold and wet, it didn't much matter. Sam intended to work, not play. What did it matter if her new home happened to be situated on one of the prettiest lakes in Northern Minnesota? She wasn't there to have fun.

Her new home. It still struck her as odd. When she had learned her grandfather had left her his cabin, she had been surprised. Shocked, actually. She hadn't been to Misty Lake in years, not since she was a child and all was still right with the world. Her grandfather had stopped talking about the cabin years ago, about the same time he stopped talking about much of anything from the past. Sam had assumed he'd sold the place, not wanting the reminder of happier days. So three months ago when she had arrived in Misty Lake with plans to sell what she guessed would have to be nothing more than a run-down, mouse-infested mess, she was dumbfounded. The cabin was still there, sitting now at the back of the lot. But closer to the lake, where she remembered her grandfather's cabin perching near the beach, was a beautiful four-bedroom log home complete with shiny new appliances, a master suite with a bathroom straight out of a glossy magazine, and a huge family room with a two-story stone fireplace and a stunning view of the lake.

Kathleen Melby, the local realtor she had contacted with the intention of unloading the cabin had been cryptic on the phone, only telling Sam that she shouldn't make any quick decisions before seeing the place. Besides, she would need to determine a selling price and there was paperwork that would be completed much easier in person, Kathleen had told Sam. Frustrated, but resigned to the fact that a trip was inevitable, she had made the drive from Chicago to Misty Lake, Minnesota. It had been a long, painful drive. Feeling so alone and as if her heart couldn't possibly take any more hurt, she had watched the miles tick off on her odometer while remembering the weeks she and her family had spent with her grandparents and cousins at the lake. Carefree as only a child with a seemingly endless summer vacation can be, she had spent the days swimming and skipping rocks, the evenings roasting marshmallows over the campfire and, as often as they could convince their parents, the kids all sleeping on the beach wrapped in sleeping bags and telling ghost stories late into the night. Until everything had changed.

As it had so many times over the past few months, the memory of the day she first saw the house came flooding back.

As Kathleen eased her car into the driveway, Sam stared in disbelief. This couldn't be her grandfather's house—her house—it just wasn't possible. They must be at the wrong place, she thought. But then, at the corner of the lot, she saw the cabin she remembered. Confused, she got out of the car and looked around trying to get her bearings but finding nothing she saw made any sense. She wanted to ask questions but couldn't put her thoughts into words.

Kathleen began heading for the house so Sam forced her feet to move and to follow when what she really wanted to do was run as fast she could in the opposite direction. The bubbly, chatty realtor never stopped talking as they made their way across the yard.

"From what I hear, your grandfather visited a few times over the years, occasionally someone would spot a car here. It sounds as though he would spend a few days in the cabin, never speaking to anyone or going into town, and then leave just as suddenly. As far as I know, he was only here once after the construction was completed. He met with the contractor, walked quickly through the new place, and then wanted to see the cabin."

"Hmmm." It was really all Sam was capable of saying. Her grandfather had been here? She had never known. And he had built this place without telling her, without telling anyone. Why? Sam blinked back the tears as questions swirled in her head knowing there was no one to answer them.

Sam listened to Kathleen rave about the quality craftsmanship, the ideal size and location of the lot, and the excellent fishing on the nearly eight-hundred-acre lake. She didn't care, she told herself, she was going to sell the place. She knew she could never be happy here, the very idea of it filled her with anger and sadness. While she had never wanted for the basics growing up with her grandfather, they certainly hadn't been wealthy. Yet this place must have cost a small fortune. Why build such an extravagant home and then never use it or even tell her about it? None of it made any sense and Sam had to fight the urge to run to the car and escape.

"Thank you for showing me around but I think I've seen enough. I'd really like to get going and take care of the paperwork. I definitely want to put the place up for sale as soon as possible," Sam said after a few minutes inside. She was desperate to leave, wanting to put the experience behind her.

Kathleen gave Sam an odd look and said, "Before you make your final decision I think we should take a look at the cabin."

Sam wanted to argue but sensed it would be futile. Fighting to keep her emotions in check she nodded her agreement and quickly made her way out of the house.

As they walked back through the yard and toward the cabin, Kathleen listed features of the lake and surrounding area while Sam simply tuned her out. She didn't care about the house, about the lake, or about the town. This had been a mistake. She should have just insisted Kathleen handle the sale, forwarding any paperwork that needed signatures.

As Kathleen opened the door to the cabin, Sam tried to decipher the look on the realtor's face. Kathleen had been almost giddy with excitement at the thought of listing the property—she had nearly bounced right out of the shiny blue pumps she was wearing as she had walked Sam through the house—but now that excitement didn't quite reach her eyes. Sam continued to study Kathleen as she stepped across the threshold. She thought she caught a look of resignation in the woman's eyes but it disappeared just as quickly as

4

she turned her bright smile back on Sam. Shaking her head slightly, Sam braced herself for her first look at the cabin she remembered so well.

She froze in her tracks as she took in the space around her. Gone was her grandmother's tiny kitchen where she had baked chocolate chip cookies and popped popcorn for her grandchildren. Gone, too, were the small bedrooms where the adults had cozied into creaky old beds at the end of the day while the kids sacked out on the floor or the beach. Her grandfather's favorite little corner window, where he would sit in his rocking chair calling out the names of the birds he spotted, was no more. Instead what greeted Sam was the last thing she ever expected.

Along the walls were shelves, cabinets, and pegboards designed, she knew, to hold her tools. There were long, smooth workbenches with plenty of electrical outlets so extension cords wouldn't be stretched across the floor. In one corner was a fancy dust collection system, a must, in Sam's opinion, in any woodshop and something she had never been able to afford. And light. The room was filled with natural light from the skylights and from the windows facing in all directions. But what Sam could hardly tear her eyes from was sitting in the middle of the room, bright and shiny and beautiful. It was the panel saw she had longed for. Her tears almost blinded her as she made her way to the machine. She slowly reached out her hand to touch the cool steel, needing to convince herself it was real.

She remembered the hours she had spent with her grandfather in his small garage workshop, first as a child watching and learning and later as an adult working along side him. He had given Sam her start and had taught her the joy that comes from making something yourself. They had talked about getting new equipment, new tools, but it was never in the budget and the shop really wasn't big enough anyway, they'd reasoned. The panel saw was always the one piece of equipment, though, that they had both dreamed about. Like a chef may want the latest new cookware or a photographer a new lens, they had longed for the saw. The fact that her grandfather had built this place and bought her the saw was too much. Sam collapsed onto one of the stools in front of the longest workbench and sobbed.

She wasn't sure why, but obviously her grandfather wanted her to stay here. They had often discussed her future. Why hadn't he told her about this place? They could have come here together, set up the workshop and started on all the projects they had talked about one day tackling. Now she was here, their dreams a reality, but she was alone.

Sam wasn't sure how long she sat before Kathleen had quietly cleared her throat. Sam had forgotten she was there and jumped up quickly, embarrassed by her behavior. Wiping her eyes and trying to compose herself, she saw Kathleen looking as though she knew what she was going to hear. Sam couldn't sell the place. For some reason her grandfather had wanted her here and since there was no longer anything tying her to Chicago, she would try to start over in Misty Lake.

Rigi's bark jolted Sam out of her reverie. A car was pulling up her drive and Sam remembered Kathleen was stopping by this morning with the final papers for her to sign to complete the transfer of ownership of the house. She rinsed her coffee cup, set it in the sink, and gave a quick twist of her wrist to secure her long hair into a ponytail. With a deep breath she went to greet the realtor.

Rigi beat her to Kathleen. She poised to jump, but Sam's sharp 'off' had her instead quivering at Kathleen's feet, hoping for a pat or belly rub. Silly dog. She drove Sam crazy sometimes but she was a loyal friend and had helped Sam through some very dark days during the past year. Funny how a dog always knows when you need a hug, Sam thought.

For her part, Rigi couldn't be happier with her new home. She had had a small backyard to romp in at their suburban Chicago home, but it was nothing compared to the acres of woods and the stretch of lake shore she had staked claim to in Misty Lake. The dog was positively in heaven chasing birds, squirrels, and butterflies through the yard or splashing in the lake and fetching the sticks Sam threw off the dock with the exuberance only a Golden Retriever can muster.

"Come on, Rigi, leave her alone," Sam called. Rigi gave Kathleen's hand one last little nudge then bounded happily toward Sam.

"Good morning, Sam. How are you today? Feeling settled in your new home? It sure is a beauty. And the location is prime. You're a lucky girl."

As usual, Kathleen's words came out fast and furious. The woman had a way of squeezing so many thoughts into one breath, it made Sam's head spin. Before she could answer, Kathleen was reaching into her briefcase and drawing out papers. "This should be the last of it, Sam. Then this stunning place will be all yours."

Kathleen headed toward Sam, gliding over the gravel drive in a way that seemed impossible given she was wearing three-inch, hot pink heels today to match her equally pink business suit. The heels still only brought the top of Kathleen's head to Sam's chin. Her blonde hair was done up in some sort of complicated twist Sam couldn't accomplish if her life depended on it. There was gold dripping from her ears, hanging heavily around her neck, and dangling at both wrists. Honestly, how did she have the time to put herself together like that every day? Sam wondered. Didn't the woman own a pair of jeans?

"Thanks for coming over, Kathleen. I could have come to your office, though. And thank you again for handling all the paperwork."

"Oh, don't worry about it," she said with a little wave. "Your grandfather's lawyer drew up most of the paperwork, I'm just handling signatures and filing the appropriate papers with city hall. And I always love a reason to drive out to the lake, it clears my head. Besides, I'm sure you're busy with the kids. How's it going?"

"It's going well. Really well," Sam said with a rare, genuine smile. "I'm so glad you told me about Project Strong Start."

And it was going well, she thought to herself. Sam remembered her first meeting with Kathleen and how the topic of Project Strong Start had come up when Kathleen mentioned she would be working with a couple of girls over the summer. Sam's interest had been piqued and she had pressed the realtor for details.

Project Strong Start was a program started ten years ago with the goal of giving disadvantaged and at-risk kids from the Twin Cities a chance to spend the summer at a camp on Misty Lake. However, it wasn't just a twelve-week resort stay. The kids chose from a variety of work/study courses and were expected to spend three hours a day, four days a week, learning a skill or trade. Some kids worked with Clyde, the town's auto mechanic, while others worked at the hardware store, the bank, the clinic, or learned culinary skills from Sally, the owner of the town's best steak house. This would be Kathleen's second year with the program. Last summer she had mentored two girls. They shadowed her while she scheduled appointments, showed houses, and prepared documentation. More importantly, according to Kathleen, the teens learned that options existed for girls to succeed and even own their own business.

Some of the kids had spent their lives shuffled from one foster home to the next, never having a role model or anyone to tell them they could do something with their lives. Those who lived with a parent often did so in fear. Many lived with drug addicts or alcoholics. Too often, these kids wound up on the streets, becoming alcoholics or drug addicts themselves. Gangs also posed a serious threat, preying on kids who were looking for a place to fit in and ready to latch on to the first person who showed them some attention, even if that person was a gang member.

Sam had contacted the leaders at Project Strong Start and after a series of interviews, background checks, and training sessions, Sam's Woodworking was added as an option for this summer's campers. Today would be the start of week three with her six students.

"The kids are doing so well," Sam gushed, "especially a couple of them. They are really taking to woodworking and are showing a lot of promise. I have them using power tools and am down to only about a dozen near heart attacks a day," she joked.

"I have three girls with me this summer. One is a return from last year. I was so tickled when I found out she'd be back and wanted to work with me again. She's such a bright girl. She told me she'd done some reading on real estate practices over the winter and it shows. She's even doing some of the simpler office work on her own."

Kathleen was beaming.

"You're making a difference with her, with all of them, Kathleen," Sam said passionately. "These kids just need a break. Someone to tell them they're important, they're smart, that they have a future and it's not drugs!" Sam's voice rose and the words poured out. "Keep showing her new things, keep teaching, and let her know she's capable of learning. Let her know there are endless possibilities in her future. She can do whatever she wants...go to college, start a business, raise a family. People care about her, love her, and will be there for her, even if she makes mistakes along the way! She—"

Rigi's whining caught Sam's attention and she stopped suddenly, realizing she was shouting now and on the verge of tears. Rigi was pressed against her leg, looking up at her, upset because Sam was upset.

"It's okay, girl." Sam soothed and stroked the dog's head. "It's okay." When she looked at Kathleen she saw the confused and concerned look on the woman's face. "I'm sorry, I shouldn't have gone on like that," Sam murmured.

"Are you okay, Sam?" Kathleen asked quietly as she reached for her hand. "You're shaking."

"I'm fine...really. I...I guess I just got a little carried away. Let's get those papers signed, shall we?"

Sam turned and headed somewhat unsteadily toward the house. She needed a minute to calm herself without Kathleen's eyes searching hers for answers. Sam wasn't about to give any.

Kathleen paused a moment then followed Sam into the house. She'd let it go, she decided. It was apparent Sam wanted to drop the subject so she wouldn't pry. At least not right now.

He woke early. Not his usual behavior but last night hadn't been a usual night. She'd be heading outside soon and would find the surprise he'd left for her. He wanted to be there to watch but knew that would have to wait for another time. For now, he contented himself with imagining her reaction and his lips slowly curled into a wicked sneer. He knew she'd be scared. And she should be, he thought. She should be.

2

By the time the paperwork was completed and Kathleen was on her way, Sam had herself back under control. She headed to her shop to put a little time into a repair job Kathleen had sent her way. The realtor knew everyone in Misty Lake, it seemed. She had spread the word there was a new business in town and had already directed a few clients Sam's way. She had repaired an antique rocking chair for the town's high school principal who was anxiously awaiting the birth of his first grandchild and wanted his daughter to be able to rock her baby in the same chair he had rocked her. She had built a small table and matching mirror for the entry of Kathleen's sister's home with her sister claiming she had wanted something in that spot for years. For Kathleen herself, she had designed a bookshelf to fit in the corner of her office because, as Kathleen had wailed, bright yellow-clad arms flying and resembling a bird as she flitted around her office, the clutter was out of hand and something had to be done about it.

She now had a cabinet belonging to Kathleen's mother-in-law awaiting new doors. Sam had to smile. She wondered how many more favors Kathleen would be able to call in. It was working though, Sam had to admit. Her clients had all been pleased with the results and assured Sam they would recommend her to their friends. That's how it worked, Sam knew. No amount of fancy advertising would ever beat word of mouth, especially in a small town.

While the cabinet repair wasn't a big job, Sam could hardly wait to get at it. Making the new doors would give her a chance to try out her new panel saw. She had played with it a little to get a feel for it but hadn't yet had an actual project to test it on. As she made her way across the yard planning out how she would cut the wood for the doors, she caught sight of Rigi already at the shop door and sniffing at something with her hackles raised. Curious, Sam called to her and quickened her pace.

Greeting her at her shop were a broken window and a pile of dead raccoons in front of the door.

"Rigi! Come!" Sam called to get the dog away from the dead animals. Confused by the scene, Sam glanced around trying to find some clue as to what had happened. Obviously three raccoons didn't just die in front of her door and the window didn't break on its own. More annoyed than anything, Sam took Rigi by the collar, stepped around the mess, and went inside to investigate the damage.

Shattered glass was strewn across the floor in front of the broken window but aside from that, Sam didn't notice anything else broken or out of place. Just a prank, she reasoned. Not a very funny one, in her opinion, but the local kids were on summer vacation and too many of them had too much time on their hands. Still, it was unsettling to be a target.

She clipped Rigi's collar to the leash she kept attached to a workbench and set about cleaning up the glass. She'd have to put a board over the window for the time being until she could get some glass to repair the damage. She fetched the broom and dustpan and made quick work of the mess. She spent a few minutes cutting a piece of plywood to the correct size then nailed it up over the broken window. It cut down on the natural light in the room which was too bad, the more light the better with the room full of kids, but she'd get the window taken care of as soon as possible. Next came the less pleasant task of disposing of the dead raccoons. She grabbed her spade and wheelbarrow from the garden shed and braced for the job ahead.

Her uneasiness increased as she went about picking up the animals. They hadn't just been killed, they had been mutilated. One had its tail and all four feet cut off. The tail had been tied tightly around its neck. Another was missing its eyes and tongue, from what she could tell. She certainly didn't want to study it too closely. The last one had been gutted with the innards left under the body.

Sam leaned against the side of the building, breathing slowly and deeply until the queasiness passed. This wasn't the work of bored school kids, she knew that much. Either someone very sick just happened upon her place or someone was trying to scare her. She wasn't sure which option was less upsetting. She glanced nervously around then chided herself for being foolish. Of course no one was going to be standing in broad daylight waiting to jump out at her.

Pushing her apprehension aside, she grabbed the spade and went about getting rid of the animals. After burying them in the woods far from her home, she got the hose and a scrub bucket and began cleaning the front step. Not the way she wanted to start her day. There would be no time now to get a start on the cabinet doors, the kids would be arriving soon.

Just as she was finishing, she heard the van pulling in her drive. When it stopped in front of her door and the kids started climbing out, her smile was back in place.

"Morning, Miss Taylor," Jimmy, the first one out, shouted. Maybe not the most gifted when it came to woodworking, he more than made up for it in enthusiasm.

"Good morning, Jimmy, how was your weekend?"

"Awesome! We got to go waterskiing!"

"Well, that sounds adventurous. How did it go?"

"Oh, it was hard, but fun. It took me about a hundred tries to get up and then I fell a bunch of times but I did it! I skied a whole circle around the lake and back to the dock," he answered proudly, his red hair and freckles glowing in the sunlight.

Sam could picture Jimmy refusing to give up and the driver of the boat probably wishing he would. Jimmy was the type of kid who would try anything and keep trying until he could do it. He was always the first to volunteer when she asked for someone to try working with a new tool and always the last to put his tools down at the end of the day. Sam knew his life at home was tough, she had been given a brief biography of each of the children she was working with, and his was a sad story. His mom was hardly ever around, more concerned with getting her next hit than with the well-being of her kids. He had a younger sister who he did his best to watch out for and who was also at camp this summer. There was also an older brother who was always in trouble of some sort. According to the report Sam read, he would show up sometimes looking for money, knock Jimmy around, then disappear again. The brother reportedly belonged to a gang and was after Jimmy to start hanging around with them. So far Jimmy had resisted but sometimes resisting wasn't an option.

"Well, I'm proud of you," Sam said, "that's quite an accomplishment. And how's everyone else?" she asked, looking at the group in front of her. She greeted all of them, being sure to ask at least one question of each in hopes of making everyone feel comfortable. It had been a challenge with a couple of the kids. They simply didn't trust anyone and their natural reaction was to shut down. She was making a little progress, though. She got smiles and nods and a few responses to her questions. One step at a time, she told herself.

"All right, head inside. Get your projects out of the cabinet and put on your aprons. Remember, no tools until I get there," she said with an eye on Davis. He liked to make his own rules, she had quickly learned.

"Good morning, ma'am," Stu tipped his baseball cap and greeted Sam as the kids headed in to get started. Stu had driven a school bus in Misty Lake for years before retiring and was now a volunteer driver for the camp in the morning. His snow-white hair, long white beard, and ample mid-section had also secured him the position of Santa Claus at the town's Christmas pageant for twelve years running. He was a sweet man and Sam adored him.

"Hello, Stu, how are you? And how's Molly?" His wife of fifty-five years had been ill and Stu's concern was obvious though he tried to hide it.

"She's better, Miss Taylor, thanks for asking. Doc says she just needs a little more rest and she'll be as good as new." His smile as he answered her added more crinkles to his red cheeks and Sam had to fight the urge to reach out and squeeze them.

"I'm glad. And I asked you to call me Sam, remember?"

"Yes ma'am, I mean Sam, I remember. Sorry." He turned his eyes to the door where the concrete steps were still drying and the bucket and spade rested. He took in the boarded up window and concern spread across his face. "Trouble ma'am, ah, Sam?"

"Oh, it's nothing, just a prank." The confidence she tried to put into her voice didn't quite reach her eyes and Stu noticed.

Stu narrowed his eyes, squared his shoulders, and asked, "What happened? Do you need help with anything? I worry about you out here all by yourself. If someone's giving you trouble, you let me know."

Sam had to smile at his chivalry. Did they still make men like Stu? she wondered. She finally relented under his stare and gave him a quick recap of the morning's events.

His unease was evident as he started walking around the shop, examining the ground under the window, and staring out into the woods. "You need to let Sheriff McCabe know about this."

"Oh, Stu, it's nothing, really," Sam said with more

conviction than she felt. "There's no need to trouble the sheriff with this."

"Hmpf. Nothing, she says," Stu mumbled, shaking his head. Looking her in the eye he said, "It's not nothing when someone tortures animals then leaves them for you to find."

"Tortured? You think they were tortured?" Sam asked, horrified. That thought hadn't crossed her mind. She had assumed the animals had been killed then mutilated, not made to suffer.

"Well, seems to me someone sick enough to do those things probably wanted to see the critters suffer. Not everyone's wired exactly right, Sam."

Sam was silent for a moment then straightened and said, "I need to get inside to the kids. Everything will be okay, Stu. Thank you for your concern but I'm fine. Please don't worry." She gave him a quick kiss on the cheek and dashed inside to her waiting students.

Stu looked after her for a moment then climbed back into the van and pulled away. His next stop would be at the sheriff's office whether Sam liked it or not. And he'd be back later to fix that window.

3

"Your birdhouse looks fantastic, Jackson," Sam encouraged the seventeen-year-old. Jackson was a tough one to get to know. While he was slowly coming around, he had barely grunted responses during the first two weeks of classes. From his file Sam knew he had been in and out of juvenile detention centers, had been mixed up with drugs, and wanted to be anywhere but Project Strong Start for the summer. In Jackson's case, it was his mother who had pushed hard for the camp to give him a chance. Unlike so many of the kids, he had a parent fighting bitterly for him to succeed. Every time he had fallen, she had been there to pick him up and from what Sam read, she wasn't about to quit.

And he was so talented. Sam had been amazed at how naturally he held the tools. For most, the first time they held a screwdriver or a saw it was awkward and the tendency was to hold it like a pencil, spoon, or other familiar object. His cuts were even, he had just the right touch when it came to sanding, and had the patience needed to measure and plan carefully so things were done right the first time.

She had tried too hard with him at first, she realized that now. He needed time, so she had given it to him. This morning when she complimented his nearly-completed birdhouse she saw a trace of a smile as he grunted his, "Thanks, Miss Taylor," before lowering his head again leaving her to look at the back of his head.

All the kids had started with a birdhouse after the initial few days of learning their way around the shop and learning how to handle the tools. It was an easy project, silly, some of them had thought, but Sam wanted them to be successful and this was a way to be sure that happened. When Mario had grumbled he didn't have anywhere to put a 'stupid birdhouse' at his apartment, she had told him she'd be honored to have it in her yard. At first he had looked at her as if she was making fun of him—oh, that had broken her heart—but once he determined she was sincere, he had seemed pleased. Right now he was etching his initials on the bottom of his just-completed robin house.

"What do you think you'd like to try for your next project?" Sam asked in an effort to engage Jackson. She was letting them choose from a few different projects and while she knew she'd have to steer Jimmy and a couple others toward the easier designs, she was really hoping Jackson would choose the jewelry box. It was a lovely piece and she knew he could handle the detailed work needed for the divided drawers, door hinges, and heart cutouts if he'd be willing to try.

"Dunno," he mumbled, "maybe the jewelry box, I guess. My mom would probably like it. She likes earrings and stuff."

Sam's heart gave a little lurch and she had to clasp her hands together behind her back to keep from reaching out and hugging him. It was exactly what she had wanted to hear. She knew from experience that getting an at-risk teen to think of others was an important step. "I think that's an excellent choice, Jackson. I know your mom will love it."

Jackson gave a little half-nod, half-shrug but kept his head bent over his birdhouse. Sam moved on, not wanting to push too hard. This was the most he had said to her thus far. She had to try to be patient and celebrate the small success.

Sam checked on each student's progress then announced cleanup time as, like usual, the morning had slipped by too quickly. "It looks like everyone should have their birdhouse finished tomorrow so think about what you want to try for your next project. I'm anxious for you to get started on something new."

Sam watched as Katie, the only girl in the group, carefully brushed sawdust from her area at the workbench into the trash bin. Such a sweet girl, but so sad. She was a beautiful girl with long, curling hair so brown it was almost black. She had huge chocolate brown eyes that Sam noticed frequently darted from one thing to the next as if she could never quite relax. Katie's mom had died when Katie was a baby and her dad, who had done his best to raise her and her brothers, was sick. The kids had been shuffled between Child Protective Services and foster homes recently as her dad had been in and out of the hospital. Her brothers had gotten into some trouble with their last foster family so the kids were awaiting yet another family to take them in.

Sam could understand the sadness and anxiety. The fear of losing those you love the most was crippling. In Katie's case, Sam wondered if she wouldn't be better off closer to her dad where she would know what was happening with him, be it good or bad. The not knowing was taking a toll on her, that much was apparent.

As stools scraped against the floor and cabinet doors opened and closed, the camp van pulled up and Bev, the afternoon driver, hopped out and up the steps to the workshop. "Everyone ready to go?" she asked brightly.

While the kids finished cleaning up and started for the van, Bev leaned her head in and muttered to Sam, "I heard you had some trouble out here."

"Oh, it's nothing, Bev. Just some kids with too much time on their hands," Sam tried to convince both of them. The last three hours spent working with the campers had taken her mind off the events of the morning but they came crashing back. "How did you hear about it?" Sam asked, curious.

"Well, Ted over at the gas station was talking to Peggy from First National, who had coffee with Elaine, Frank's wife—Frank's the mailman in town—who heard from Kathleen about your trouble this morning."

"What?" Sam asked as she tried to unravel the chain of events. "How did Kathleen…oh, it doesn't matter," she shook her head. "Things are fine here, all cleaned up. I'm sure it was just a one-time thing."

Bev looked uncertain. "I hope you're right. Ted said he heard Kathleen thinks you should put in a security system. She said the owners of all the fancy houses on the lake are doing it."

"I didn't realize crime was so rampant here in Misty Lake," Sam teased.

"It's not, Sam, it's not, but you're here all alone. Maybe Kathleen's right…"

"Bev, I'm fine. I can take care of myself. Besides, I have Rigi."

Sam grimaced as both women looked over at the dog, currently running in circles around a pine tree, barking and tripping over her own feet at she tried to look upward at the squirrel well out of her reach and looking like anything but a watchdog.

Bev raised a brow. "Yes, well, I'm sure she's a great comfort. You watch yourself, Sam," she said as she patted Sam on the back and headed for the van.

As Sam watched the van pull away and she was alone for the first time since discovering the morning's vandalism, she had to shake off the chill that threatened. Just kids, she told herself again and tried to believe it.

4

After a quick lunch and a little time spent throwing sticks for Rigi, Sam was back in the shop finally getting to the cabinet doors. Her saw was humming away beautifully and thoughts of the morning were long forgotten. As Sam ran her hand over the smooth oak she smiled. While her favorite projects were those she designed and brought to life, reviving and saving a piece of furniture from the fire pit was rewarding as well. "A little more sanding right here," she mumbled as she slid her hand along the edge and headed back to the workbench. After wiping a little sweat and sawdust from her brow, taking a swig of Diet Coke, and cranking up her iPod, she set to work with the sandpaper.

That's how Jake found her, standing with her back to the door, gently sanding and hips swaying along with The Rolling Stones. The music was loud and she hadn't heard when he'd knocked and called her name. Not wanting to startle her, he decided to wait the song out and enjoy the view. It was her hair he noticed first, well…after her hips. It was brown with hints of gold and deep auburn twining through the ponytail that curled half way down her back. He could see tendrils of curls that had escaped the hair band and hung alongside a long, slender neck. His eyes made their way down a graceful back to the narrow hips that had picked up the pace and to some of the longest legs he had ever seen. He felt an inexplicable desire to loosen her hair band and let those curls spill through his fingers. He wanted to run his hands along her arms and feel the skin he knew would be like silk.

Ah, hell, what was he thinking? He was here to do his job and check on a resident of Misty Lake who had been the target of vandalism, not to behave like a schoolboy taken with the cutest girl in the class. He tried to put his less-than-professional thoughts out of his head and as Mick finished belting out one last 'start me up' and the song faded, he gave a soft rap on the door and announced his presence. "Excuse me, Ms. Taylor?"

Sam jerked and whirled around at the interruption. "How long have you been standing there?" she demanded when she saw the uniformed man in her doorway. All at once she noticed his dark hair, broad shoulders, trim waist, and casual stance. Sheriff McCabe, no doubt. She wasn't surprised, it seemed as though half the town knew her business, and she had expected the sheriff to show up sooner or later.

"Just a minute or two. I knocked but you didn't hear me over the music," he answered with a glance toward her iPod.

"Well, yes, I, maybe…" Since she didn't seem

capable of forming a coherent sentence, she turned her back and lowered the volume. And knocked over her Diet Coke. Damn, what was wrong with her? She hated being caught off guard, that was all.

"I just wanted to stop by and make sure everything was okay out here. I heard you had some trouble this morning. Heard it from several people, as a matter of fact."

Slightly calmer after a few deep breaths, she turned back to face him. "Sheriff, it appears your town's residents are looking for some excitement. Nothing happened here except a little vandalism. I'm not happy to be the target but I'm also not terrified to stay in my home, as some people seem to think I should be. I'm perfectly capable of taking care of myself and I'm sorry to have troubled you. Samantha Taylor, by the way," she added, extending her hand.

"Ms. Taylor, a pleasure to meet you. Jake McCabe. And it's no trouble. Would you care to go over the details with me and let me make my own decision on whether I wasted my time with a drive out here?" The jolt he felt when he shook her hand was real, he felt it down to his toes, and from the look of surprise on her face she felt it, too. He gave her a curious look as she quickly pulled her hand away.

"Call me Sam, please," she said, wondering what the hell was happening. She glanced briefly at her hand as she shoved it in her pocket. The last thing she needed was some local cop doing things to her head. She had no time for anything other than her work, her students, and her dog. And she didn't need anything else. Especially anything like the man standing in her doorway. The man

26

who was at least 6'-2" and all lean muscle. The man with hair that looked like fine walnut and that curled at the top of his collar. The man with eyes like brown gems flecked with gold. The man whose handshake almost had her knees buckling. Oh, for crying out loud, she silently scolded herself, get it together.

In an attempt to break the tension, Sam headed for the broken window explaining how she had found it shattered. She then went on to explain about the raccoons, even though it made her stomach churn to do so.

"Have there been any incidents before this?" Jake asked, aware of both Sam's uneasiness talking of the events of the morning and her reaction to him. She really was striking, he thought as he watched her move around her shop, straightening and organizing as she walked. Her eyes were as blue as sapphires and sparkled as brightly though they appeared wary when looking at him.

She hesitated, he noticed, and seemed to be debating with herself on how to reply. "Well, I'm sure it's not related but there have been a couple of things..." her voice trailed off and she turned toward the window facing the lake. "The garbage cans were tipped over one morning with the trash spread all over the yard but I'm sure that was just animals. My mailbox was knocked off its post but maybe that was just a passing truck or something? An accident?" she responded, trying to convince herself.

"Could be just coincidences but could be more. Anything else, even if you don't think it could be related?"

"Well, there are dead fish on the beach almost every morning," she answered jokingly, trying to lighten the mood. "I'm sure that's something devious, right Sheriff?"

"I will certainly look into the dead fish, you're not the first to report something similar," he deadpanned.

Sam smiled in response and felt herself relax. Just business, she told herself. Answer his questions and that will be the end of it.

"Why don't I take a look around and see if I notice anything. You're alone here, is that right?"

"Why is everyone so concerned about the fact that I live alone?" she asked, her voice rising. "I am perfectly capable of taking care of myself as I have had to explain to everyone who's been out here. What, just because I'm a woman I'm helpless? Really, this isn't the nineteenth century anymore. And, I bet those women were a lot more capable than men gave them credit for," she added, well on her way to working up a head of steam.

"I'm not suggesting you can't take care of yourself," Jake replied, being certain to keep any trace of a smile off his face or risk, he was sure, another barrage. "I just wondered if there was anyone else I needed to talk to who may have seen something." And wanted to find out if there was a man in the picture, he admitted to himself.

"There's Rigi. My dog," she added, noticing his slightly confused expression. "She'd let me know if there was anyone suspicious around. Should I fetch her so you can interview her?"

"The Golden who ran up to greet me then proceeded to roll over on her back waiting for a belly rub? Yes, I can tell she's quite the watchdog."

"She's friendly, that's all," Sam defended the dog. "I'm sure she'd rise to the occasion if necessary." Right, she thought to herself. Rigi was afraid of the garbage disposal but she wasn't going to tell the sheriff that.

"It's good to have a dog around. It's a fact that prowlers tend to avoid houses with dogs. I've known a couple people who have gone so far as to buy dog dishes and dog toys to leave lying around their yard to give the impression a dog lives there in the hopes of deterring potential criminals. Not a bad strategy, really." When she didn't reply he realized how badly he wanted to keep her talking, just to hear her voice. "So, Riggy, did you say? Like Ziggy?"

"It's Rigi, R-i-g-i, sounds like Ziggy, though."

"Interesting name. Is there a story behind it?" Anything to keep her talking.

He watched her hesitate, seeming to fight some inner battle, then turn back to the window. "I went to Switzerland once," she started, and he noticed a sadness creep into her voice. "It was a long time ago. We stayed in Lucerne. Have you ever been to Switzerland?" she asked, but didn't wait for a reply. "One day we went up a mountain, the Rigi, on a cog-wheel train. We wound up the mountain past cows grazing, past hikers. You could see for miles and miles from the top, even into Germany and France. I had never seen anything like it and I couldn't get enough. The ride down was on a cable car, another first for me and absolutely thrilling. That day was one of the best I had had in a long time and it's stuck with me over the years. When I brought Rigi home, she was this clumsy little ball of fur with giant feet she kept tripping over but she headed right for some big landscape rocks in the yard and tried and tried to climb up. She'd slide down, tumble head over tail, and try again. My grandfather called her a little mountain climber so I came up with the name Rigi. It just seemed to fit." Her voice quieted and she seemed lost in her own thoughts.

"I like it. A name that reminds you of something happy is a good name."

"Thanks, I think so too," Sam smiled turning back to Jake.

He stared at her for a minute, inexplicably drawn to her and wanting the moment to last. As she shifted from one foot to the other and looked curiously at him, he gave himself a mental slap. "Well, I'll just go have a look around."

She followed him out the door, pointing out where the dead animals had been left and answering his questions as to their condition. Jake walked around the shop in front of the broken window, checked the door locks on both the shop and the house, and walked across her lot down to the lake. "So, this is the scene of the mysterious dead fish, I assume, " Jake joked with her.

"Yes, Sheriff, and if you could solve the mystery I would be forever in your debt. Seems my silly dog likes nothing better than to start her day with a good dose of dead fish. I can't tell you how many times I've hosed her off and given her a bath since we've been here."

"The smellier the better with dogs, it seems." As they headed back toward the house a pickup truck was pulling into the drive.

Sam squinted to see who it was but didn't recognize the truck. "Busy place today," she muttered.

"Looks like Stu. He's probably here to take care of your broken window. He told me he'd be back out here this afternoon when he stopped by the office this morning."

"He doesn't have to fix my window! I was going

to get some glass later today," Sam said, realizing it was nearing evening and she hadn't given the new glass a thought. "Stu, what are you doing here?" she asked as he climbed out of his truck.

"Just got a piece of glass, ma'am, figured I could help you with that broken window. Jake, give me a hand?" he asked looking toward the sheriff.

"It's Sam," she mumbled out of habit, "and I was going to fix it. You've got Molly to worry about, you don't need to be running back out here."

"Molly's doing fine, she told me I was 'hovering' and shooed me out of the house. Said she can't rest when I'm there asking her what she needs."

Sam studied the old man and guessed Molly probably had a point. Some of the worry seemed to have disappeared from Stu's eyes so he must be feeling confident of Molly's recovery. "Well, thank you, Stu, that was really very kind of you. What do I owe you? And please don't say nothing."

"Nothing. I'm just doing a favor for a friend. Since the sheriff is here, I'm sure he won't mind lending a hand. We'll have this window taken care of in no time."

"I'm not letting you do this for nothing. How about I put together something for your dinner tomorrow night? You can pick it up tomorrow morning when you drop off the kids."

"Well, now, that'd be mighty kind of you," Stu grinned. "Molly's still not up to doing much cooking and I'm not very gifted when it comes to things in the kitchen. I'm afraid Molly's getting tired of canned soup and my famous grilled cheese sandwiches. The lasagna you sent with me last week? Now that was something special. Molly ate more that night than she had in a long time."

"Then it's settled. I'll have something for you tomorrow. Thank you, Stu. Now, let me get you two some lemonade if you're going to be out here working in the sun."

As Sam headed to the house, Jake and Stu got to work on the window. "What do you think happened out here, Jake?" Stu asked.

"I'm not sure. I agree with you that it sounds like more than just kids but I don't want to worry Sam unnecessarily. I'm going to ask around a little. Usually if it's kids, one of them can't keep his mouth shut and pretty soon word gets around about who's responsible. I'm also going to check into the kids at the camp. Many of them have had some trouble in the past and it's possible one or more of them was able to make their way out here with the idea of doing some damage."

"Sam won't like to hear that, she really cares about those kids," Stu cautioned. "And I can't see it being one of her kids, I think she's getting through to them, Jake."

"I hope it's not the case but it's something I need to look into. Part of my job, Stu. The thought of someone around here torturing animals makes this more than just a case of vandalism."

"The way Sam described it to me, it was pretty bad. Know anyone around here who'd do something like that?"

"I've been giving that some thought since you stopped by this morning and no, I really don't. Most of the folks I know are serious about their hunting and fishing and with that comes a certain respect for animals."

The men let the conversation go when Sam

returned with lemonade and the offer to lend a hand. "It looks as good as new," Sam proclaimed when the new glass was in place. Thank you, Stu," she said, reaching out impulsively to give him a hug. She found the blush rising on Stu's cheeks impossibly sweet but turned to keep from embarrassing him further.

"And thank you, Sheriff McCabe, I appreciate the help." And she did, even if her heart had raced a little every time she'd caught a glimpse of Jake stretching to hold the window in place. She didn't realize she was staring until Stu climbed in his truck and the creaking of the door snapped her out of her daydream.

"See you tomorrow, Sam, Sheriff," Stu said waving out the window as he pulled away.

"Is there anything else, Sheriff, or will you be getting back to the office?" Sam asked, sounding a little snippier than she intended but needing to put some distance between herself and the man who was getting under her skin.

"A few more questions for you, Ms. Taylor," Jake answered, aware of the change in Sam's demeanor.

"Oh, for crying out loud, call me Sam," she almost shouted. Then, more calmly, "What can I answer for you?"

"Do you recall Rigi fussing at all during the night, maybe due to the fact that she heard something outside? It might give us an idea of what time the damage occurred."

"I don't. She usually sleeps in my room, I keep a bed for her in there, but when it's warm she likes the tile floor in the bathroom better. Still, she would have been close, I think I would have heard if she growled or barked."

"Okay. The shop is far enough from the house

33

that it's likely she didn't hear anything."

Sam paused, a chill making its way up her spine. "You were thinking whoever did this was up at the house, too, weren't you?" The thought hadn't entered her mind before and it was unsettling.

"No, not necessarily. In fact, probably not. I think the dog would have heard someone had they gotten very close."

"Hmmm," was all she could say as she considered the possibility.

"I need to ask a little more about the animals you found. I'm sorry," he added at her pained expression, "I'll be as brief as possible. Can you give me an idea of how much blood was on the steps?"

"What? Why would need to know that?" she asked, horrified.

"Again, I'm sorry, it will just give me a better idea of what actually happened. Was there blood pooled on the step? Had it dripped down onto the ground? I know it's not pleasant but it will help. Really."

"Okay, okay." Sam looked off into the distance. "There really wasn't that much blood, come to think of it. The top step in front of the door was bloody, I had to scrub it, but I wouldn't say the blood had pooled there. And no, there wasn't any blood on the ground around the step or dripping down onto the other steps."

Jake made a quick note on his pad and decided it was enough for today. She had probably told him everything she could and he could tell she needed a change of subject. "How about I help you carry these glasses back up to the house?"

She was grateful for the reprieve. She handed him

the glasses as she turned for the house.

"Quite a place you have here," Jake said as they climbed the wooden steps up to the double front doors. "I have to admit, I've been a little curious."

"It is quite something," Sam agreed. "Sometimes I still can't quite believe I'm living here."

They were in the kitchen now, all shiny stainless steel and granite. The rough-hewn wood floor was a perfect fit for a lake home, Jake thought. Something he would have chosen.

Sam noticed him examining the cabinets. "They're cherry, custom-made. Gorgeous, aren't they? I wish I could have made them myself," she said as she ran her hand along the smooth wood and admired, for the hundredth time, the excellent craftsmanship. "I'm a little jealous, I have to admit. I often wonder who did make them. There are so many things I just don't know." She grew quiet and her eyes had a far-off, hurt look.

"So you really didn't know about this place until you got here?" he asked, unable to hide his curiosity.

"No, I really didn't. I expected to find the old cabin, though I didn't even know my grandfather still owned that until after he died." She looked at Jake, leaning against the counter, one booted foot crossed over the other. He looked so at ease, so confident. She wondered how long it had been since she'd felt that way. The past year and a half had shaken her to the core and it was a long climb back. "Can I get you something to drink, a beer, glass of wine, soda?" As she saw Jake glance at his watch she added, "Or do you have to get back?" She realized she wanted him to stay.

"Actually, I'm off duty so I'd take you up on that

beer if it's not too much trouble." He wanted to stay, wanted to know everything there was to know about her.

She grabbed a beer from the refrigerator, poured a glass of wine for herself, and led Jake to the living room. The soft, chocolate brown leather sofas were arranged to take full advantage of both the cozy fireplace and the view of the lake. When Jake took a seat on one of the sofas, Sam hesitated before sitting down on the opposite end of the same sofa.

"You were close to your grandfather," Jake said, more a statement than a question.

"Yes, he raised my brother and me. My parents were killed when I was twelve, Danny had just turned eleven."

"I'm sorry, Sam, I didn't mean to pry."

"It's okay, it was a long time ago."

"That doesn't make it any easier," he said softly.

He was right. So often people assumed the passing of time made the hurt go away. It didn't. Dulled it, maybe, but it would always be there. Along with the questions. What if they hadn't died? What would her life be like? Would Danny still be alive? Would her grandfather? She looked at Jake, saw the kind and patient look in his eyes, and was pleased. He knew it wasn't pity she needed, just someone to listen. With him, she felt like she needed to talk.

"My parents were on their way to my school for a program. My grandmother was in the car with them. It was early winter, one of the first snowfalls, and the roads were getting icy. The driver coming toward them lost control and hit them head on. My parents were in the front seat and were killed instantly. My grandmother was in the back, she was very seriously injured but was alive when the ambulance arrived."

Sam took a deep breath and continued in a monotone voice, unable to stop the words. "My grandfather was a doctor, he was semi-retired but one of his patients had been hospitalized and had asked for him. That's the only reason he was at the hospital that day instead of in the car with my parents. When the ambulance arrived with my grandmother he was able to see her for a minute. She was unconscious but he had the chance to hold her hand and tell her he loved her. She died in surgery. In one afternoon I lost my parents and my grandmother. My grandfather lost his son, his daughter-in-law, and his wife of nearly fifty years. And became responsible for two scared and confused children."

Sam paused and Jake moved closer to take her hand. "He did his best but he had his own grief to deal with. It was rough for a while, even at twelve I could see that. My uncle and aunt came back for the funerals and tried to talk my grandfather into letting them take us back with them. I wasn't supposed to hear their conversation but I did. It was the first time I had ever heard adults really yell at each other. My uncle argued his brother would have wanted him to raise his children. I'm sure he was right. But they were living in Switzerland at the time, a temporary transfer for his job, and my grandfather was adamant that we weren't going to be uprooted from our friends, our school, and everything we knew when we were already dealing with so much. It went on for a long time, they argued back and forth, and I know my uncle wished things could have been different. In the end, we stayed with my grandfather."

Sam sighed and looked at Jake. "I'm sorry, I shouldn't have gone on like that." She looked down at their hands, fingers intertwined, and while she couldn't quite remember it happening, realized it felt right. That was something she would have to think about later.

"Don't apologize, Sam. Never apologize for speaking what's in your heart." He squeezed her hand and shifted a little closer. "Was it your uncle you went to visit in Switzerland?"

It took her a moment to remember mentioning her trip and was touched he had listened so closely. "Yes, the summer after my parents died my brother and I spent a couple weeks with them. My grandfather thought we needed to get away. I remember fighting him bitterly. I didn't want to go, I was terrified something would happen to him while we were away. It turned out to be a good trip, though. Spending time with my cousins helped and things seemed almost normal again for a while. My uncle joked Switzerland would never be the same after having so many Taylors there," Sam smiled at the memory.

"Just how many cousins do you have?"

"Oh, only four," she laughed, "but I guess when we're all together we have a way of making it seem like more. We've always been close and when they came back to the States I was thrilled...and relieved. It was hard having them so far away."

"How about your mother's side of the family?" Jake asked, selfishly wanting to keep her talking to make his time with her last longer.

"No," she replied wistfully, "my mother was an only child, a surprise born long after my grandparents had accepted they would never have children. They both died when I was a baby."

"So, that's your past," Jake began after a moment, "what about now? You're in a strange place with no family around. What's your brother doing? He stayed in Chicago?"

Sam tensed, her eyes clouded, and Jake knew instantly he had said something wrong. Sam turned away and answered softly, "He died."

Jake desperately wished that he could take his words back. "Oh, Sam, I'm so sorry. I had no business asking you so many personal questions." It just wasn't fair, he thought to himself, one person shouldn't have to deal with so much loss.

"My grandfather died of a heart attack about six months after Danny died. Sometimes I think his heart just simply couldn't take any more hurt."

He wanted to hold her and comfort her, to do something to take away the hurt he could see on her face but he knew it wasn't what she needed. Instead he sat, holding her hand, while dusk began to settle over the lake.

Sam was thankful for his silence. Sometimes she thought if she heard one more 'I'm sorry' or 'what can I do' she might snap. Of course people cared and were trying to help, but she wished more of them would realize sometimes all she needed was someone to sit next to her and hold her hand. Like Jake was doing right now.

Eventually Sam spoke again, softly. "I still have so many questions. Why did my grandfather build this place and never tell me? Why leave it to me? He has a son, other grandchildren. I feel guilty sometimes."

He could sense frustration, anger even, in her voice and understood. So much had been taken from her.

"He had never spoken to your uncle or your cousins about this place, either?"

"No, no one knew. He left them letters, though. They all got letters after he died, everyone but me, I got this," she said, lifting her hands and letting them drop. "I didn't want to read them, they all offered, but it was too hard. They told me a little. He mentioned the lake place but gave no details, just that he wanted me to have it. Same with his money. I didn't even know he had money, he didn't tell anyone about that, either. We lived comfortably enough but there was never much extra. According to his lawyer, he had money from insurance policies and from retirement accounts and investments stashed away. He left some to the others but, again, the bulk went to me. I just don't understand, Jake."

It was the first time she had used his name, he realized. He liked how it sounded but wished she didn't seem so heartbroken. "I think sometimes we're not meant to understand. We just have to accept."

"I guess you're right," and because the urge to lean into his shoulder was so great, she jumped up from the sofa. Time to change the subject, she decided. "Enough of my life story, you must be starving," she said with an enthusiasm she struggled to feel.

Sensing she needed a distraction, he stood up with her. "I could eat something if you're offering."

She smiled, putting her earlier thoughts out of her mind for the time being, and headed to the kitchen.

As they sat together eating the salad she had thrown together along with some cheese and crusty French bread, Sam turned the tables and asked Jake, "So what about your family? Are there a lot of McCabes running around Misty Lake?"

"Enough," he answered with an exaggerated eye roll. "My parents live in town, my dad grew up here and my mom just a few miles away. I have three brothers, a sister, and more cousins than I care to claim."

"Big families are nice. Are your brothers and sister all in town?" Sam asked, fighting off the hurt that threatened.

"Yeah, there're all here. Makes my mom happy. She's been wanting grandchildren since my sister left for college and lets us know about it on a regular basis," he said, shaking his head.

"Oh, so the McCabe men are all single?" Hard to believe if they all looked like Jake, she thought.

"My brother Joe married his high school sweetheart, Karen, last year. Mom's afraid to pester them so she asks the rest of us, every time she sees us, if we know what their plans are as far as children. She doesn't seem to get the fact that I'm not about to ask my brother if he's trying to make a baby," Jake said with a baffled look.

Sam chuckled. "No, I don't suppose that's a subject that comes up too often between brothers."

It was dark when they finished clearing the dishes and when Sam suddenly realized things were starting to feel far too comfortable. Trying to hide her sudden panic, she started to guide Jake to the front door when it seemed he was ready to head back to the sofa. "It's getting late and I have kids coming tomorrow morning," Sam began in a brisk tone.

Jake, surprised at the sudden change in Sam, raised a brow questioningly when she handed him his keys.

"Sam, I wasn't planning on moving in, I thought we were having an enjoyable evening."

"We were. Now it's over." She didn't enjoy being rude but needed to get him out. Nothing could happen between the two of them and she was determined to make that clear.

When he reached for his keys he grasped her wrist and was pleased at the heat he saw rise in her cheeks. He pulled her close and took a handful of her hair the way he had wanted to do since he first saw her that afternoon standing at her workbench. She gasped. He ran a knuckle down her cheek. "Oh, Ms. Taylor, it's far from over."

The desire to fall into his arms warred with the voice in her head that said run. She tried to pull back but Jake held on, his eyes darkening as he looked into hers. "Jake…" she protested, on a shaky breath.

He saw the determination, and fear, in her eyes. What was it about this woman that had him acting like a fool? He released her and ran his hand through his hair. Pulling a card from his wallet he slapped it on the counter. "Call me if there's anything out of the ordinary. And I mean anything, Sam." With that, he strode out of the door.

Sam closed the door softly then collapsed against it. Putting a hand against her cheek where he had touched, she allowed herself a minute to imagine. But only a minute. Because she wanted to run after him, she headed to the kitchen. Making dinner for Stu and Molly would eat up part of her night. She knew sleep wouldn't come easy.

5

Jake twirled his pencil between his fingers and looked across his desk at his brother, Joe. "I still don't know the real reason for your visit," and glancing at his watch, added "and before eight o'clock? It seems a school teacher on summer vacation wouldn't need to be bothering me this early." He heard the stiffness in his voice but seemed unable to stop it.

"Mom tells me you're 'edgy', says she doesn't know why, tells me to check up on you, so here I am. You know how Mom works."

"I'm not edgy. Everything's fine," Jake snapped but he knew he wasn't fooling Joe any more than he was fooling himself. He hadn't heard from Sam in three days and it was eating at him. He'd been tempted to drive out to check on her but was afraid without a reason she would likely be nothing more than annoyed.

"Tough case you're working on?" Joe asked, trying

to read the look on his brother's face.

"Nah, it's nothing. Mom's overreacting. She's done that once or twice before, you know," Jake scowled.

Before Joe could answer, Marc, Jake's youngest deputy, stuck his head in the door. "Haven't been able to find out anything about that trouble out at Ms. Taylor's, Sheriff." Then, noticing Joe, added "Sorry, didn't know you had company."

"It's ok, Marc. Joe's not company, Joe's a pain in the ass. So, no word on anyone raising hell at the lake?"

"Nope, Sheriff, no one's doing any talking."

"Thanks, Marc, that's about what I expected."

When Marc left, Joe shot a questioning look at his brother. "What's going on out at the lake?"

"Just some vandalism, thought it might be some kids seeing that they're on vacation, but we usually hear about it within a couple days if it's some of the local kids. They like to talk about what they've done."

Joe gave a knowing nod. "I remember bragging about a few stupid things we did as kids. Seems that half the fun is telling your buddies about it after the fact."

As Jake shook his head at the memories, Joe added, "And about this Ms. Taylor? I take it she's the new owner of the Taylor place everyone's been so curious about. What's her story?"

Jake bristled at his brother's casual attitude and regretted it when his brother noticed his reaction.

"Hmmm, maybe Mom's radar isn't so far off after all?"

Jake gave Joe a withering look. "Get off it, okay? She had some trouble out at her place, I went to check it out. It is my job, if you'll recall."

"Fine, fine, calm down," Joe held up his hands.

Jake ran his hand across his eyes and ordered himself to do just that. "Sorry," he mumbled. "She's out there by herself, looks like someone was trying to spook her. She's tough but she's been through a lot. She needs a chance at a fresh start, not someone pulling crap like breaking windows and leaving dead animals on her doorstep."

Joe studied his brother and was smart enough to hide his smirk. So, big brother's taken with the new girl in town, he thought to himself. To Jake, he asked seriously, "Just the one incident? If it's not kids, any ideas what's going on?"

"A couple other things Sam, er, Ms. Taylor, doesn't think are related but I'm not so sure. We're checking into the kids from Project Strong Start. She's working with some of them, teaching them woodworking. We'll see…"

Joe watched Jake stare off into space for a minute then shook his head, grinning. "Any plans for Saturday afternoon? Karen wants you to come out on the boat with us, says it's been too long since we've seen you."

"Saturday?" Jake considered and decided flying around the lake on Joe's boat might be just what he needed to clear his head. "Saturday's good. Tell Karen I'll see her then…and if she wants to ditch you, that's fine by me."

Joe gave a whoop of laughter as he walked out of the office. "That'll be the day, big brother, that'll be the day."

Sam breathed in the heady scent of pine and wildflowers as

she headed to the shop to start her day. She loved the early mornings at the lake, the quiet that was so different from her mornings in Chicago. Here there was no sound of traffic racing on the nearby highway. The birds greeted her with their cheerful chirping as the breeze tickled the leaves. Occasionally, she would hear the lonely call of a loon though she hadn't spotted one of the birds yet.

The week was flying by with the camp kids filling her mornings and her own projects keeping her busy well into the evening. She liked it that way. The busier she was, the less time she had to think. Because when she had time to think, her thoughts turned to a certain sheriff and she was determined not to let that happen.

Sam threw an old tennis ball for Rigi as they made their way through the yard. She had been a little apprehensive every morning as they approached the shop, not able to get Monday's events completely out of her mind. However, there hadn't been any more trouble and she was trying mightily to convince herself it was a one-time thing.

This morning Sam wanted to finish the cabinet doors before the kids arrived. She was pleased with the way the doors had turned out and the fact that they looked like the originals. That was her goal when doing restoration work. A final coat of varnish this morning and she could install the doors that afternoon. Sam smiled. Completing a project, no matter the size, was incredibly rewarding.

As she walked through the main room to the smaller room in her workshop, she wondered again at the time her grandfather must have put into the planning of the place. Dividing the workshop into two separate rooms meant a designated spot for staining and varnishing and no time lost when a piece was drying. In the small Chicago shop, there was mandatory down time when something was in the finishing stages, as it wouldn't do to be cutting or sanding one piece while another was drying. Wet varnish and sawdust simply don't mix.

And remodeling the cabin's small bathroom was genius, too. No more trips back and forth to the house when she was in the middle of something. Being able to rinse brushes and rags without having to drag them to the house or the hose was incredibly convenient. She sighed and once again started to wonder about her grandfather's motive for keeping everything a secret.

Nope, she told herself, not this morning. She wasn't going to get caught up in whys and what ifs...she'd already spent too much time thinking on it without any answers and it wasn't getting her anywhere.

As she slowly and carefully applied the final touches, she heard the camp van. The kids' projects were coming along well even if she did have to tell Jimmy every few minutes to slow down so he didn't lose a finger and convince Mario he'd have plenty of use for the step stool he was working on.

As the kids filed in, she noticed Katie was more distracted than ever, sitting down at Zach's spot instead of her own and staring out the window. Sam watched her for a moment then called, "Katie, will you come over here for a minute, please?"

Katie's head snapped around and she looked up as if surprised to realize she was in the workshop. Her eyes flitted from one thing to the next as she made her way across the room.

"Katie, would you be willing to help me out with

some staining today?" She needed some distance from the rest of the group, Sam decided, and distance from power tools that, if she remained so distracted, could be a real danger.

Katie nodded and mumbled, "Sure," obviously not really caring what she did for the next three hours.

Sam led her into the adjacent room, gave her some boards along with a gallon of stain and a brush. "Put this jacket over your clothes, Katie, you don't want to be covered in stain. Since you're ahead of the other kids making step stools, I'd like to give them the chance to catch up today. And, I really need these boards stained so appreciate you helping me out."

Katie nodded and Sam got her started on staining. Katie didn't need to know the boards were scraps. "Is everything okay today?" Sam asked gently.

Katie was quiet for so long Sam thought she wasn't going to answer. Finally, she said softly, "I talked to my dad last night, he said he's better and will be able to leave the hospital soon."

"That's wonderful news!"

"I don't believe him, I think he's just saying that so I don't worry about him." Her voice hitched and her eyes filled.

"Oh, honey," Sam took her hand, "he wouldn't lie to you. I'm sure he really is better." Sam made a mental note to call the camp director and see if she could get any information, she would hate to be giving Katie false hope.

"Do you really think so?" Katie asked, and the desperation in her voice had Sam taking her into her arms.

"I do, I really do," she soothed and stroked the girl's hair. She had been cautioned about getting too close to the kids, told repeatedly that her job would be educating the kids on what she knew best, and leaving the emotional counseling to those trained to handle it. Well, warnings be damned. Katie needed her and Sam wasn't about to turn her back.

She held her and reassured her until Katie seemed to relax and until the volume in the other room demanded her attention. Sam left Katie to the staining and went to manage the chaos in the adjoining room.

Jackson was busy measuring small strips of wood to form dividers. His jewelry box was going to be stunning. That was really the only word for it, Sam decided. Once he had decided to tackle the project, he threw himself into it and gave every detail his utmost attention. He had modified the design slightly, saying his mom likes earrings more than bracelets so he wanted another drawer with small dividers to keep the earrings in pairs. When he asked about adding a darker wood to the oak he was using to offset the edges of the box, Sam had been thrilled and happily gave him some of the walnut she had been saving until a special project came along. This definitely qualified. The work he had done so far was outstanding.

Since Jackson was always careful and worked competently on his own, Sam often let him, guiding and suggesting when it seemed appropriate. Jimmy and Davis, on the other hand, were giving her a run for her money. Davis had a fondness for finding a loophole in most all the instructions she gave and managed to find ways to wreak havoc. Just yesterday he had taken the small electric drill and drilled a hole in one of Jimmy's boards because, as Davis had succinctly explained, she had said 'the drills can be used on the projects, only,'—her attempt to keep him from drilling holes in her workbenches—but hadn't specified 'on *your* projects only.' Jimmy had been in a panic, certain his project was ruined, that there would never be time to fix it, and had tried his best to convince Sam she should let him drill a hole in Davis' project as it was only fair. It took her the better part of an hour to diffuse the situation. Today the boys were on opposite sides of the room.

Zach was doing well with his table. It wasn't an especially complicated design but it's size made it a little more involved than the step stool while it was still far from the complexity of the jewelry box—a perfect fit for Zach. He was capable of doing the work, had a good touch with the tools, but lacked interest. Sam was concerned about Zach. He was quiet, frequently pulling out his cell phone when Sam, and the camp directors, had told the kids phones were allowed only during free time and only at camp. He would put it away when he saw Sam look, but several times she had seen him texting furiously under the table. Sam knew she wasn't making much of an impact on him. She made her way to Zach, both to check on his progress and to try to see what he was crouching over that was so interesting.

"Hey, Zach, how's the table coming," Sam said as she came up behind him. Zach jumped, hurriedly shoving something into his pocket before turning to face her.

"What?" he almost shouted at Sam, his cheeks burning and his eyes unable to meet hers.

"What's wrong, Zach?" Sam asked calmly even though it looked an awful lot like a knife he tried to hide from her.

"Nothing. I'm fine. Why does everyone always think something is wrong with me?" he shot back.

"I don't think there's anything wrong with you, Zach, I just wondered if something was bothering you. It doesn't look like you've gotten much work done today," she added, nodding toward the wood and tools lying untouched on the workbench.

"I...I just have a headache."

Sam hesitated, wanting to try to get him to talk, but decided to let it go. She would ask about Zach, too, if she was able to speak with one of the camp leaders later. "Okay. If you don't feel up to working today why don't you go ahead and put your things away. It's almost time for everyone to wrap up anyway."

Zach mumbled something Sam didn't catch and, holding his jacket close to his chest, began to clear his work area.

Later that afternoon, long after the kids were gone and she had finished putting the new doors on the cabinet and had delivered it to Kathleen's mother-in-law, Sam grabbed a pencil and paper and decided it was time to tackle a project she had dreamed of for years. Designing and building a china hutch may seem silly, she didn't even have any china, but it was something she needed to do.

When Sam was just a child, her grandfather had often told her grandmother he was going to build her the finest china cabinet she had ever seen. Sam could remember her grandmother laughing, saying, 'That will be the day!' Her grandmother had had a beautiful set of china, stashed away in boxes and brought out only on very special occasions. Sam had always thought that was a waste but her grandmother had insisted it was too special to risk.

Her grandmother had died without ever getting her china cabinet. Sam's cousin, Susan, had the china now, Sam had insisted she take it, but the urge to build the cabinet was still there.

Lost in her memories, Sam began to sketch. It was relaxing letting the ideas flow. Usually she was designing following specifications from a customer but now, it was only herself she had to please. She drew, erased, and tossed aside attempts that didn't seem quite right. It would have to have glass doors, display shelves for china as well as crystal, drawers to store silver. It should be pretty but not fussy, a piece that would fit in with different decors and that would stand the test of time. Something a grandmother would hand down to a granddaughter who would love it as much as her grandmother had, Sam thought wistfully.

Finally, Sam had in front of her the cabinet she knew she had to make, the cabinet she would have loved to make for her grandmother. She felt oddly content as if this was something she had needed to do for a long time. Surprised to see that it was getting dark, she roused Rigi and headed inside, knowing, this night, she would sleep well.

6

Calls from the office before he could make it out the door in the morning were never a good thing, Jake thought to himself as he answered his cell phone. When the dispatcher told him he was putting Sam through his heart started to pound and he grabbed his keys and ran to his car. Even after years on the force, the fear that something had happened to a family member, a friend or a...well, he wasn't quite sure how to categorize Sam just yet, but the fear was almost paralyzing. He had seen things during his career that had left him angry, shocked, disgusted, and so sad that he had cried at the end of the day. Fear had him running as he answered her call.

Sam's voice was shaky, her words jumbled together, and Jake had to strain to make sense of what she was saying. "The door was smashed, kids' things are everywhere, stain and nails...floor is covered," she managed between sobs. "I don't know who would do this.

It hurts, Jake, it hurts…" her voice trailed off.

"Sam, are you hurt? Where are you?" Jake almost shouted into the phone. He was tearing out of his driveway, driving as fast as he dared toward Sam's house.

"What? Hurt?" Sam answered, sounding confused. "No, I'm not hurt, it just hurts that someone would do this. Why would someone do this?"

"Tell me what happened, Sam. And tell me where you are."

"I'm in my shop. Someone broke in during the night, I guess. Things are broken, spilled. I thought before it was just someone playing games. I don't think this is a game."

"Sam, I want you to go back to the house. Take Rigi and lock the doors." When she didn't answer he started again, "Sam, are you listening? I want you to go to the house. Stay on the phone with me but start walking. Right now, Sam, please."

"Do you think someone is still here?" she asked, her voice barely more than a whisper.

"No, I don't," and he wanted to believe it. "I just want you out of there. Don't touch anything, just leave everything where it is. I'm on my way."

"Okay, I'm going," Sam answered as she called Rigi to her and scanned the yard before running toward the house. She locked the door behind her and let out the breath she had been holding as her knees gave out and she sank to the floor.

"Sam, I need you to listen to me. I want you to check and make sure the other doors are locked. Check the windows, too. Get everything closed up for me, Sam."

"I think everything should be closed and locked.

It was so hot last night I had the air conditioning running so all the windows are closed," Sam said more to herself than to Jake.

"Just go check, Sam." He kept talking, wanting her to stay focused on him and not give in to panic. Sam seemed to calm some and they talked about the hot weather and other easy topics as Jake continued to drive.

After what seemed to take twice as long as it should have, he pulled into her driveway. "I'm here, Sam, I'm heading to the front door," he said as the car door slammed behind him.

As Sam opened the door for Jake and saw the concern on his face, embarrassment started to replace fear as she realized how ridiculous she must have sounded on the phone.

"I'm sorry, Jake," she began as Jake said at the same time, "Are you okay, Sam?"

"I'm fine. Really," she added in response to his skeptical look. "I'm sorry I reacted the way I did and I'm sorry I worried you."

"Don't apologize, you were right to call. Let's sit down and you can tell me what happened," he said leading her to the kitchen. Her pale complexion had him filling a glass of water and placing it in front of her. "Drink this," he ordered gently. "Have you eaten anything?"

He found some muffins on the counter and put one on a plate along with some fruit and tried to convince her to eat something. As Sam picked at the muffin he began to question her.

"I woke up early and headed out to the shop. Since it's Friday and I don't have the kids I wanted to get a start on a project…" She paused for a moment then seemed to deflate. "Oh, God, the sketch."

"What sketch?" Jake asked, alarmed at the devastated look on her face.

"I worked all night on it, something I've been wanting to make for a long time. I finally got it right, it was just what I had pictured in my mind for years. I didn't see it this morning. Do you think someone took it? Why would someone do that?" she asked helplessly.

Jake didn't want to tell her that if this was personal, the person responsible would do whatever he thought would hurt the most. "Maybe we should go take a look. Do you feel up to going out there with me?"

Sam took a deep breath and looked Jake in the eye, some color returning to her cheeks. "Yes. I do. I want to figure out who did this," she said, her voice getting stronger. "Let's go."

As they made their way to the shop, Jake looked around the yard, hoping to see something out of the ordinary that might give him a clue as to who was responsible. Nothing seemed out of place to him and Sam agreed. "You didn't hear the dog barking at any time during the night? She didn't make a fuss?" Jake asked.

Sam shook her head. "No, I didn't hear her," she said, realizing this was at least twice someone had been on her property and the dog hadn't made a peep. "But, like I said, the air conditioning was on so with all the windows closed and the shop a bit of a distance from the house, Rigi probably didn't hear anything."

At the sound of her name, the dog jumped playfully at Sam, tennis ball in her mouth. Sam threw the ball and the dog loped happily after it. "I know she's not really a watchdog, but if she heard something I'm sure she would have made some sort of noise. She barked the other day when a couple of deer wandered through the yard," Sam added hopefully.

Jake didn't reply as they approached the shop. It was obvious from the damage that whoever had done it hadn't worried too much about being quiet, maybe having noticed the house was closed up and the air conditioning running and realizing it was unlikely he would be detected. The doorknob was hanging loosely on the door, smashed with something heavy, probably a hammer. The inexpensive lock had given way easily, Jake was sure. Splinters of wood hung on the doorframe and littered the step in front of the door.

Jake turned to Sam before pushing the door open, wanting to make sure she was ready to face the damage again. She looked straight ahead, her jaw firmly set. When she looked at him, he saw only the briefest flash of pain in her eyes before they turned steely and she opened the door herself.

The shop was a mess, Sam hadn't exaggerated. Stools were overturned, stain was spilled on the floor, tools were strewn about, and pieces of wood littered the benches and floor. Sam wavered for a moment and reached for Jake's arm but there was determination in her voice as she started walking around the room listing off the damage for Jake.

"I wanted to start cleaning up but thought you should see it as is so I called." She walked to the longest workbench and picked up what looked like a broken step stool. "The kids' projects are all damaged, I think that's the worst part. How am I going to tell them? They have been working so hard," she said, heartbroken.

Jake didn't want to but he knew he had to bring up the possibility of one of the kids being responsible. "Sam, we have to start thinking about who might have done this. What can you tell me about the kids you're working with?" he began gently.

"The kids? What do you...oh, no! You're not suggesting one of them did this? They're good kids, Jake! They may have had a rough start and found some trouble along the way but that doesn't mean they're criminals!" She was working up a head of steam. "Don't you dare accuse them, you don't know anything about them. They just need someone to give them a chance, not to start blaming them the first time something goes wrong."

There was fire in her eyes as she glared at Jake, almost daring him to contradict her. "Sam, I'm not accusing anyone, I just need to look at all the possibilities. My guess is the person, or persons, responsible for this is also responsible for the other things that have gone on here. We need to figure out if this is personal or if you're a random target. It's the type of thing that happens sometimes with gang initiations..." He stopped himself deciding against telling her that if it was a gang issue, the violence would likely escalate. That could wait.

"It's not the kids," she said again but less forcefully. She looked sad and Jake wondered, not for the first time, if she wasn't getting too involved with the kids from Project Strong Start.

"Tell me about the kids. How are things going with them?"

Sam sighed, resigned to the fact that, as the sheriff, Jake needed to look into the kids from camp. "There are six of them," she began, "each one has so many good qualities, they just need to believe in themselves and have someone believe in them."

When Jake was silent, she continued. "Jackson is by far the most talented. He has taken to woodworking like he was born to do it. He doesn't talk a lot but he's starting to open up a little. He told me he had a woodshop class in school once but said he didn't learn much. From his file, it looks like attendance at school was an issue, he's been suspended more than once for drug use and," she paused, reluctant to go on but knowing Jake would find out for himself, added, "and there's been some evidence of gang involvement."

Without waiting for Jake to comment, she continued. "Jimmy is a sweet kid, kind of an accident waiting to happen in the shop, but he tries hard and wants to please. I know his older brother who's heavily involved with a gang has pressured him. He's spending the summer here to put some distance between him and his brother."

"Davis is a little troublemaker, I'll admit, but it's harmless stuff. He just tries to push my buttons. He's looking for attention, that's all. He likes to rile up the other kids, especially Jimmy who's the perfect target, but I can't believe he'd be involved in something so serious."

She looked at Jake, realizing she was giving him ample reason to suspect the kids and hating herself for it. "I know this sounds bad, but you don't know them like I do. They've had problems in their past but they wouldn't do this, I know they wouldn't."

"I'm not ready to accuse anyone of anything, I just want to get your feelings on the kids you've been working with. And I don't think they're bad kids, Sam. I've spent some time out at Project Strong Start over the past few years. The department has made an effort to go out to the camp and interact with the kids, trying to show them that not all cops are out to get them. You're right. I've found most of them to be great kids once you break down the barriers."

Sam nodded, pleased with what Jake said, and continued the run down of the campers. "Mario puts on a tough façade but really just wants someone to care. It's sad how he thinks I'm poking fun at him when I try to compliment him, like no one has ever taken the time to tell him he's good at anything. I have never gotten the impression that he's in any way violent," she added.

"Zach, I admit, worries me. He's on his cellphone whenever he thinks he can get away with it and always seems to be trying to hide something from me. I'm not saying I suspect him," she added quickly, "because I don't, but I do think he's up to something."

"Katie wouldn't hurt a fly. She's just a sad little girl, really. Her mom died when she was young so she and her brothers were raised by their father. He's been sick; she's so worried about him and so afraid no one is telling her the truth about how he's doing. She wants to go home and I think she should. She's not getting anything out of camp, it's just making her miserable. I said as much to the camp director I spoke with yesterday."

Jake looked up. "You talked to the camp director? Why?"

Sam wished she could take back her words. The suspicious look on Jake's face had her wincing. She blew the hair out of her eyes with a huff and tried to explain. "It was mostly about Zach. I know he's been hiding something or is mixed up in something. He's been kind of," she paused as she searched for the right word, "sneaky, I guess, ever since he started coming here. I see him texting under the table, he spends a lot of time in the bathroom, and yesterday he had something with him he was very anxious to keep hidden from me."

She looked at Jake, debating with herself about how much more to tell him. Her desire to protect Zach warred with the need to let Jake do his job and figure out who was responsible. "Yesterday he had something, he shoved it in his pocket when I came close. I think it might have been a knife, I don't really know, it was silver and shiny…"

"Okay, Sam, that's good. It sounds like you've really gotten to know the kids. They're lucky to have you. I will have to do some checking but I hope it's not one of them. I really do," he added in response to her skeptical expression.

She remained silent, lost in her own thoughts. Jake walked around the shop some more, checked the outside and made notes in his notebook.

"What about anyone else, neighbors you may have had a run-in with, angry customers?" he asked as Sam eventually joined him outside.

Sam had to laugh at that. "Well, I don't really have any neighbors as you can see. The closest ones are on the other side of those trees," she said pointing. "It's a young family from the Twin Cities, I've only met them once. I don't think they're here very often."

"My property extends pretty far on the other side so I don't even know who is closest to me in that direction. I remember when we were kids there was a family with a cabin next door, the Andersons. They had a few kids around our ages and we'd hang out together sometimes swimming and goofing off. The place is gone and I guess my grandfather bought the property at some point. I was surprised when Kathleen first walked me around the lot and showed me how far the property line extended. It looked so different without a cabin there."

Jake didn't know the details of what happened with the cabin or if there was even anything to know. He'd have to check with his father on that one. If there had been problems or disputes, the former sheriff would know, he was sure of that.

"As far as customers, I haven't had many and I think they've all been happy. Certainly none of them have been angry, unless you count Max Foster," she said with a chuckle.

"What happened with Max?" Jake couldn't imagine the old man getting angry about work Sam had done for him. He was a crotchety sort but didn't have a temper.

"Oh, I'm kidding, he wasn't angry. He was just a little put off when he came to 'Sam's Woodworking' looking for someone to make him a new mailbox in the shape of a train car and found out Sam was actually Samantha. He mumbled a few things about a woman doing a man's job but I showed him a few things I've done and finally convinced him I could handle making a mailbox."

"That sounds like Max. I'm pretty sure he's still of the opinion that women shouldn't do much other than cook and clean and raise children."

The conversation lagged as Sam watched Jake poke around outside the shop, walk up and down the drive, and even take a look in the trash cans. When they headed back inside and she was forced to face the destruction once again, grief threatened to take over.

"I don't know if I can repair all of the kids' projects," she said dejectedly. "Some pieces are so damaged I'm afraid they're a total loss." She walked toward the cabinet where the projects had been stored and began to pick up pieces from the shelves and from the floor in front. "There's so much cleanup, I'll have to try the power tools and make sure they're all still working properly and aren't dangerous. I'm just glad I delivered the cabinet I was repairing last night or that probably would have been destroyed, too.

"You didn't tell me you went out last night. What time was that?"

"I think it was around six o'clock but I came back to the shop after making the delivery. Nothing was out of place then. I stayed in here until well after dark working on the sketch."

Being reminded of the sketch made her heart sink even further. Would she be able to recreate it? She thought so, but the idea of the entire evening's work lost was a lot to bear. And it had been so perfect.

Shaking off the sadness, she told herself she needed to get to work. "Well," she began in an upbeat tone Jake knew was forced, "this place isn't going to clean itself so unless you have more questions, I really need to get to work."

"I think I have everything I need for now but I may have more questions for you later." He liked thinking about there being a later, another chance to spend time with her.

"Okay, Sheriff, then you better get back to work. I don't suppose crime in Misty Lake will come to a halt because you're busy here."

The teasing in her voice didn't reach her eyes. She looked devastated and exhausted already from the stress. As he watched her begin straightening and putting tools back in their proper places he said impulsively, "Come with me tomorrow. It's Saturday, I have the day off, and you need a break."

"What?" she said, tilting her head in confusion as she turned to face him. "What are you talking about? Come with you where?"

"It's a surprise," he answered, getting into the spirit of things and wanting desperately to lift hers. "Just wear a swim suit."

"Are you crazy? I have hours and hours of work to do," she said, waving her hands around the room. "I don't have time for a break. I need to try to repair the kids' things before Monday, I really don't want them to see this."

That was the worst part for her, he understood. She didn't want the kids to be disappointed. As he looked at her standing there in an old pair of cut-off shorts and a faded Minnesota Twins t-shirt with sawdust clinging to it, his heart gave a lurch. He was going to put a sparkle back in those eyes no matter how long it took.

"You have today, tomorrow morning, and all day Sunday to work on things. And I'll help. I may not be able to do what you do with a hammer and saw but I'm pretty handy with a broom."

She considered him, standing there looking at her with—well, she wasn't exactly sure what—in his eyes. And she liked what she saw. He was fidgeting like a child at Christmas waiting for her reply. Because she couldn't stand to see him suffer, she agreed.

"Okay, a break Saturday afternoon. I can do that." The look of relief on his face had her heart softening even more. "But a swim suit? Really?"

"Trust me, you won't be sorry," he grinned as he rocked back on his heels. "Now, where's that broom?"

7

They swept, sorted, organized, and repaired. Jake had done his best to clean up the stain spills on the floor and had been helpful with the lifting needed to right an overturned cabinet. He had watched as Sam carefully went over the panel saw inch by inch and shared in her joy as she announced that, other than some dents and cosmetic damage, it looked as though the machine was undamaged.

Jake decided it was time to get back to the office and to leave Sam to start some of the repair work that was ahead of her. As he was washing his hands in the bathroom that had remained, for some reason, mostly untouched by the vandal, he noticed a crumpled up piece of paper behind the wastebasket. He headed back to the main workshop as he opened it, trying to decipher what it was he was looking at.

"Sam, I found this in the bathroom," he began as he headed to where she was working on assessing the damage to Jackson's jewelry box.

"Hmmm?" she answered, her attention on the jewelry box.

Jake laid the paper on the workbench and smoothed it out. Sam's hands stilled as she realized what Jake had lain in front of her. "The hutch!" she shrieked, grabbing the paper and throwing her arms around Jake before she realized what she was doing.

Caught off guard, it took Jake a moment to realize he was holding Sam in his arms. Deciding not to let the moment pass, he held her tighter and felt his pulse quicken as he inhaled her scent—the hint of coconut from her shampoo mixed with the soft floral scent of her perfume.

Dammit, Sam thought, what was she thinking? That was the problem, she rationalized, she hadn't thought. When Jake laid the sketch in front of her she'd over-reacted to the first bit of good news she'd had all day. Nothing more, just a knee-jerk reaction. Then why did it feel so right? She stiffened, telling herself she needed to back away, that this was a mistake she wasn't willing to make. As she started to shift, Jake tightened his arms around her and she felt her knees threaten to give out. She held on and allowed herself, just for a moment, not to think, just to feel.

When Jake felt her give in and melt against him he stopped the celebratory cheer that was threatening to escape by pressing his lips to hers. He felt her shock when their lips first met and then her slow warming and response to him. Maybe there was some truth to the whole stars and fireworks thing, he thought. If someone told him the town's Fourth of July celebration was happening right now in Sam's yard, he wouldn't doubt it for a moment.

Warning bells sounded in Sam's head as Jake pulled her closer and kissed her. She needed to stop this before it went any further. Then why was she kissing him back? She needed to concentrate on the fact that this was a really bad idea. Then why did it feel like the most natural thing in the world?

Like a bucket of cold water over his head, the realization suddenly hit that this wasn't the way he wanted things to happen with Sam. He was taking advantage of her when she'd just been through something traumatic and needed a friend. Slowly, he drew away, taking a deep breath and using one hand to steady himself on the workbench. He was shakier than he cared to admit.

Sam kept her eyes closed for a long moment, then looked up at him with a combination of desire and confusion. It took all of Jake's willpower not to grab her again.

She found it took more brainpower than she was currently capable of harnessing to form a rational thought. Later, when she was alone, she would try to make sense out of what just happened but for now, she needed to diffuse the situation. But looking at Jake seemed to turn her into a mindless bundle of desire and she had to clasp her hands tightly behind her back to keep from embarrassing herself further.

"Look," she finally managed, "that was my fault, I'm sorry. It shouldn't have happened. I guess I just over-reacted to you finding my sketch. Stupid, really..."

Jake studied her for a minute, oddly pleased at the blush rising in her cheeks. So, it had affected her, too, he thought. "You sure spend a lot of time apologizing. Why do you think that is?"

It wasn't the response she had expected and she didn't know how to reply. If he had shot back with a smart comment about her only doing what she knew they both wanted or some such nonsense, she could have handled him. As it was, she just stared.

"Listen, Sam, I'm more to blame than you are but you can't deny there was...something there. It might take some time to figure out what, but we have plenty of time," he said with a smile so sweet it almost had her throwing herself back into his arms.

She had to get him out of there. Now. She decided to ignore the whole situation and act as though nothing had happened. "Well, I would imagine you need to get to work. Aren't people wondering where the sheriff is?" she asked briskly.

"My office knows where I am and that I'm working on a case. They can handle things without me." He studied her and watched her fight the urge to squirm under his gaze. God, she was gorgeous. He gave himself a mental shake. "But, I should be getting back. I want you to give Mike Jameson over at the hardware store a call like we discussed. He'll come out here and install some decent locks for you. You may want to consider a security system, too. Misty Lake's a safe place but you're pretty isolated out here and with you living alone..."

Before he could finish, she straightened her spine and sputtered, "I've told you and everyone else who's been out here that I can take care of myself. I'm not going to be scared off by some nut job who thinks it's funny to damage what's mine."

"I know, Sam. I don't for a minute think you can't take care of yourself but I also think it only makes sense to do what you can to stay safe. Get new locks and give some thought to a security system. I can give you a name of someone who will do a good job if you decide to go ahead with it. And, I've been meaning to ask you, do you have a phone?"

"What do you mean, do I have a phone? I called the sheriff's office, didn't I?" she scoffed, still miffed at him for thinking she couldn't handle herself.

"I mean do you have a landline in the house? Cell phone reception can be spotty out here, it would be a good idea to have a backup phone."

"I guess you're right about that. There have been a couple of times when I've been down by the lake or walking around the yard with Rigi when the reception has cut in and out," she admitted. "I'll look into it. I will!" she added when he raised a brow.

"Good. Now, I really am going to go. Take it easy out here, you don't need to get everything done today. And remember, I'll be here around noon tomorrow to pick you up," he added with a devilish grin.

"I'll remember. Thank you for your help, Jake, I really appreciate it," she said sincerely.

He nodded as he got in his car to leave. If she only knew he felt like the one who should be saying thank you. In spite of the circumstances, it was the best morning he had had in a very long time. He called out the window as he backed out, "Keep Rigi with you!" then sped away before she could tell him again she didn't need anyone watching out for her.

She stood and watched his car until it was out of sight then watched nothing for a good five minutes more. When she finally turned and went back inside the shop, she had convinced herself anything that had happened earlier was a one-time thing, chalked up to her emotions running high, and it would certainly never happen again. She was far too sensible to let her emotions reign supreme over her common sense. Getting involved with a man, giving her heart to someone only to have it shattered, as it surely would be, was simply out of the question. She had dealt with enough hurt and loss to know steering clear of potentially painful situations was a must. Nobody, not even a sexy sheriff who apparently was capable of turning her bones to liquid, was going to change her mind. Tomorrow she would make it clear they were friends and friends only. With that, she tackled the work ahead of her with a vengeance.

Jake didn't stop to talk on his way into the office, merely waved away questions with the flick of a wrist and spent the next two hours hunched over his desk making notes and trying mightily to focus on the case and not on Sam. He made a call to Project Strong Start and scheduled an appointment for later that afternoon to speak with Tom Lindahl, the head of the camp. He was determined to dig deeper into the kids' pasts.

He had also spoken with a couple colleagues in the Twin Cities who were very familiar with a few of this year's campers. Sadly, several of them already had long records of run-ins with the law, documented drug use, and gang involvement. Jake was waiting to hear back from a friend on the Minneapolis police force who knew as much as anyone about the current status of gangs in the city. He was out of town until Monday so there wasn't much Jake could do but wait.

Jake had hated leaving Sam alone. It was obvious whoever was responsible for the trouble at her place was becoming more violent. There was no longer a question in Jake's mind that all of the incidents were related. From tipped over garbage cans and a broken mailbox to the vicious destruction of her shop, the seriousness of the attacks was escalating. The fact that everything had occurred at night told Jake a couple things. First, the guilty party hadn't yet reached the point where harming Sam personally was part of his plan. He was sneaking around under cover of darkness hoping to frighten her. Second, he was afraid of being seen. There was no indication he had come near the house, focusing his efforts on the shop and areas out of sight of the house. Jake's best guess was that he was far away during the daylight hours. Usually in cases like this, the perpetrator was someone with a personal grudge so the victim would be able to identify him if he were spotted. Third, and most unsettling, was the likelihood that things would continue to escalate until he achieved his goal, whatever that may be.

The fact that Sam knew so few people in town made Jake think it likely that one or more of the kids from Project Strong Start were responsible. As much as Sam didn't want to believe it, not all of the kids could be helped by a summer at camp. Many had been forced to attend the camp or had had it offered as an alternative to juvenile detention. Sam wanted to believe that deep down, everyone was good, and as much as he'd like to agree, he had seen too much throughout his career to know it wasn't a reality.

Jake also searched back in the police records for cases of vandalism at the lake. There were a few scattered over the years, most taking place in the winter when many of the cabins were closed up and there were fewer people around. There had been a string of small thefts a few summers ago but a drifter had been caught with the stolen goods in his possession and the case closed. Serious crime in Misty Lake was almost unheard of. The one murder had been a domestic situation twenty years ago and still came up in conversation from time to time among those who were old enough to remember. Jake knew they were fortunate. It was a community where neighbors looked out for one another and people still felt comfortable leaving their doors unlocked although Jake had been doing his best to convince them to do otherwise.

Jake finally leaned back in his chair and looked at the ceiling. He would need to talk to his deputies and order extra patrols around Sam's place at night. He'd be taking a turn or two himself. He was going to send Marc back out to talk to some of the kids he knew would confide in him to see if there had been any talk yet of someone pulling pranks or causing damage. Fred, the oldest member of his team, was good at listening to gossip in the town's bars and restaurants and there wasn't a person in town he didn't know and know well. If there was something to hear, he'd hear it. He pushed back from his desk, grabbed his notepad, and went to talk to his team.

Later that afternoon, Jake pulled his patrol car into the lot in front of the lodge housing the offices of Project Strong Start. As he got out of his car, he was aware of the stares and whispers from the kids milling around the outdoor rec area. The volleyball game came to a halt as Jake made his way toward the sand court. "What's the score?" he asked.

It was quiet for a few seconds until a short boy who looked to be about fifteen and sporting bright red hair and freckles answered, pointing to the other side, "They're winning but it's cuz they have one more player than we do."

"Oh yeah, that's why," a tall, thin girl on the other team laughed.

"Well, how about we even up the teams?" Jake suggested, joining the losing team.

The kids looked at one another, unsure of what to do. Finally the boy holding the ball muttered, "Whatever," and went back to serve.

It took a few points, but the kids gradually loosened up and Jake worked up a sweat. "Hey, nice shot, Cop Man," one of the boys on the opposing team jeered as Jake's hit flew out of bounds.

"Just a little rusty," Jake shot back, "wait 'til I really get going!"

"Ooh, now we're scared, ain't we guys!"

The heckling intensified and Jake sensed the kids relaxing. He decided it was well worth the sweat he felt running down his back to see the kids having fun and forgetting it was a cop on the court with them. A few other campers had gathered around and were cheering on the teams. Jake noticed two boys he guessed to be in their late teens hovering around the tree line, keeping to themselves. Without being obvious, he committed descriptions of the two to memory and decided he would ask the director about them during their talk.

Finally, after winning the game he joined in progress and then losing the second he had been convinced to play, Jake held up his hands in mock surrender. "I'm done. I'm too old to keep up with all of you," he panted and wiped sweat from his brow. He took a seat at the nearby picnic table and most of the kids joined him, either sitting at the table or flopping on the grass.

"Having fun here this summer?" he casually asked the group.

He got a few nods and murmured responses. The redhead who was the first to talk earlier and who Jake had already figured out was Jimmy from Sam's class almost shouted, "It's so great! We get to swim and waterski and play games and I'm learning how to make stuff out of wood! It's awesome!" A few of the kids just rolled their eyes, obviously used to Jimmy's exuberance.

Since Jimmy had opened the door to talk about the classes the kids were taking, Jake took advantage of his opportunity. "Anyone else in the woodworking class?"

He looked around as most shook their heads no. A quiet girl who hadn't been part of the game but had joined the group watching said softly, "I am."

Katie, Jake remembered from Sam's run-down of the class. "How do you like it? Is it really as cool as he says?" Jake asked, hooking his thumb toward Jimmy.

"It's fine," she replied. "Miss Taylor's nice," she added. Sam was right, he thought. Katie looked sad and distant.

When no one else volunteered anything more, he asked about the other classes the kids were taking and continued to chat with them for a few more minutes before telling them he needed to get going. "I'm already late for a meeting with Mr. Lindahl, I better run before he comes looking for me. Maybe we can have a rematch one of these days? I'll come ready to play next time," he said, indicating his sweaty uniform.

He got a few smart comments and some challenges shouted at him as he made his way to the lodge. He checked the tree line for the boys he had noticed earlier, but they had disappeared.

The camp director didn't waste any time getting to the point. "I understand there's been some trouble on the lake and you think some of the kids are responsible," he challenged.

Jake took his time responding, sizing up the director, a short, grey-haired man with keen eyes Jake guessed didn't miss much. He was new to the camp and to the area. "I don't have any suspects at this time, Mr. Lindahl, I just hoped you could answer a few questions for me," he said slowly, looking the man in the eye.

"Okay, what can I answer for you?" he shot back.

"Mr. Lindahl, I'm not here to accuse anyone of anything. There have been some incidents of vandalism and since the victim is one of the volunteer instructors for the camp, my investigation naturally brought me here."

"One of our instructors?" the director asked, genuinely surprised. "I didn't know that. I was just told you wanted to speak with me about some possible trouble with the kids."

"Samantha Taylor, who is teaching a few of the kids woodworking, has had some vandalism out at her place. She lives on the lake, doesn't seem impossible that one or more of the kids could make their way over there," he said, and let the thought hang.

"Please, call me Tom," the director said, removing his glasses and rubbing his eyes. With a sigh, he added,

"I'm sorry, Sheriff, I don't mean to be uncooperative. It's just that after years of working with kids who don't always follow all the rules, shall we say, I've learned to expect that visits from law enforcement will be less than pleasant."

Jake gave a brief nod then asked, "How did you end up with Project Strong Start, Tom?" deciding to let the man talk a little before delving back into his questions.

"I've been working with at-risk kids most of my life, spent time in Milwaukee, Chicago, Minneapolis, even went to Texas for a while. I'd like to think I've helped a lot of them," he said with a half-smile, "but I'm tired. It's not an easy job. Wouldn't have wanted to do anything else, mind you, but my wife is on me to retire, says I'm an old man in a young man's job. She may be right but I'm not quite ready to walk away. When a former colleague of mine called out of the blue about this program it seemed like a good way to step back gradually, keep both my wife and myself happy for the time being."

"It's a good program. I try to spend a little time out here every summer, the department likes to be a presence in a positive way. I've met a lot of good kids. Some today, in fact."

"I saw you playing volleyball," Tom said with a chuckle. "Did Jimmy talk your ear off?"

"He had a lot to tell me. Seems like a good kid, happens to be one of the kids working with Ms. Taylor. Why is he here? Doesn't seem like the type to get into too much trouble."

Tom's face grew serious, accepting the change in the direction of the conversation. "In Jimmy's case it's not him so much as it's his brother. The goal this summer was to put some distance between the two. His older brother

77

William, or Blade as he's known to his 'friends,' is bad news. And believe me, I don't say that easily. Blade has been involved in a gang in Minneapolis for years, been in jail a couple of times for theft, aggravated assault, other offenses. The police like him for two gang-related murders but haven't been able to get the evidence they need to charge him. The older Jimmy gets the more the brother is pressuring him to join his gang. Jimmy's resisting but the pressure and the threats are getting stronger."

Jake thought over the information. He didn't see Jimmy as the gang type but knew what pressure could do to a kid who didn't have a strong support system. "Do you think Jimmy could be fulfilling some kind of gang initiation here by doing damage out at Ms. Taylor's place?"

"No. No, I really don't think that's a possibility. I've spent quite a bit of time with him and I'm convinced that, at this point, he has no interest in the gang and is determined to keep his distance. I don't think he's figured out yet how to do that, but he doesn't give any indication that he's leaning toward joining."

Jake nodded, agreeing with the director's assessment based on what he had seen himself and what he had heard from Sam about Jimmy. "What can you tell me about the rest of the kids in her class?"

Tom shuffled through his desk drawer and pulled out a file. "Let's see, in addition to Jimmy she has five other kids. Katie Jacobson, a quiet girl who wouldn't hurt a fly. She keeps to herself, mostly. Has a couple brothers who are troublemakers but nothing serious, mostly just do their best to annoy the foster families who take them in. I don't think we need to worry about her."

"I met her outside, definitely not high of my list of

likely suspects."

"Davis Philips," Tom continued, "been in quite a bit of trouble at school, suspended and eventually kicked out of his first high school. He has a history of vandalism," Tom said, leafing through the pages in Davis' file," but it looks like it's been limited to the schools he's attended and a church where he was supposed to be part of a youth group."

"Sounds like a definite problem with authority." Jake considered what Tom had said. "If he's looking at Ms. Taylor's class as another school setting, it might not be such a stretch for him to want to do some damage."

"I guess it's a possibility," Tom conceded, "but there's still the issue of one of the kids getting to her place. We don't just hand them car keys and let them run wild. They are supervised at all times."

Jake raised a brow but said nothing. "Let's go through the rest of the kids before we start thinking about how they might get over there."

Tom looked like he wanted to argue but continued with the list of kids. "Mario Ramirez has a history of drug use, nothing too serious yet, but he has trust issues. He doesn't have much of a home life, has a hard time letting anyone close. I've seen it far too often when kids like him turn to serious drug use as a way of escaping. There's no mention of violence or vandalism in his file."

Jake let Tom continue. "Jackson Rogers. An interesting case, caught my attention when I first read his file. Said to be a good student when he bothers to show up for school. There's also mention of some gang involvement, nothing for sure, apparently he's just been seen with some known gang members. What Jackson has going for him is a mother who simply won't give up. Believe me, that's not common with most of the kids I've worked with over the years. His mother attends every school conference, checks on his attendance, even drives him to school to see that he gets there in the morning. She fought hard to get him into Project Strong Start. I've spoken with her a couple times when she's called here to check on her son. I can tell she's a good mother."

Again, Jake nodded but stayed silent. He had heard a similar story from Sam. He watched Tom grow uncomfortable as he stared at the file in front of him, obviously struggling with what to tell Jake.

Finally, Tom began slowly. "The last student in Ms. Taylor's class is Zachary Fields. He's…something of an unknown, I guess. He ended up here as an alternative to time in juvenile detention in St. Paul. He was caught stealing from a convenience store, not for the first time. It was the first time with a weapon, however. He had a knife on him when he was arrested. He hadn't used it but it was in his possession. He's always acted alone, from what the police reports say, which is unusual for kids. Most times when kids get started stealing they do so in a group, feeding off one another and afraid to look like a chicken in front of their friends. Zach doesn't seem to have many friends but according to school reports, has been in trouble countless times for texting and using his phone when it's not allowed. That's something of a red flag for me."

"Any idea who he's texting or calling?" Jake interrupted. "Heavy cell phone use could be a number of things. Dealing drugs comes to mind."

"No, no mention in his file that anyone is aware of who it is he's contacting. I agree with your guess at drugs, dealers tend to be glued to their phones. And before you ask, there's nothing to indicate he's active in any gangs. What worries me most about Zach is the only person he's had anything to do with here at camp is Tyler Loomis. Tyler has the most serious record of any of our campers this year. He really didn't qualify for camp, he has convictions in his past that make him ineligible, but his probation officer argued long and hard that the serious crimes are in his past, he's been doing well for almost two years, and deserved a chance. The final decision was made before I was hired so I didn't have any input, but I have to say, I would have tried to keep him out."

"What sort of things in his past?" Jake asked.

"Convictions for arson, robbery, destruction of property, accused of rape but never convicted. He's been getting into trouble for years."

Jake gave a low whistle. "That's quite a record for a kid. The alleged rape is nothing to take lightly."

"I don't take any of it lightly, Sheriff," Tom said forcefully then backed off again. "Look, I'm here to watch out for and advocate for these kids. That doesn't mean I'm not vigilant or I'll look the other way if I suspect anything illegal. I believe most of them still have a chance to turn their lives around. Some of them, unfortunately, won't. After thirty years of working with kids, I have a pretty good idea of the ones who won't."

"Is that your feeling about Tyler?"

Tom answered with a frown and a nod.

"And you're worried he'll get to Zach," Jake said more as a statement than a question.

"Yes, that's my concern. Zach seems impressionable and as I said, Tyler is really the only other kid he's spent any time with."

Recalling the two kids lurking around the tree line during the volleyball game, Jake gave descriptions to the director.

"That sounds like Zach and Tyler, both the physical description and the behavior fit."

"Can you give me a run-down of your security procedures? How do you assure the kids are where they're supposed to be?"

Tom described a typical day with the kids spending their mornings at their chosen field of interest, returning for lunch, some free time, chores, and structured activity until lights out at eleven o'clock. He stressed that at no time were the kids left unsupervised.

"And overnight?" Jake asked.

"The sleeping quarters are locked with a staff member on duty in each building at all times. There are alarms and monitors. It would be very difficult for anyone to leave during the night."

"But not impossible."

Tom was quiet and Jake could see the anger starting to burn in his eyes. He finally answered, "No. Not impossible."

Jake let the idea fester for a couple minutes before changing the subject. "What about the safety of your volunteers? They are alone with a group of kids. Who or what is ensuring their safety?"

"The kids here aren't perfect, they've made their share of mistakes, but we don't take kids who have a history of violence and place them with volunteer mentors.

Now, I know what you're thinking—Tyler. He doesn't work with a community volunteer, I wouldn't allow it. He's spending his mornings with the maintenance man here at camp, learning some basic plumbing, repair work, that sort of thing. Jeff, our maintenance man, is a former Navy SEAL and is trained in working with kids. I don't have any worries for his safety."

"Supposing one of the kids is responsible for the damage at Ms. Taylor's place, do you still feel comfortable having her working alone with them four days a week?"

"Honestly, I was reluctant to take her on as a volunteer from the start and told her as much during her interview. I'll admit the thought of a woman alone and more or less isolated with a group of teenage boys with troubled pasts concerned me. She's a hard woman to say no to, though," he added, shaking his head. "She just insisted this was something she wanted to do and that she knew what she was getting in to."

Silently, Jake agreed. "Did you discuss safety with her? Tell her what to do in the event something might happen?"

"Of course, it's part of the required training for all of our volunteers. We also do periodic visits with all of our volunteers, stopping in when they're working with the kids to see how things are going. We've been out to Ms. Taylor's once already, early on, and will be visiting again…" he paused as he checked his calendar, "next Wednesday."

Deciding he'd gotten all the information from the director he was going to get for the time being, Jake rose to leave and extended his hand. "Thank you for your time, Tom. If you hear any talk around the camp or notice any unusual behavior, I'd appreciate a call."

"Of course, Sheriff. I'll be meeting with my staff this evening and will brief them on our meeting. If there's anything to hear, one of them will hear it and will let me know."

After a few more words, Jake headed back to the office, making a swing by Sam's place on his way.

8

Just before noon on Saturday, Sam found herself standing in her kitchen wearing shorts and a t-shirt over her swimming suit and wondering for the hundredth time why she ever agreed to spend the afternoon with Jake. She had been tempted to call him and cancel telling him she had too much work to do but she figured he'd show up anyway with a crazy offer to help. As she threw a hat, towel, sunscreen, and sunglasses in an oversized bag, she let a combination of nerves and melancholy get the better of her.

She assumed Jake had plans for them to be on the lake and Sam wasn't sure she could face it. Moving here had been hard enough but she had convinced herself the new house wasn't a part of her past and had been doing her best to block out the often-painful memories. Aside from throwing a stick into the water for Rigi to chase, Sam had avoided the lake even though she had been itching to swim. It was silly, she knew, but the lake held even more memories for her than the old cabin did.

She had spent countless hours in the water with her cousins. She couldn't help but smile to herself as she remembered the diving and cannonball competitions they had forced their parents to judge. There had been an old raft, really nothing more than some plywood mounted on barrels with a couple cinder blocks for anchors, that the kids had dragged out first thing every year. They had spent hours playing their version of King of the Raft, wrestling and pushing each other off in the hopes of being the last one standing and having that moment of glory, raising your arms in victory before someone climbed back up and sent you flying into the water. Sam could remember being so tired and so out of breath, climbing back onto the raft had been almost impossible. At least one of the parents had always been on lifeguard duty, sitting on the beach counting kids, and always seeming to know when it was the right time for a break.

Sam had learned to swim here and had fallen in love with the sport. She could still remember the summer when she was first able to beat everyone else in a race, even her older cousins. The boys had insisted she'd cheated and had called for do-overs until they were forced to admit Sam was faster than they were. After that summer she had pestered her parents until they finally let her quit dance class and join the local swim club.

She supposed somewhere in one of the boxes she had moved into an extra bedroom and forgotten was her box of ribbons and trophies. Her grandfather hadn't let her quit swimming after the deaths of her parents and grandmother even though she had cried and stomped her feet and said she wouldn't go. He had let her have some time, then one day put her in the car and drove her to the pool. Once she was in the water, some of the sadness had started to slip away and Sam threw herself into the sport that became an outlet for her grief.

She missed the water. Before she moved to Misty Lake she had spent at least three mornings a week at the local health club, swimming laps to stay in shape. As she stretched her arms over her head, her muscles almost begged for a workout. Maybe it was time, she thought to herself as she stared at the lake, lost in her memories.

A sharp knock at the door had Sam whirling around and tripping over the dog dozing contentedly at her feet. Pulling herself together, she opened the door to Jake, grinning and looking more relaxed than she had ever seen him in his swim trunks and baseball cap.

The casualness with which he took her hand then leaned over to kiss her cheek had her swallowing the much less intimate greeting she had planned. "And how's Rigi?" Jake asked as he leaned down to pat the dog and received a wet nose in the face as a reply. When the dog flopped over on her back in anticipation of a belly rub, Jake obliged and it gave Sam a moment to collect herself.

"You know, Jake, I really have a lot of work to do. I don't know if it's a good idea to go anywhere, I should try to—"

Jake stood and cut her off. "Oh, no, you don't. You need a break, it's already been decided. No backing out now," he warned. "Are you ready?" he added before she had a chance to argue.

Blowing a breath out, Sam mumbled, "Fine," and turned to grab her bag.

Once they were in the car and pulling away, Sam asked, "Just where is it you're taking me?"

"It's a surprise. One I'm sure you'll enjoy," he added in response to her doubtful look. "You do know how to swim, don't you?"

"Yes. I know how to swim," she replied and left it at that.

Ten minutes later they pulled up to a comfortable looking home on the other side of the lake. The weathered siding and shake shingles were brightened by red geraniums spilling from window boxes. The lawn was precisely mowed and dotted with trees and shrubbery. A whimsical wishing well gave the place a charming, homey feel.

"Is this your house?" Sam asked, thinking it wasn't at all what she had expected and then wondering why she had given any thought to what Jake's home would look like.

"No, I'm afraid I can't take credit for this. It's my brother Joe's place. Although it looks a lot different since Karen got her hands on it."

"Your brother?" She wasn't quite sure how she felt about meeting Jake's family. It seemed too personal and she was regretting her decision yet again.

"Come on, he doesn't bite," Jake said seeing the apprehension on her face. If Jake knew his brother, or better, his sister-in-law, they were peeking out the window right now, waiting to get a look at Sam. When he had called his brother yesterday evening to tell him Sam would be coming with him, he had heard Karen in the background firing questions at Joe. Since Jake hadn't brought a woman to a family function of any sort in years, he was sure word had spread and his parents, as well as all his siblings, were curious.

Sam gave Jake a withering look then headed to the door with him. Damn, she wished she had known they were going to be spending the day with his brother. She wasn't sure what she would have done differently, probably nothing, she decided, but at least she would have been prepared.

She put a smile on her face as the door opened and she was greeted by Jake's brother and his wife. Sam caught the look between Joe and Karen and their attempts to hide their grins. Hadn't Jake ever brought a woman around before? she wondered, but found that hard to believe. Surely he must have dated, and with a family as close as he had made his sound, it seemed only natural that he would have brought her home to meet his family.

With the introductions out of the way, during which time Sam had learned Joe was a high school science teacher and Karen a nurse, they headed to the back and towards the lake. Sam still wasn't sure what the plan was until she saw a huge, shiny boat bouncing softly next to a long, sturdy dock. Even with her limited knowledge of boats, it was hard not to be impressed. "Wow," she managed, glancing at Joe as they reached the dock.

He seemed to stand a little straighter and square his shoulders as a wide grin spread across his face. "Thanks, Sam, I'll take that as a compliment. She is a beauty, isn't she?" he said almost reverently.

"It looks brand new," Sam said taking in the sleek lines and smooth upholstery. There wasn't a scratch or ding anywhere that she could see.

"Just got her this spring. We'd been wanting a new

one for some time, right, honey?" Joe replied with a look to his wife who only raised her eyebrows. "I've got the motor broken in, she's ready to fly."

Sam leaned back a little and craned her neck to peek at the part of the motor sticking out from the back of the boat. It looked huge. "Just how fast does this thing go?"

"Well, that depends upon the conditions," Joe replied, his voice slipping into what Sam could only describe as teacher mode as he started educating her on horsepower, aerodynamics, and weather conditions.

When Karen gave a sigh and murmured, "Here we go," Joe stopped the lecture and suggested they get in the boat and she experience it for herself.

After a lot of loading, arranging, and situating, they pulled away from the dock, the boat fully stocked with drinks, snacks, water skis, and a giant, rather intimidating-looking tube strapped to the back. They started out slow, cruising along the shoreline with Joe and Karen pointing out the homes of a couple people Sam had met and explaining features of the lake. The weather was perfect with just the lightest breeze and not a cloud in the sky. The water sparkled and as Sam gazed across the lake, she felt herself relax.

Jake sat with Sam in the front of the boat, pleased that she seemed to be enjoying herself. He had noticed the flash of anxiety when she first glimpsed the boat but it had seemed to pass quickly. As he watched her look out over the lake, her eyes hidden by the sunglasses she wore, he realized how little he really knew about her. Was there something in her past that made her fear the water? he wondered. Or was it just the memories of her time spent here as a child that had caused her to hesitate?

Sam noticed the gradual increase in speed as Joe guided the boat further from the shore. Soon they were racing across the open water, the boat seeming to barely skim the surface. The wind whipped her hair back while the sunlight warmed her skin. Sam hadn't felt this free in a long time, as if she could outrace any memories that threatened to sneak into her consciousness. She closed her eyes and ordered herself to enjoy the day for what it was, a fun afternoon spent with friends. She wouldn't allow thoughts of either ghosts from the past or vandals of the present to interfere.

When she looked over at Jake she found him watching her, his head tilted slightly as if trying to figure her out. She smiled and impulsively took his hand and gave it a squeeze. "Thank you," she mouthed, knowing he wouldn't hear her over the roar of the engine and the whip of the wind.

After a while, Joe slowed down then stopped the motor completely and let the boat drift. Karen passed around snacks and offered drinks. The men each grabbed a beer with the women both opting for bottled water.

"Well, now that we can hear each other, maybe we can get to know you, Sam," Karen said with a look toward her husband.

Sam grew uncomfortable, not wanting to be the center of attention. "There's not really much to know," she began, determined to keep the details vague. "I grew up outside of Chicago. My grandfather owned property here and left it to me when he died this past winter."

Karen looked at her encouragingly when she quit talking, expecting more information, but Sam remained silent. Although she wanted to ask more about her past, Karen decided to let it go, for now. "How do you like it here?" she asked instead.

"Truthfully, I feel like I haven't had a chance to decide yet. I've been busy since I got here, unpacking, then getting my business going and working with the group of kids from Project Strong Start. There hasn't been time for much else," she said with a shrug.

"You're enjoying working with the kids?" Karen asked although she already knew the answer based on the look on Sam's face when she mentioned them.

"Oh, yes. What's not to enjoy? They're amazing kids. Talented, funny, sweet...it's incredible working with them," she gushed.

"Have you had any more trouble at your place?" Joe asked.

"The kids aren't responsible for anything that has happened there! They wouldn't cause that sort of damage, especially to their own work." Then, seeing the surprised look on Karen's face and realizing she was practically yelling, Sam calmed and apologized. "I'm sorry, I guess I've just gotten in the habit of defending them," she said with a sideways glance at Jake.

"What sort of damage are you talking about?" Joe asked slowly. "I thought it was a broken window, dead animals, and a couple other minor things."

"Oh." Sam let out a breath. "I assumed you knew when you asked about trouble..." Her voice trailed off as she glanced at Jake, unsure what she should say.

"There was some vandalism overnight Thursday night," Jake said. "Her shop was pretty badly damaged. We don't have any suspects yet."

"Oh, Sam, that's terrible!" Karen said, shocked. "Were you home? Did you hear or see anything?"

"I was home but no, I didn't see or hear anything. The shop is on the other side of my lot so not real close to the house and I had the air conditioning running, the house closed up…I guess I just slept through it."

Karen gave Jake a long look, clearly implying that he had better do something about the problem.

Sensing Sam was uncomfortable with the conversation, Jake decided she needed a distraction. "Look," he said pointing. "Your place looks pretty good from here."

Sam turned and saw her home. The boat had been drifting with Joe starting the motor a couple of times and slowly directing the boat away from shore. Not really knowing the lake well at all, she had lost her bearings and had no idea they were in front of her property.

This was the first time she had seen her house from the water and she couldn't help but stare. It was stunning, there was no denying it. The windows sparkled and reflected the lake. The log construction coupled with the wide stone chimney and coordinating stone accents gave the home a sturdy yet warm and inviting feel. Sam was quiet as she studied it, once again fighting the melancholy that threatened.

"It's beautiful," Karen said softly. "We watched it being built, curious what it would look like when it was finished. It's more incredible than I even imagined it would be."

Sam nodded. The fact that everyone seemed to know more about her house than she did bothered her. She wanted to ask questions, find out how long construction took, when it started, if anyone had seen her grandfather when he visited, but she didn't know if she really wanted the answers so she remained silent.

They floated for a few minutes, studying the house. When Sam didn't say anything Joe gave Jake a questioning look, tilting his head toward the open water. Jake answered with a short nod and Joe announced, "Hold on!" before he started the boat up again and they took off flying across the lake.

Sam appreciated the gesture. At the moment, she just wanted to put some distance between herself and the house she knew so little about. She lifted her face to the wind and let it blow the tension away.

"How about a ride?" Joe asked as he slowed the boat once again. Sam was about to ask what he meant when Jake got up and went to unstrap the giant tube from the back of the boat.

"I'm ready," Jake said.

"We'll see," Joe answered.

The look that passed between the brothers wasn't lost on Sam. She had spent enough time in competition with her brother and her cousins to recognize a challenge when one was given. The men continued to grin and eye one another as Jake wiggled into a life jacket and Joe secured the rope to the hooks on the back of the boat.

Karen moved up to the front of the boat next to Sam while Jake and Joe continued their preparations. "You should see it when all four of them are together," she said with an exaggerated eye roll. "Everything from who can eat the most hotdogs to who can tell the best joke to who's driving the fastest car is a contest with them."

"I remember doing the same thing with my

cousins when we were kids. I guess we eventually outgrew it," Sam said with a laugh.

"Maybe when you have three brothers the competition never ends. I don't get it but they seem to thrive on it."

"Sounds like a close family," Sam said soberly.

"Very close. Joe and I started dating in high school. Once they realized I wasn't going anywhere they started treating me like a sister. The McCabes are a crazy bunch but there's nothing they won't do for one of their own," Karen said looking lovingly at her husband.

Joe, catching her looking at him, came over and planted a kiss on her lips. "Love you, baby, now hold on, I'm going to give my brother a ride he won't soon forget."

Jake looked at Sam as he stood on the edge of the boat. "He's going to try his darnedest to get me off that tube. In case I decide to let go and let him think he succeeded, make sure he doesn't leave me in the middle of the lake." With that, he was in the water swimming for the tube.

Joe threw his head back and laughed and Sam couldn't help joining him. This afternoon was just what she needed, she decided. She watched Jake skim and bounce across the water holding on to the tube for dear life. Joe sped up, slowed down, drove the boat in tight circles and, as Jake had predicted, did everything he could to throw him from the tube.

Sam saw Jake bounce several feet into the air only to come crashing back down again. At times, when Joe took the boat into a tight spin, he slid so far off to the side of the tube she had no idea how he managed to hold on. It looked horrible to Sam but Jake laughed during the entire ride.

Finally, Joe slowed the boat and Jake let go, sliding into the water. He was floating on his back, breathing heavily when Joe circled back around to pick him up. "Looks like that's one for me, little brother," Jake grinned as he heaved himself back into the boat.

"Hmpf. I took it easy on you, didn't want you to embarrass yourself in front of Sam," Joe shot back. "Now give me that jacket and get behind the wheel. It's my turn out there."

The brothers switched places and Jake gave Joe a ride as wild as the one he had just had. Joe slid, bounced, and even flipped over once on the tube but, like his brother, managed to hang on. Sam was convinced they were both crazy.

"I guess it's a draw today unless you're up for another round," Joe said as he toweled off back on the boat. "Or a go on the skis?"

"No, once is enough for me," Jake replied, subtly rubbing the marks on his legs where the tube had done a good job of scraping up his skin. "What about you, Karen, are you ready for a spin?"

"No, not today," she replied looking toward Joe. Sam caught the look that passed between the two but couldn't quite figure it out.

"I'll give it a try," Sam said earning her curious stares from the others.

"Really, Sam? Have you done this before?" Jake asked, sounding unsure.

"Oh, nothing like the rides you just gave each other," she said, "but the neighbors here on the lake used to take us once in a while when we were kids. The boat was much smaller, I'm sure it didn't go nearly as fast as this one, and the tube was nothing more than a rubber ring," she continued with a look at Joe's tube complete with a nylon cover and cushioned hand grips, "but it was fun. I'd like to go for a ride. You have to tone it down a little, though," she said pointing at Joe.

"Don't worry. My brothers are the only ones who get rides like that. Well, maybe my sister if she gets a little too big for her britches."

Sam tossed her hat and sunglasses in her bag and peeled off her t-shirt and shorts. It had gotten hot and she could hardly wait to cool off in the lake. As she stepped up onto the side of the boat preparing to jump in, Jake stammered, "You, ah, um, the life jacket…have to wear one."

Jake thought he might have to jump back into the lake himself to cool off when Sam took off her clothes and he got a look at her in her swimsuit. The electric blue bikini didn't leave much to the imagination. Her long legs were capped off at her hips by blue strings holding the suit bottom together. The top was more strings with two tiny blue triangles covering her breasts. He struggled mightily not to stare as he held the life jacket out for her.

"In a minute," she mumbled quickly. Then, before Jake knew what was happening, she dove into the water and swam with long, sure strokes away from the boat.

The cool water felt heavenly on her burning cheeks. Sam had forgotten she was wearing the silly bikini. It had been the only suit she could find in the few minutes she'd left herself to get ready for the afternoon with Jake. The far more sensible racing suits she wore when she swam laps were packed somewhere along with her goggles and other swim equipment but without digging through countless boxes, she didn't know where. The bikini had been a gift from her cousin Susan when she had dragged Sam to Florida last winter for a long weekend following her grandfather's death.

Now, she wished she had thrown the ridiculous thing away. The weekend had been a disaster, neither one of them had really enjoyed it, the only consolation being they were able to spend time together. She had only put the suit on once and had shoved it in a drawer when she returned from the trip. Remembering the look on Jake's face, she swam harder trying to swim away the embarrassment.

What must Joe and Karen have thought? she wondered. Probably that she was trying to seduce Jake when that was the farthest thing from her mind. She pounded out a few more strokes before flipping and heading back to the boat. She'd just ignore the whole thing, she decided, then put her clothes back on once she got out of the water.

Jake was still standing in the same spot and holding the life jacket when she swam up to the side of the boat. He seemed a little dazed as she treaded water and looked up at him. When he didn't say anything she asked, "Can I have the life jacket?"

Jake snapped out of his stupor when she spoke. Realizing he was acting like a fool standing there holding the jacket as she waited, he muttered, "I'll help you," and jumped in beside her.

Both sensed the other's unease as Jake helped Sam get her arms in the life jacket and tighten the straps. Desperately trying to come up with something to say, Jake asked, "So, are you a swimmer?"

What? she thought to herself. What was he asking her? She couldn't seem to make sense out of anything. Something about swimming. "Um, yes," she finally replied, hoping her brief answer fit his question.

"I could tell," Jake said awkwardly.

After they looked at each other for a minute, both unsure what to do or say, Joe saved them further humiliation by waving his arm and shouting, "Tube's that way!"

They both looked up at him as if they had forgotten anyone else was there. After a moment, they both turned and swam for the tube. Once they were away from the boat Karen looked at Joe and burst out laughing. Joe just shook his head and said sadly, "Oh, God. What an idiot."

Jake helped Sam up onto the tube, showed her where to position her hands, and asked again, "Are you sure about this?"

"Absolutely. I'm already wet, what's the worst that can happen?"

With one last look, Jake turned back for the boat. When he was back on board he looked out over the lake and told Joe, "Be sure to take it easy. The lake's busy, I'm willing to bet there are more than a few careless drivers out there."

"Don't worry, I'll give her a nice, easy ride," Joe answered. Jake was right, he thought, seeing the number of boats nearby. It was always a little trickier pulling someone when there were this many boats on the water. Noticing Jake's nervous look, he said again, "Don't worry, she'll be fine."

Joe turned and called back to Sam, "Ready?" When she gave the thumbs up sign he pushed down the throttle and sped off.

Sam felt the pull on her arms as the front of the tube submerged slightly before popping out of the water and skimming along the top. She moved her legs and readjusted her grip trying to find the best position to stay atop the tube. It was harder than it looked, she thought, as she slipped from one side to the other before figuring out how to balance her weight and steady herself.

Then she looked out and enjoyed. If the boat ride was exhilarating, this was doubly so. It was the closest to flying she had ever come, she decided, as the tube picked up speed and slid across the wake when Joe turned the boat sharply. It was incredible.

Jake felt like his head was on a swivel trying to keep one eye on Sam and the other on the nearby boats. He wasn't sure why he was so nervous, he'd been in the boat countless times when his brother was pulling skiers or tubers. He was an excellent, and careful, driver. It was the other drivers he was worried about. He could tell Joe was just a little tense, as well. He saw his eyes dart from one side to the other then skip to the rearview mirror to check on Sam.

For her part, Sam seemed to be having the time of her life. Jake could see her grin as she flew across the water and he watched as she tentatively let go of one of the grips to give a quick wave. Just as he turned back to look off the front side of the boat, he caught a flash of color as a boat full of loud teenagers whizzed past. They cut far too close to Joe's boat and were now turning back their way, oblivious to the boat in their path.

Jake turned to scream at Joe but Joe was already yelling to Karen to hold on as he had no choice but to turn sharply into the other boat's wake. Jake looked back at Sam, still smiling, unaware of what was happening up ahead. He saw her expression change instantly to one of confusion as the boat jerked sharply to the left and her tube zipped across the water to the right. Jake saw the wave before she did and was on his feet pulling his t-shirt over his head. There was no way she was going to be able to hold on when the tube hit the swell head-on.

Sam didn't know at first what Joe was doing when the boat suddenly veered sharply to the left, but then saw the boat heading toward them. She could tell Joe had turned in time to avoid a collision, but could also see the giant wave the wakes of the two boats combined had produced. She held on with all her might as she was thrown into it.

She felt first like she hit a wall and then felt weightless as she tumbled head over heels above the water. She was pretty sure she skipped across the surface at least twice before coming crashing down on her back. It was like hitting solid ground and she felt the wind rush out of her lungs.

For a moment she was unsure of which way was up. She tried to open her eyes but was met by water and closed them again. She started to move her arms and kick her feet as the life jacket did its job and slowly righted her. When her head finally emerged from the water the first thing she saw was Jake, swimming furiously toward her.

As she struggled to catch her breath, Jake grabbed her around the waist and eased her onto her back. She rested her head against his shoulder and slowly started to relax and breathe deeply.

"Are you okay, Sam?" Jake asked, panic written all over his face. He was brushing the hair out of her eyes and willing her to answer him.

"I think so," she replied slowly, moving her neck gently from side to side. She felt a little sore and was sure tomorrow would be brutal, but she seemed to be in one piece. "I...that was a little scary," she finally managed. And then she began to shake.

Joe had pulled the boat around and was slowly maneuvering toward them. Karen was on her feet, throwing out a life ring which Jake grabbed and used to pull them both to the side of the boat. With Joe's help, he got Sam in and onto the seat. Karen gathered towels and covered Sam who was shaking even harder. Jake kneeled beside her and gently dried her face and hair. "Where does it hurt, Sam? Can you move your arms and legs okay? Are you dizzy?" His fear that she was badly hurt had him firing questions at her faster than she could possibly answer.

"Jake," Karen said softly and gave him a warning look as she laid a hand on his shoulder. She squeezed in next to Sam and took her hand. "Look at me, Sam. How are you feeling?" she began, and ran through a quick series of tests to rule out a concussion or broken bones.

Slowly, color seeped back into Sam's cheeks and the trembling quieted. She looked at Joe. "What happened?"

Joe looked angrily out over the lake before answering. "A boatload of fools, that's what happened. I'm sorry, Sam, I had to try to avoid their boat. I never would have done that to you if I could have helped it." He looked miserable.

"I know, don't worry about it. I'll be fine. Really," Sam added when he looked at her doubtfully. "Do you have any idea who it was?"

Both Jake and Joe shook their heads. "I just caught a glimpse of them, a bunch of teenagers I think, but I didn't recognize any of them," Jake answered, clearly frustrated.

"No, neither did I. Didn't recognize the boat, either. Probably just here for the day," he said with an odd look at his brother.

"If no one's on the lake patrolling today I'm going to get someone out here right now," Jake snarled, grabbing his cell phone from the glove box and punching in the numbers for his office.

While he barked instructions to whoever was unlucky enough to answer his call, Joe started up the boat again and headed for home taking care to stay close to shore and avoid what waves he could.

Sam sat wrapped in a towel feeling almost back to normal. She could detect some stiffness in her neck and shoulders and one wrist was giving her some trouble, probably due to her futile attempt to hold on to the tube but, all in all, she felt fortunate Joe had handled the boat so well and the outcome hadn't been much worse.

Karen, noticing how gingerly Sam was moving her wrist, brought some ice from the cooler and wrapped it around Sam's wrist.

"Thanks, didn't mean to cause so much trouble," Sam said to Karen but kept her eyes on Jake.

How long is it going to take for her to realize she's in love with him? Karen wondered to herself. She could remember looking at Jake's brother the same way years ago. She'd been a teenager at the time but love was love, she reasoned. She smiled at Sam. "No trouble, no trouble at all."

When they got back to the dock Karen and Joe waved off the offer to help unload the boat. "Sit down and relax," Karen said, indicating the chairs lined up on the beach. "Can you stay for dinner? I have some steaks in the fridge."

Sam turned to Jake with what she hoped was a look indicating she really wanted to get going but he was already answering. "Thanks, Karen, but I think I should get Sam home. I'm just going to make one more quick call to the office and then we'll head out."

While Jake paced around the yard, well out of earshot of the rest, Sam thanked Joe and Karen and reassured Joe, again, that she was okay. They chatted for a few minutes while Jake finished his call then headed for the car. As Sam loaded her bag in the back seat and started to climb in the front, Joe called Jake aside.

"What's with the calls to the office?" he asked, narrowing his eyes at his brother.

"Just making sure I have someone out on the lake today, I already told you that," Jake snapped. "If someone is going to drive that carelessly, I want someone out here to put a stop to it."

"I don't disagree but it seems like there's a little more to it. You're thinking it wasn't an accident," Joe stated, reading his brother well.

Jake sighed. "I don't know what to think. There have been too many things happening involving Sam to brush this aside as just another coincidence."

Joe studied his brother. "There have always been

jerks on the lake, always will be."

Jake took a long time in answering, gazing out at the water before looking his brother in the eye. "If that's all it is, then that's all it is. But I'm going to be damn sure I do all I can to find out if it's something more." With that, he strode to his car and sped away.

9

After a ride home during which not much was said but Sam caught Jake glancing nervously at her again and again, they arrived at her place and Jake walked her to the door. "I'm glad you took my advice," Jake said, indicating the heavy-duty dead bolt lock Sam was working to open.

She huffed and stabbed again at the lock with the key. "I just hope I don't have to get in quickly," she said, clearly frustrated, "it takes me ten minutes to get the damn thing open."

At last, the door swung open and she turned to him. "Thanks for today, Jake, it was fun. It's been a long time since I've been on the lake."

"I'm sorry it ended the way it did. Are you sure you're all right? How's your wrist?" He hadn't missed the way she'd winced when she turned the doorknob.

"Fine, fine," she waved his concern aside. She paused in the doorway and studied him, considering.

"Would you like to come in?"

Very much, he thought to himself, but reigned in his pleasure at the invitation and settled for an easy nod as he stepped inside.

The house was blessedly cool, a relief from the day that had gotten warmer and muggier as the afternoon passed to evening. Clouds were gathering over the lake and it appeared as if a storm was on its way.

"I was going to spend the evening in the shop getting a little more repair work done but I think maybe I'll leave it until tomorrow. I've actually accomplished more than I thought I would, most everything is cleaned up and I've made some progress with the kids' projects..." She stopped herself, realizing she was rambling to cover her nerves.

Jake moved to the windows and looked out over the lake. Sam looked at him, unsure of what to do or say. Her idea had been to make it clear to Jake that today was just about friendship. She was pretty sure she had failed...miserably. As she remembered the look on his face when he'd seen her in her swimsuit and then his concern when he thought she was seriously hurt, she worried he had entirely different ideas. Since she felt like she needed a little distance she said, "I think I'll run upstairs and change."

Jake turned and caught the brief look of panic that flitted across her face. "Let's take a walk down to the lake first," he said as he held out his hand for hers.

Sam debated with herself then took a step forward and took hold of his hand. That same little jolt she'd felt the first time she touched him was back and had her tensing. Determined not to make a fool out of herself yet again, she kept her hand in his and led him outside towards the lake.

Rigi followed them out the door and quickly found a tennis ball in the yard. She ran circles around them with the ball in her mouth until Sam relented, took the ball, and fired it—as best she could with her left hand—across the yard. The dog was off like a shot, running so fast she was unable to slow herself and had to double back to pick up the ball she overran. Sam gave the ball a couple more tosses before walking out onto the dock with Jake and sitting on the bench overlooking the lake.

Clouds continued to gather, swirling and darkening. Many of the day's boaters had taken notice, as the lake was much less crowded than it had been earlier. The few that remained, Sam figured, would wait for the first raindrops or clap of thunder before heading for shore.

"Could be a bad storm tonight," Jake said, looking up at the sky.

"I used to love storms when I was a kid. I remember hoping the power would go out so we could light candles and play with flashlights. I still kind of love them but now I think about things like damage to the house and what will happen if the power stays out for a long time. Sometimes it's no fun to grow up."

"But sometimes it is." Jake leaned over and kissed her, something he'd been wanting to do all day.

The kiss took Sam by surprise. She started to resist then gave in, melting against Jake as he put his arms around her and took the kiss deeper. She wasn't sure how much time passed before Jake slowly pulled away and positioned her so her head rested on his shoulder. They sat quietly, both lost in their own thoughts, until Rigi decided she'd had enough lying on the dock and it was time to play. She dropped the tennis ball in Jake's lap and looked up expectantly.

"Oh, Rigi, knock it off," Sam scolded. "I'm sorry, she's rather selfish and quite convinced everyone loves her," she said with an exasperated look at her dog. Rigi just panted and tilted her head, quivering with excitement when Jake took the ball in his hand. He threw it far into the yard and the dog dashed happily after it.

Jake and Sam slowly made their way back toward the house with Jake continuing to entertain the dog by throwing the ball in all different directions. "One more time," he told her as they reached the door. He threw the ball into the trees and they watched Rigi wind her way into the wooded area.

"Can I take you out to dinner tonight, Sam?" Jake asked, not wanting the evening to end.

"I don't feel much like going out." The disappointment in his eyes didn't surprise her but her own disappointment at the thought of him leaving did. "How about staying and helping me grill some hamburgers? Do you think we can beat the storm?"

"Sounds like a good idea. I'll get the grill started and we'll have burgers on the table before the first raindrop falls." He smiled and threw an arm around her shoulders.

"Where's Rigi?" Sam asked, realizing she hadn't returned after Jake threw the ball into the trees. "Rigi!" she called then whistled loudly for the dog.

Soon she appeared, trotting happily out of the trees with something other than a tennis ball clamped tightly in her mouth. "What have you got there, girl?"

Sam was reaching for what looked like a dirty rag when Jake ordered, "Wait!" Sam stopped in her tracks and looked curiously at Jake who was heading for the dog, talking softly with his hand held out.

"What is it? What are you doing?"

"That's a good girl," Jake crooned, rubbing Rigi on the head and gently easing the rag from her mouth, taking care to hold it by the corner only.

"Jake, what's up? What do you want with some dirty old rag? It's covered in mud."

"I don't think it's mud," Jake said as he carefully held up what turned out to be a t-shirt. "I think it's blood."

"Oh, well, it's probably been here for ages…" She couldn't help it, she glanced around nervously.

"From the looks of it, the blood is relatively fresh, that's probably why Rigi found it. It was twisted up pretty tightly like it was wrapped around something," Jake continued, more to himself than to Sam. "Hold on to the dog, I'm going to take a quick look around."

Sam held tight to Rigi's collar and waited less than patiently while Jake made his way to the tree line and disappeared from sight. Her anxiety increased as the minutes passed and Jake didn't return. She was just ready to follow after him when he emerged, brow furrowed and clearly deep in thought.

"Jake…?"

"Let's go inside." He took her by the hand and led the way.

"What is it? What did you find?" She couldn't keep the fear from bubbling up and knew he heard it in her voice.

"When we're inside."

She wanted to argue but sensed it would be futile.

"Stay put for just a minute, I'll be right back. Please, Sam," he added when he saw her eyes flare.

Annoyed, she cursed under her breath and paced the kitchen while Jake went out to his car. She saw him put the stained t-shirt in a plastic bag and make a call on his cell phone. The arguments she had ready died on her lips when he returned and she saw the look on his face.

"Jake, tell me what's going on," she said, half demanding, half pleading.

"Sit down." Looking over her shoulder at him, she moved to the sofa. When she sat, he sat next to her and took her hands. "I called the office to get someone out here to take a look around the woods. Someone was out there recently, there's an area with some blood on the ground and, in addition to the t-shirt, I found a knife."

She gasped. "What kind of knife? Where is it?"

"For now, it's where I found it. I didn't want to disturb the area more than necessary. Marc's on his way out here with evidence bags, a camera…we'll take a closer look around when he gets here."

Sam stood and began pacing again, her mind racing. "So, you're thinking whoever vandalized my shop was in the woods and left behind a bloody t-shirt and a knife? That seems pretty stupid. What, he leaves clues full of his DNA so you can catch him? Wants to make it as easy as possible for you?" She was nearly shouting, her anger at being a target fueling her tirade.

Since he understood how quickly anger could, and often did, turn to fear and panic, Jake spoke calmly. "First of all, I don't know for certain the shirt and the knife belong to the same person. Even if they do, I don't know

111

if that person is the one responsible for what's been going on here. Second, using DNA to catch someone isn't quite as easy as television would make it seem. If a person has no prior criminal history, their DNA isn't part of the database so there's no way a sample obtained at a crime scene will match any existing data."

She studied him, trying to decipher the look on his face. "Then what do you hope to find out there?"

"It's standard procedure. We'll take a look around, see if there is any additional physical evidence, distinguishing footprints." He looked out the window and frowned. "The rain won't help." Raindrops had begun pelting the windows and the sky seemed to darken as they watched.

"Who do you think is doing this?"

"I don't have any suspects yet. Hopefully we find something in the woods that will help me get closer."

Sam jumped at the knock on the door then berated herself for doing so. She simply refused to be frightened in her own home. She waved away Jake's offer to answer the knock and, after a quick glance out the window at the young man in uniform, opened the door to Marc. Jake introduced the two, made a few notes in the incident book Marc had brought with him, then the two men donned rain gear and headed out leaving Sam to stew.

As much as she didn't want to, she couldn't keep her thoughts from drifting to the kids from Project Strong Start and wondering if one of them could be responsible. She would defend them with her last breath but knew she had to be reasonable and if Jake found evidence suggesting one of them, she'd have to accept it. She ran her students through her mind again and couldn't find anything that worried her. Except Zach.

Oh, how she didn't want to believe he could be responsible but his behavior had her second-guessing herself. He was so secretive, so unwilling to talk to her— or to any of the other kids, for that matter. And there was the fact that it had looked an awful lot like a knife he had tried to hide from her in class. What she couldn't come up with was a reason. Why target her? Did he think he could steal from her? Was it just to be hurtful?

Realizing she was coming close to assigning blame where she had no reason to, she decided she needed to busy herself so quickly showered and changed clothes then set about making sandwiches for Jake and Marc since the planned barbecue was obviously not happening. She had a plate of sandwiches, fruit, vegetables, a pitcher of iced tea, and a pot of coffee ready when the two returned from the woods. "So?" she demanded when they got inside and out of their rain jackets and boots.

"There wasn't much to find, I'm afraid. We bagged up the knife and took some soil samples we'll send to the lab along with the t-shirt but that's about it. Between the dog and the rain, any footprints that may have been there were long gone."

Sam ran her hand through her hair, clearly frustrated. "Do you think you'll learn anything from what you did find?"

"It's possible. I'd like to know if the blood on the shirt matches the blood on the ground. And, I'd like you to look at something."

"What?" she asked slowly, eyes darting from Jake to Marc. Marc dropped his gaze to the floor and Sam's stomach twisted.

"The knife. You said you thought maybe one of the kids had a knife with him during one of your sessions. Do you think you'd recognize it?"

"Jake!" she hissed and looked toward Marc who still had his head down, clearly wishing he were someplace else. She wanted to shout that he shouldn't have said anything, that she had told him those things in confidence because she simply wasn't sure of anything, then realized of course he'd tell his deputy. "Fine, I'll look at it but I doubt I can tell you anything. I just saw something silver that I thought *could* be a knife."

While Jake went for the bag he had left by the front door, Sam told Marc to help himself to the food spread out on the kitchen table. "Thank you, Ms. Taylor. Maybe just a cup of coffee." He looked toward Jake before continuing. "I have a date tonight, taking Sarah out to dinner...soon, hopefully."

Softening at the blush rising on Marc's cheeks, Sam smiled. "Is Sarah your girlfriend?"

"Been together almost five years now. She's amazing, just about finished with her degree in social work."

"Good for you, that's nice," she replied sincerely. "Is she from Misty Lake?"

"No, she lives about fifteen miles away in Fox Grove. She has cousins here in town, that's how I met her."

Jake returned with the knife, safely encased inside a plastic evidence bag, and held it out for Sam. She didn't take it but inched closer to get a better view. It was silver, the blade anyway, the handle black. The blade was extended but looked like it would fit into the handle. "Is this a switchblade?" Sam asked, not exactly sure what a switchblade even was.

"That's one name for it. And it's illegal in Minnesota. Could it be what you saw?"

"I don't know. I really don't know. I told you, I didn't see much more than a flash of something silver. It was small, could have been a knife but I'd have said it could have been a phone, too, if I hadn't seen Zach's phone a dozen times before and known he has a green case on it. I'm sorry I can't be more help."

"It's okay, it was a long shot."

The conversation stalled and Marc cleared his throat. "If there's nothing more here, Sheriff, maybe I'll head back?"

"Sure, Marc. Take this stuff back to the office and lock it up until we can ship it out on Monday then take off. You're already pulling overtime tonight."

"Thanks, Boss. Ms. Taylor," he tipped his hat at Sam as he grabbed the gear and made his way back out into the rain, a little spring in his step if Sam wasn't mistaken.

She was smiling when she turned to Jake. "Nice kid. He's in love, you know."

"In love?" Perplexed, he looked at Sam. "Who? You mean Marc?"

"Yes, I mean Marc. He has a date with his girlfriend Sarah tonight so he was anxious to get out of here. They've been dating for five years and from the impression I got, he's head-over-heels in love with her."

"And you learned all that when?"

"Just a minute ago when you were digging the knife out of your case over there." She waved toward the door while Jake continued to stare at her.

"He told you all that in the two minutes it took me to get the knife?"

"It doesn't take long to learn about someone. Don't you ever ask him about his life outside of work?"

"Sure. I know he likes to fish, both in the summer and in the winter. Puts a fish house out on the lake every winter as soon as the ice is thick enough. He may have mentioned a girl going fishing with him…" He scratched his head trying to remember if he had ever asked about a girlfriend and decided probably not. That was personal, not like talking fishing or baseball.

"Oh, Jake." She shook her head and chuckled. "Have a sandwich. Those burgers are going to have to wait for another day."

After they had eaten, cleaned up, and agreed to stop discussing police business for the evening, they sat in the living room and watched the storm rage. Lighting crackled in the inky sky and thunder shook the house. Rigi paced nervously, returning frequently to Sam for a reassuring pat.

Jake loved this, sitting in the dark, watching the storm with Sam snuggled next to him on the sofa. He imagined them doing the same when the leaves changed to crimson and gold, when the snow fell, when the ice turned black before it melted into spring. He caught himself. Since when did he think about being with a woman and imagine just sitting on the sofa? He wasn't quite sure what it was about Sam that made him think of those things, of doing the everyday things together, but it seemed natural. To get his mind away from bizarre domestic fantasies, he asked, "Was today really the first time you've been on, or in, the lake since you moved here?"

"Yes, I guess I just didn't want to face it and all the memories. I need to get past it, it's just taking some time."

"Did you learn to swim here? Looked to me like you could have kept going clear across the lake this afternoon."

Sam smiled at that, recalling her embarrassment and the fact that the thought had crossed her mind. "Learned to swim and learned to love it here. My older cousins didn't know what hit them the year I outswam all of them. It was fun having something I was the best at, we were pretty competitive."

"I get that. Growing up with three brothers, and a feisty little sister, more or less everything we did was a contest. I don't think any of us could ever come close to keeping up with you in the water, though."

"I guess I was fast, once. Now it's more for exercise. My days of competing are long behind me."

"Tell me about it. Where did you compete?"

"You don't really want to hear my boring stories," but she continued when he nodded his encouragement. "I started swimming competitively when I was about eleven, I guess. Age group stuff with the local swim club. I swam all through high school, went to state, got a couple medals, then went down to Florida at my grandfather's insistence and swam one year in college. That's about it."

"Why just one year?"

She sighed. "I didn't want to go...didn't want to go to college or be away from home. I told my grandfather I would make a living doing woodworking. He wouldn't hear of it. I was offered a scholarship to swim in Florida, he insisted I go, give it a try. It was a long, miserable year for me. I didn't swim well, mostly because I didn't want to be there, and I needed to be home with my grandfather and my brother."

Jake noticed the sadness creep back into her voice when she spoke of her brother and grandfather and gave her hand a squeeze. "When you came home after the first year did you start a woodworking business?" He was curious about her past, the good and the bad.

"No, not right away. My grandfather and I argued fiercely about school. He felt so strongly I should have an education that I finally gave in. We compromised on a technical school that offered classes in woodworking, among other things, along with business classes. It ended up being a good thing. I even told my grandfather so…after about five years." She laughed at the memory. "I couldn't let him know too soon that he had been right."

It didn't take much imagination to picture Sam ten years younger and fighting with her grandfather about her future. If she was half as stubborn and determined as she was now, her grandfather must have been a hell of a man to have won the argument.

"How about you, Mr. Sheriff? How'd you end up doing what you're doing?"

"I guess I always wanted to do what my dad did. I watched him go to work every day dressed in his uniform, carrying a gun, and I thought he was so cool. Pretty heady stuff for a kid. What I didn't see was the worry my mom dealt with on a daily basis. Looking back, I can see that she did a good job of hiding it from us. Being the wife, or mother, of a cop isn't easy. I didn't learn that until I told her I wanted to go to school for a degree in law enforcement. It took me, with a lot of help from my dad, weeks to convince her it wasn't the dumbest idea I had ever come up with."

She sat up straighter and looked at him. "I didn't know your dad was the sheriff before you. How didn't I know that? It seems like everyone I talk to is more than anxious to share town lore and gossip."

He nodded at her assessment of the town's residents. Pretty accurate, he figured. "It's no secret, I'm not sure why it hasn't come up until now. My father retired about three years ago, I ran for sheriff and was elected. My brothers would tell you the only reason I won was that half the people who voted saw the name McCabe and assumed they were voting for my father again. I suppose there could be something to that, not that I'd ever admit it to them."

Sam laughed as she considered this new information. She wasn't sure why, but the fact that Jake followed in his father's footsteps made her look at him a little differently. She had always viewed cops as distant, tough, if not harsh, cold, and unemotional. They would have to be in order to do their job. Even without having met his father, she felt certain he wasn't like that. It would take loving parents to raise a big family with children like Jake…and Joe. And a child didn't want to be like his father unless he admired his father.

"What are you thinking so hard about?" Jake asked, taking in her furrowed brow and slightly narrowed eyes.

"Nothing," she lied. Then, before he could ask any more questions, "Did you work with your dad before he retired?"

"I worked as a cop for a couple years in the Twin Cities after I got through school then came back up here and, yeah, worked as a deputy for my dad. I learned a lot from him in a few years. Things are different here than in the Cities, a slower way of life, but people still do stupid and dangerous things. My dad taught me how to separate the stupid but harmless from the stupid and not so harmless."

She nodded and leaned her head on his shoulder, gazing back out the window at the lake, lit up with frequent flashes of lightning. She was starting to see him, and maybe all cops, in a little different light. She had always respected police officers, realized their job was a difficult, dangerous, and often thankless one, but had had some negative experiences that weren't so easy to put behind her. It was easier to think of them not as fathers, mothers, sons, and daughters but rather as autonomous, even faceless, individuals. Not fair, she decided.

She turned her head, looked into Jake's dark eyes, barely visible in the dark of the storm, and made a quick decision. She was lonely, had been for a long time, and the companionship of a man, a good man, didn't seem like such a bad idea any more. Nothing serious, she told herself, she'd see to that, but maybe a date here and there, someone to spend a warm day on the lake or a stormy evening with, someone to talk to, surely there wasn't any harm in that. Keeping her eyes on his, she slowly leaned her head down and pressed her lips to his.

The fact that this was the first time Sam had initiated any sort of physical contact other than the simplest hand holding was not lost on Jake as he put his arms around her, ran one hand up her back and into her long, thick hair. The kiss deepened and Jake fought for control as he fisted his hand in her hair and gently pulled. His lips traced a line down her neck and he felt her tremble under his hands.

The lightning and thunder had nothing on the feelings pounding through her, Sam thought, as Jake trailed kisses down her neck, onto her shoulder. A soft moan escaped her lips as his hand found its way under her shirt and caressed her back. She shifted her weight to mold herself more tightly to Jake when all at once the room lit up in a flash, thunder cracked so loudly the pictures on the wall shook, and Rigi propelled herself from the floor onto the couch landing right on top of Sam. Whining and panting, the dog wedged her way between Sam and Jake and buried her head in Sam's lap.

Sam couldn't help herself, she started laughing. Jake's expression went from shocked to frustrated to annoyed in a matter of seconds. He let his head fall back onto the pillow and blew out a deep breath before looking at her and shrugging. Still laughing, Sam settled the dog between them and stroked her silky fur until she calmed. Together, the three watched the storm run its course until, at some point, all three relaxed enough to fall asleep.

He sat in the car, far enough around the curve in the road that he couldn't be seen from the house. He tipped the bottle to his lips again, and fumed. He'd seen the kid from the sheriff's office show up, knew they were heading back out to the woods. Damn, he should have realized before today that he'd left the t-shirt and knife behind. But when that stupid mutt had come charging into the woods when he had been there with the raccoons, his only choice had been to run. He figured he was lucky it had been late and the woman had called the dog back inside quickly or he may have had to act sooner than planned.

No more mistakes, he promised himself. He'd be more careful. Besides, what could they learn from the knife and an old t-shirt? He had worn gloves, there'd be no fingerprints. He was smarter than they were, he knew that. Idiot backwoods cops, he'd outsmart all of them. Just like he had outsmarted the big city cops. His confidence buoyed as the bottle emptied.

10

Sam let herself sleep in a little on Sunday morning. She wasn't sure who had stirred first last night, although she knew it wasn't the dog. Sometime around one o'clock Sam had realized she could no longer feel her leg below the point where Rigi had decided she needed to lie. She squirmed to free herself and had discovered Jake looking at her in the dark. The night had cleared and the moonlight lit his face enough for her to make out the sharp angles and sleepy eyes. Once they untangled themselves from the dog, Jake had decided he had better head home. It had been a good night and Sam smiled remembering the long, slow kiss on the dock and the brief, but passionate one, on the sofa.

It was the in between that had her frowning, climbing out of bed, and wincing as her sore muscles reminded her of the terrifying tube ride. The discovery in the woods concerned her, more than she had let on the night before. Easier to act angry than have Jake worrying she was going to collapse into a helpless heap. She hoped he had some answers soon as the uncertainty was starting to take its toll.

The morning was clear, all traces of the previous night's storm gone, and as she made her way to the shop she couldn't help but pause to take in the fresh, clean smell and the sounds of the birds chirping happily in the trees. The temperature had dropped considerably and the oppressive humidity had vanished along with the storm. The lake shone a brilliant blue again, a far cry from the dark grey churning monster of the night before. Sam unlocked the door to the shop and couldn't stop the sigh when she took in the chaos…much more orderly chaos than a couple of days ago, but chaos nonetheless. Well, no point in crying over spilt milk, as her grandfather used to say. She pushed up her sleeves and got to work.

She spent a couple of hours repairing and rebuilding parts of the kids' projects. After discussing it with Jake, she had reluctantly agreed not to try to hide the vandalism from them, rather tell them straight out what had happened and watch for reactions. She still didn't like it, it seemed like setting them up, but he had convinced her that finding out who was responsible was the main priority right now. She was going to do some repairs to their projects but decided to leave some of the work for the kids themselves. A good lesson, she figured, as there was always something that needed fixing and knowing how to do it was not only satisfying, it was just plain smart.

She hammered, sawed, sanded, and glued, working not only on the repair work for her class, but also further repairing her workbenches and cabinets. Tired and ready for a lunch break, she muttered an oath as the last bolt she needed to reattach the vise to the workbench slipped out of her hand and rolled out of sight. Sighing heavily, she got down on her knees to locate the errant bolt. Out of reach, of course. She crawled under the bench, stretched, and got it with her fingertips. Pulling back, her head brushed the underside of the bench and something rustled. Paper, probably a receipt or warranty document, she figured. Feeling her way above her head, she ripped the paper loose, stole a glance, and froze.

She recognized the writing immediately, she had seen it her whole life. And her grandfather had always called her Samantha, never Sam. Her hand shook and she sat where she was, still half under the bench. How long she looked at the envelope, she would never recall. A thousand thoughts flashed through her mind and nearly as many emotions. She wanted to tear it up, almost did, but deep down knew she wouldn't, couldn't. It had to be her 'letter,' the one she had wanted so badly eight months ago.

Why here? Why hide it from her? The answers were inside, she guessed, but wasn't sure she was ready for them. She finally crawled out from under the bench, shoved the envelope in her pocket, and headed for the house.

Sam made herself a sandwich, sorted her mail, tidied the kitchen, and brushed Rigi. And gave the letter a wide berth. Sure she glanced at it when she passed the table, who wouldn't? And she may have picked it up and held it up to the light when she was wiping down the table but it had to be moved in order to clean and it wasn't her fault the sun was shining so brightly through the kitchen window. But, she didn't open it. Eventually she went back

125

to the shop and worked, hard, trying to put it out of her mind.

Later that evening after she had finished everything in the shop she wanted to get done before morning, played in the yard with Rigi, showered, and fixed herself some dinner, Sam found herself unable to relax. The movie she tried watching held her interest for all of fifteen minutes before she turned it off. The numbers in her checkbook may have as well been hieroglyphics for as much sense as they made when she attempted to pay bills and balance her accounts. She thought about going for a swim since yesterday had made her realize how much she missed the water and since swimming was always a guaranteed way to zap her stress, but it was getting dark. She considered calling her cousin, Susan. They hadn't talked in a couple weeks and Sam missed her. But Susan would tell her to open the envelope and get it over with and Sam didn't know if she could face it alone.

That was it, really. She didn't want to be alone when she read whatever it was her grandfather had to say. It hit her like a brick to realize how alone she really was. And how much she missed her girlfriends. She hadn't let herself think about them much, rationalizing that there wasn't anything she could do about it with all of them in Chicago and she here in the middle of the woods in Minnesota. Sure, they talked on the phone occasionally but she missed the face to face…the girl talk, the laughs, and the unwavering support. They had been there for her when she lost her brother and then her grandfather. Even when she had been despondent, distant, and sometimes downright mean, her girls got her through. They would get her through this, too, she knew, if they could.

Tina would joke and make light of the situation even when Sam knew, deep down, her heart would be breaking to see Sam hurting. Jess would make pro and con lists, analyzing the situation to death until Sam couldn't stand it any more and tore the envelope open. And Carrie would hold her hand and support her no matter what her decision. Yes, she missed them.

The decision to keep to herself and avoid any and all personal relationships in Misty Lake seemed less sensible now than it had a few months ago. She had lost so much, all those closest to her. Everyone she had loved the most had been taken from her. If she was being completely honest with herself, leaving her girlfriends, her cousins, her aunt and uncle behind hadn't really been that hard. She loved them all dearly and realized now that putting some distance between herself and those she cared most about was her way of protecting herself from more hurt. The easy way out, really. If she didn't care so deeply, it wouldn't hurt so deeply if—no, when—something happened to another one of them.

As she looked again at the letter, she admitted that maybe she had been wrong. Not having anyone in her life meant facing everything, including this, alone. Was that what she wanted? Is that what her parents, her brother, her grandfather would have wanted for her? No, she was sure of that.

Except for hanging out with Jake a couple of times, she hadn't spent time with anyone since arriving in town. It was time to move forward with her life, deep down she knew it. Sam furrowed her brow, tapped her nails nervously on the counter, and considered. Could she do it? Could she open herself up again and risk heartache?

She poured herself a glass of wine and settled into her favorite chair to think things through, almost pleased to have a problem to chew on so as to forget the letter for a while.

So, how did one even go about making friends? What in theory seemed like something simple, in reality seemed daunting. People made friends at work but she wasn't working someplace where that was a possibility. She didn't have any relatives in town to invite her over, introduce her to people. She supposed she could ask Kathleen, the woman really did seem to know everyone in town, but even thinking about it made her laugh to herself. What was she making her out to be? Some kind of girlfriend matchmaker?

Karen, Jake's sister-in-law, had been friendly, nice. They were about the same age, Sam figured, probably had other things in common. It was a possibility. She had worked with Lynn at First National Bank when she first came to Misty Lake and needed to set up both personal and business accounts. Lynn had been pleasant and talkative, had even asked Sam if she wanted to join her at her monthly Bunco game, but Sam had declined. She wasn't sure what Bunco was but figured it would have involved socializing which, at the time, was out of the question. She should go back to church, another thing she had avoided since her grandfather's death. People at church were usually friendly, maybe she could stay for coffee and mingle a little, she'd meet people that way. She promised herself she'd think about it. What else? She knew Jake had a sister…

Then it hit her. She did have one friend—Jake. Granted, not a girlfriend, but someone who had already proven he would listen, offer support if needed. Could she call him? Was it too late? Would he make more of it than she intended? She paced and looked at the clock. Picked up her cell phone then set it down. Talked to Rigi, asked her opinion, and was rewarded with a loud snore. Finally, she picked up the phone again and, this time, dialed. The letter was making her crazy, she reasoned, as evidenced by the last hour spent dreaming up ways to make friends and then talking to her dog and actually expecting a response. Phase one of her 'Sam Makes Some Friends' campaign would start now.

11

Monday morning dawned warm and sunny, a beautiful day in Misty Lake. Jake loved his town, always had. Even when his friends had talked about getting out after high school, he had always known he wanted to stay. He loved the sense of community, a feeling that remained even as the town grew. He appreciated those who had been there for years, working hard to keep the town's economy growing. And he was proud to work for the people who had put their faith in him as sheriff.

As he walked out of his apartment on the second floor of a refurbished building on the town's main street, he took in the morning's activity. Rosie's Diner was filling up with those looking for a home-cooked breakfast or a leisurely cup of coffee. If his father wasn't already there, he would be soon. Jake remembered how, a few weeks into his father's retirement, his mother had said, in her tone that left no room for debate, she needed some peace and quiet in the mornings and his father needed a reason to get up and get moving. He was interfering with the routine she had had in place for over thirty years, she had claimed. Knowing better than to get on the wrong side of Anna's Italian temper, Sean had spent every weekday morning since having a cup of coffee at Rosie's with friends who went back to the days when they were the ones raising hell in town.

Bob Bell, the president of First National Bank, was opening up and gave Jake a wave. Further down the street Jake could see a steady stream of people filing in and out of The Whole Bean, the town's trendier, and wildly successful, coffee shop. Megan Perkins, a year behind Jake in school and his on-again, off-again girlfriend for most of their high school years, had worked hard to build the business after her husband of only two years had left her with a newborn baby. Jake and Megan had remained friends and he was proud of her and her success.

As Jake made his way down the stairs that wrapped around the outside of his apartment building and to his car parked behind, he saw Lynn from First National along with other harried-looking parents urging their kids to hurry into the church that housed Precious Ones Daycare. Lynn had one hand of each of her two-year-old twins gripped tightly in her own and somehow managed to hang on to them while juggling two backpacks, stuffed animals, and blankets. The woman was a superhero, Jake thought, shaking his head.

Yes, he loved his town. And if it seemed a little sunnier or a little happier this morning, well, that may have something to do with the call he had from Sam the previous night. There had been that brief moment of panic when he saw her name on his cell phone and his thoughts jumped to trouble, but it hadn't taken long to determine that wasn't the case. Sam had called him, he thought to himself, and couldn't hold back the grin.

She had been a little cryptic, first saying she wanted him to come over last night, then changing her mind and asking him to come over tonight. She had said there was something she needed help with but hadn't elaborated. He had tried asking some questions but she had deflected most of them. In the end, Jake had talked her in to going out to dinner since she had already fed him on two occasions and he wasn't about to let it become three before he had the chance to reciprocate. She had started to refuse and then, almost as if she was waging some kind of internal war, had done a one-eighty and agreed to dinner at The Misty Lake Lodge, Jake's favorite place on the lake. They'd have a nice dinner, some wine, candlelight, all those things women seemed to like and, he figured, she hadn't had much of lately. He hadn't looked forward to a date this much in a long time. Maybe since that first time he had convinced Megan Perkins to go to a movie with him and they had never made it into the theater. God, he thought to himself, that was a long time ago. He had had to do some quick thinking when his dad found her sweater in the backseat of his car the next day.

He was still chuckling to himself as he made his way into his office and picked up a ringing phone. Pete Griffin, his friend from the Minneapolis Police Department, greeted him in his booming voice.

"How the hell are ya, Jake? Still busy bustin' speeders and guys without fishing licenses?"

Playing along with their long-standing joke, Jake

shot back, "You know me, every illegal fisherman's worst nightmare. How about you? Still got task forces, committees, and community groups telling you what to do?"

"Same old, same old. I guess we all do what we gotta do." Then growing more serious, "So, what's going on up there? Sounds like you're having some trouble you think might be gang related?"

Jake filled Pete in on what was happening and gave him the names of the kids in Sam's class, including Tyler since he'd been tight with Zach, knowing if any of them were heavy into gang activity, Pete would know them.

Pete was quiet for a minute then began, "Well, a couple names stand out. First, the Salentine kid. Does he have an older brother, William, or Blade, as he's known?"

"Yeah, that's his brother. I've heard a little about him but tell me what you know."

"Blade's been running with a gang for about eight years. They're bad news, Jake. Blade's bad news. He disappeared about six weeks ago. I've talked to departments in Milwaukee, Chicago, Detroit, lots of places this gang of his is known to have a presence, told them to be on the lookout. So far I haven't heard anything. We like him for a couple murders but haven't had any luck getting witnesses to come forward. They're all scared. I don't know Jimmy, but these guys tend to try to get family members to join, make it hard to say no."

"I don't like it that no one knows where he is. Can you get me a photo? I want to make sure we're on the lookout here."

"Consider it done." Jake could hear him clicking

away, probably emailing a file while he talked. "Now, the other name I heard from you that raised a flag was Tyler Loomis. Not really my area as he's not a known gang member, but the kid has been in enough trouble that we all know him. He's been in and out of juvie, stands to do some hard time if we can pin a rape on him. I didn't know he was up there for the summer."

"From what I hear from the director at the camp, he shouldn't be. They normally don't take kids with records like his but apparently his probation officer finagled it. So, what's your take on this? Could one of these kids be responsible?"

"Could be, yes. But I don't think it's likely. Frankly, it'd be pretty small time stuff for either Salentine or Loomis. Seems to me the more likely scenario is that one of the other kids in this Ms. Taylor's class has something against her. I didn't recognize any of the other names but I could do some checking for you, pull some files."

Pete's suspicions mirrored his own and Jake's anxiety increased. The thought of Sam alone with the group had him more and more concerned. "Thanks, Pete, I'd appreciate it. I got an overview from the camp director but if there's more, I'd like to know."

"Not a problem, I'll get on it today."

"Let me ask you this. Assuming the older Salentine has made his way up here and has made contact with his brother, do you think the vandalism could be some kind of gang initiation?"

"Not really typical initiation stuff we see from the gang Salentine is in with, it's usually some pretty serious assault, even murder. But, if he's working on his brother and has something to hold over the kid's head to scare him, he could be easing him into bigger stuff. It's not out of the question."

"Yeah," Jake was nodding as he twirled a pencil between his fingers. It was about what he had expected to hear.

"You're looking at someone from the camp...what about locals? Someone who doesn't like this lady?"

"That's the thing, she's new in town, doesn't really know anyone except the kids she volunteered to work with. The attacks, especially the last one, have felt personal. A lot of damage, including to some stuff the kids were working on, things she's teaching them how to build. They were stored in a cabinet, had all been pulled out and pretty much wrecked. Not exactly a stretch to think one of them could be responsible."

"Makes sense. Well, buddy, gotta go protect the citizens of this fine city. Good luck, let me know if I can help you out with anything else."

"All right, Pete, thanks again. If you can dig up any information you think is pertinent, send it my way. And get your butt up here one of these days, it's been a long time. Tell you what, I'll even spring for a fishing license so I won't have to write you a ticket."

With a laugh, Pete signed off and Jake stared out his window, going over the facts he had so far on the case and hoping for a break...soon.

It had been a long day filled with routine paperwork, frustrating dead ends on Sam's case, and a particularly ugly incident of road rage that had resulted in two arrests and a shattered window on Jake's patrol car thanks to an errant swing with a tire iron. Jake was more than ready to put it all behind him as he drove to pick up Sam for their date. When she answered the door in a short, white sundress, some strappy sandals that made her legs seem to go on forever, and with her hair loose and curling riotously around her shoulders, he found it hard to remember his name let alone the miserable events of his workday. Unable to resist, he didn't even manage a hello before he grabbed her by the waist and closed his mouth over hers.

Sam's breath caught and she had to grab his arms for support. The jolt was there again along with something else she couldn't quite put a finger on. Desire, yes, but a calm at the same time. A feeling of closure, as if she had been searching long and hard for something and had finally arrived where she was meant to be. A contented sigh started in her throat before she caught herself.

Whoa! Sam jerked back and stared at Jake. Where had that come from? She definitely wasn't looking for permanent, for home, for…the L word, but damn, if that wasn't what it had felt like for a moment. A little dazed, she didn't realize Jake was talking to her.

"Sam, everything okay?"

"What? Oh, yes, fine. You just…just surprised me, that's all." Needing a minute, she turned and headed for the closet. "I need to grab a sweater," she mumbled.

Jake frowned after her. Had he screwed things up? He shouldn't have grabbed at her like that, should have at least tried to act somewhat civilized. She had just looked so good, he was actually proud of himself for keeping it at only a kiss. But Sam was smiling as she made her way back with a sweater and purse in hand. She patted the dog on the head then looked up and smiled even brighter. "Ready?"

Conversation on the drive to the restaurant was limited to small talk, the next heat wave bearing down on most of the Midwest, and the Twins' resounding win over the White Sox. All the while, Sam was struggling mightily to make sense of her reaction to Jake's kiss. She hardly knew him. Any feelings other than friendship and maybe a mild interest in a little more than friendship were ludicrous, she told herself. It was only when Jake asked her about her day with the kids and their reactions to the damage that she put personal thoughts out of her mind and focused on Jake's investigation.

"They were all surprised, confused, upset. Even though things are pretty well cleaned up, they all noticed the paint and stain spills on the floor, the dents and dings to some of the equipment. And, of course, they saw the damage to their own projects. Jackson took it the hardest, I'd say. He was angry and, even though he tried to hide it, sad. When he looked at his jewelry box his face just fell. I assured him it could be repaired, or he could start over, whatever he wanted, but he seemed upset, distracted, all during class."

"So no one had an odd reaction, anything that struck you as suspicious?"

Sam fought the urge to lash out, to insist the kids were all innocent. She gave him a long look then replied as calmly as she could, "No, they all seemed bothered by what happened. Zach reacted the least but that wasn't a surprise, he's always distant. Oh, and Jimmy wasn't there today. Stu brought a message from one of the counselors saying he wasn't feeling well so would be staying back at camp."

Jake's head snapped toward Sam. "Sick? Has he missed before because he's been sick?"

"No," Sam answered slowly. "What are you getting at, Jake? Everyone gets sick sometimes."

"Nothing. Just seems curious that he'd be out today after what happened, that's all."

"Jimmy's a good kid, Jake. He didn't do this."

Jake just nodded and let the subject drop as they pulled up to the restaurant. The dinner, candlelight, and wine seemed to relax Sam although Jake caught her looking at him kind of strangely a couple of times. When he asked, she changed the subject. The same way she did when he asked what it was she needed help with. So he kept the conversation light and enjoyed the evening.

Sam's mood changed quickly once they were back at her place. She seemed nervous, fidgety, as she let the dog out, offered him something to drink, turned on the TV, turned it off, and turned on music all the while wringing her hands and glancing towards the kitchen. Finally, Jake took both her hands tightly in his.

"Sam, what's going on?"

She took a deep breath then blurted out, "I found something in the shop yesterday. I didn't know what to do, couldn't face it alone, I guess. I didn't know who to call."

"Did you find something related to the vandalism? Something you think might tell us who's responsible?"

"No, no, nothing like that. It's...well, I found a letter. A letter from my grandfather." It sounded stupid when she said it out loud and Sam was suddenly embarrassed. "You know what? Let's just forget it."

"Why should we forget it? Did you learn

something upsetting?"

Embarrassed and uncomfortable, Sam was unable to meet Jake's eyes as she whispered, "I haven't read it yet."

Jake took her in his arms. "I can understand not wanting to be alone when you read the letter. I know you have questions, questions you thought would never be answered. It's got to be a little scary thinking some of the answers might be in there and that they might not be the answers you want."

How had he completely hit it on the head? She didn't think she could have put her own feelings into words better than Jake had just done. "Okay," she agreed, steeling herself and getting the letter from the back of the kitchen drawer where she had hidden it.

Her resolve wavered some when she held it in her hands again but she forced herself to sit down next to Jake and slide her finger under the flap easing the envelope open. Again, as if knowing her thoughts better than she did, he said, "I'll be right here. You read it, if you want to share any of it with me, fine. If not, that's fine, too."

Sam gave his hand a squeeze and unfolded the paper, taking in the lines of her grandfather's neat and precise handwriting. She had teased him, she remembered, about being the only doctor whose writing was legible. His reply had been, 'If you're going to do something, do it right, Samantha, even if it's something as simple as penmanship.' He was always teaching, giving her advice, she realized now. She told herself that no matter what she read it wouldn't change her feelings toward her grandfather. She loved him, she always had, and he had done his best raising two kids long after he thought school conferences and curfews were behind him. With a final glance at Jake, she began to read.

My Dearest Samantha,

My hope is that you're reading this when you need it the most. Since you've made your way to Misty Lake and found the home and workshop I left for you, that means I'm gone and you must be feeling very alone in the world. And, I'm sure you're angry with me as you have every right to be, but I hope you will read to the end and give me a chance to explain.

First, I love you, Samantha. You are an incredible woman and I have been proud of you since you were a child. You are kind, generous, and fiercely loyal. I love all of my grandchildren but you have always held a special place in my heart. The day we lost your parents and your grandmother was the worst day of my life but having you and Danny with me meant I still had a part of your father with me. Maybe it was selfish of me but I couldn't let you go.

I tried to give you a normal childhood, I hope I didn't do too poorly. Saying it was difficult losing your grandmother and your parents so suddenly would be a gross understatement. It was the hardest thing I've ever had to bear. But I was determined to give you and Danny as close to a normal life as I could. I know it wasn't always easy, especially when things with Danny got so difficult, but I did my best, Samantha, please know that. And there were many happy times. Try to remember them.

By now you know that I left letters for your cousins and I'm sure you were hurt when there wasn't one for you. I just didn't know how to put into words how badly I wanted you to come to Misty Lake and how much I hoped you would fall in love with the house and stay. I know you remember the happy times we had here when you were a child. I wanted that for you again. I'm sorry I couldn't talk about it years ago when you asked. It was just too painful. When you finally stopped asking, I was both relieved and sad. I didn't want your memories to fade but putting it behind me somehow made the loss a little more bearable. I know now I was wrong and hope you can forgive an old man the error of his ways.

There was some money from insurance policies and investments that I set aside, deciding to make do without it and raise you and your brother to appreciate what you had. The money that came from your parents' estates was always separate, half each for you and Danny to be held until you reached thirty years of age. None of that money went towards the building at Misty Lake. It's important to me that you understand I would never have made the decision on how to use any money that came from your parents. That was always meant for you and Danny to decide for yourselves. Now, I guess, it will be for you alone to decide.

The idea to rebuild here grew slowly. Once I saw how you took to woodworking, and how you seemed so certain it was what you wanted to do with your life, I wanted to give you what I could and instead of just refurbishing the cabin, I wanted to help you make a life here. But, I know what you do with your life is not my decision. If you decide to sell, to take the money and go someplace far away, please do so without regret. I would only want what you want. Make a life for yourself, Samantha, and make it a good one. Let yourself love again. You've had so much pain and loss in your life and I understand the desire to shut down and to shut out. I fought that demon myself but I had you and Danny to help me through. Let someone in; don't let fear keep you from happiness. It's no way to live.

I'm sure you've got to be wondering why I never told you about the home and workshop. I wanted to, especially after we lost Danny. I pictured the two of us working side by side in that beautiful shop, enough space for both of us to be working on our own projects, the separate room for painting and staining... and the panel saw! It was everything we had talked about and dreamed about. But, the truth is, I was too much of a coward. I was afraid to come back to Misty Lake with you. Afraid to face the past, the loss, the heartache. I came here a few times over the years, always unable to sell but not able to stay, either. My favorite times were the weeks we were all together at the lake and part of me wanted to come back, to make new memories, but I couldn't. I'm sorry I couldn't give that to you. Again, I hope you are able forgive me.

So, Samantha, make your decisions and do so with a clear conscience. Whatever you decide, you will make me proud. All I ask is that you let yourself truly live and love.

All my love,
Granddad

Sam read the letter twice before looking up and before realizing her face was wet with silent tears. She was a jumble of emotions, the letter having brought up feelings about her parents' death, her brother's death, her childhood, things she had tried to bury deep. As she stared out at the moonlit lake, she could imagine her grandfather feeling a lot of the same as he wrote the letter. He had never talked much about his feelings but Sam knew they were always there, close to the surface.

Did she feel better after reading the letter? A tough question, she thought. Better, in that she had some answers, at least answers as well as her grandfather had been able to provide them. Confused, as her grandfather had given her an okay to do as she pleased with the property. What did she want to do? She stared out at the lake as if it held answers. Finally, she looked over at Jake who was sitting silently, waiting. She gave him a small half smile and dropped her head onto his shoulder. She felt wiped out. His arm went around her and held on.

They talked, eventually. Sam shared some of the details of the letter but didn't ask Jake to read it. It felt too personal. She told him, though, that her grandfather talked about wanting to come back to Misty Lake but felt like he couldn't face it, with or without her.

"I guess I'm having a hard time not being angry about that. He couldn't face it yet expected me to. Rationally, I know he gave me all he had, all he could, while I was growing up and then this, at the end," she said, lifting her arms to take in all that surrounded her. "But he had to know how difficult it would be for me to come here alone."

"I think he did know, Sam, just didn't know what else to do. From what you've said, it sounds as though he struggled with how to handle things. I'm sure he didn't come to the decision easily."

"I know, but together we could have overcome the past so much easier! At least I could have," she added less forcefully.

"He was getting older. Maybe when he wrote the letter he knew he didn't have too much time left. Maybe he didn't want to throw something else at you so soon after you lost your brother and then have to face losing him in a strange place, a home that, even though it was new, held old memories. And this way it really is a fresh start. Assuming your grandfather had passed away here, at home, that would be something else you would have to face day after day."

Sam nodded. Jake made sense, she knew that, but she still felt somehow betrayed. Keeping so much from her, especially when it had been just the two of them dealing with Danny's death and struggling to move forward, seemed wrong. This would have given them something new to focus on, something to think about, something to do instead of spending endless days walking through the rooms where Danny had once lived and laughed.

Finally, she gave a sigh and stood. She wasn't going to solve everything tonight. She had things to think about, her future to think about, but it was going to take some time. A glance at the clock told her it was after midnight and she was exhausted. "Thank you for everything tonight, Jake. I enjoyed the dinner and appreciate you being here with me. It was really very kind of you and you've helped me look at some of what my grandfather said from a different perspective."

"I'm glad you asked, glad you felt like you could." Jake drew her close and kissed her, a slow tender kiss meant to soothe and relax. He wanted to ease the worry from her mind, to erase the sadness and distress from her eyes. He ran a hand up and down her back and felt the tension slowly leave her muscles. Reluctantly, he drew back and looked into her eyes. "I'll call you in the morning but promise me you'll call me earlier if you want to talk."

Sam nodded and gave her promise. She could share the worry, the unknown, with Jake. That's what friends were for, she reminded herself. And Jake was her friend. She would let him in and let him help. She smiled a little to herself as she thought back to the night before and her determination to find some friends and how her grandfather's letter had asked her to do just that.

12

The rest of the week was a blur for Sam. The temperature continued to climb and along with it, tension in her class. The kids' tempers were short, they were frustrated with their work and with each other. Jackson had started to repair his jewelry box but had been so unhappy with the way it looked, had started over and now was rushing to make up for lost time. Davis needled everyone, barely working on his project but finding fault with everyone else's. He managed to have both Katie and Jimmy in tears during one particularly long morning. Sam found herself looking forward to the end of the week and the midsummer break over the Fourth of July. The kids would be spending the week in the Boundary Waters and Sam would have a week to herself. They all needed a break.

The bright spot of the week came on Thursday morning when Katie came to class smiling and with a bounce in her step. She was going home. When the rest of the kids left on Friday for their camping trip, Katie would be heading home to her father who was out of the hospital and doing well enough to care for his children. Sam was happy for Katie. She helped her finish up her step stool and listened as Katie chatted excitedly. Even Davis couldn't dim her spirits as she told Sam about her apartment, her friends, and Blackie, the cat she hoped they would be able to get back from the neighbor who had taken him when her dad had first gotten sick. Sam gave her a hug when Bev came to pick up the kids. Katie called out promises to email and send pictures of Blackie as she skipped into the van for the last time.

It was with a sigh of relief that Sam turned back to the shop. She had the rest of the day and the next ten days to work on the china cabinet and a few other small jobs she had in her queue. The china cabinet was coming along nicely and working on it gave Sam a sense of calmness. She had been a little hesitant at first as the beginning stages had been difficult. Memories bombarded her as she remembered her grandmother bringing out her beloved china for a special Christmas dinner when her grandmother's sister visited from Germany. She remembered countless other holidays and family dinners when her grandfather suggested she bring it out only to have her grandmother skillfully deflect the idea saying the kids were having fun, she didn't want to have to tell them to slow down just because the nice dishes were on the table.

Eventually, though, she concentrated on the words her grandfather left her in his letter, asking her to be happy, to remember the good times, and to move forward with her life, making of it whatever she wanted. And once she tried to do as he had asked, working on the china cabinet became both a tie to her past and a window to her future. As she ran her hand over the smooth oak she smiled and reached over to turn on the music.

Sam worked well past dark, pausing only to grab a quick bite and to exercise the dog. When she finally wrapped things up and stood back to assess her progress, she was pleased. The frame of the cabinet was done, sitting in sections to be put together later, but done. She had the wood cut for the doors and would start gluing tomorrow. The drawer fronts would be next, cut to match the raised design of the doors. There was still a lot of detail work as she intended to add scallops around the top and bottom as well as incorporate sectioned drawers, wine glass holders, and plate racks. It was a big project and Sam still didn't know where she'd put it or what she'd put in it when it was done, but building it was cathartic.

As she showered and got ready for bed, Sam realized her plans to get out and meet people hadn't exactly been realized. It had been a crazy week, though, she reasoned. With the coming Fourth of July holiday she'd have time to get into town, maybe call Karen and see if she was free for coffee or lunch, stop in at the bank and check in with Lynn. She could do those things, she told herself. It wouldn't be weird to call someone, stop in to say hi, people did it all the time, right?

She was doing a pretty fair job of psyching herself up when her cell phone buzzed. She glanced at the time, her heart jumping as she reverted for a moment to the days when phone calls at night almost always meant bad news. She took a deep breath. It was only ten o'clock and it was only Jake. And this was now, not then. She thought her voice sounded reasonably normal as she answered the phone.

Fifteen minutes later when she hung up, she was wishing she hadn't answered. No, that wasn't entirely true. She had enjoyed talking to Jake, hearing about his day, and sharing hers with him. It was the invitation he had extended, that she had tried to turn down but had eventually agreed to, that had her panicking. A family picnic at his parent's house sounded downright intimidating. Yes, she wanted to meet people, she really did, but so many at once? It would mean answering the same questions over and over, people wanting to know how she ended up in Misty Lake, wanting to know about the house they watched being built on the lake. Questions she either couldn't or wouldn't want to answer. She had tried using Rigi as an excuse, saying she couldn't possibly leave her home alone all day, but Jake had assured her she could bring the dog along.

Sunday. The annual McCabe family Fourth of July picnic. Only a couple days to mentally ready herself. She'd meet his entire family, from the way it sounded. His parents, siblings, cousins, aunts, uncles, even a couple of great aunts. Not to mention half the town. According to Jake, his parents had been hosting a picnic for years and it seemed to grow bigger every summer. Sam had never been much of a drinker. She considered starting.

Jake picked her up on Sunday, a gesture she appreciated and he had insisted upon even though it meant he had to drive from town out to the lake then back to town to his parents' house. She really hadn't wanted to arrive alone.

She had insisted on bringing something even when Jake assured her there would be more food than could ever be eaten, so she was juggling a platter of brownies and a pasta salad as they made their way to the front door. Jake tied the dog outside then walked in and led her to a kitchen that was a beehive of activity.

Sam stood a moment and took it all in. Buns were being sliced, crockpots stirred, and hamburger patties formed. Someone let go with a booming laugh and there were somewhat more subdued chuckles all around, Jake and Sam having apparently just missed the punch line of a particularly good joke. Sam spotted Karen standing at the sink washing fruit. When Joe walked up behind her and kissed the top of her head, Karen turned and noticed Sam. She gave a smile and a wave that Sam clumsily attempted to return without dropping the food she was carrying. When Joe spotted them and said loudly, "Welcome to the jungle, Sam!" it quickly grew quiet and everyone seemed to stare. Sam felt her cheeks heating as a striking woman with short, shiny black hair and eyes that were identical to Jake's came forward with her arms extended.

"Sam, welcome to our home. I'm so happy to meet you, Jake has told us so much about you." Then, in one swift move, she had the dishes out of Sam's hands and her arms around her in a welcoming hug.

Sam, a little taken aback at the intimate greeting, stammered out her hello and thank you. As Jake's mother drew back, Jake put his arm around Sam's shoulders and said, "Sam, my mom, Anna McCabe. Mom, Samantha Taylor." When a smiling, red-haired man with bright blue eyes approached, Jake repeated the introductions with his father.

"Mr. and Mrs. McCabe, it's a pleasure to meet you both. Thank you for having me today."

"Please, it's Sean and Anna," Jake's mother insisted. "And don't you look lovely!" she added, stepping back to look at Sam. "Jake, you didn't tell us she was beauty queen material."

Sam didn't know how to respond but was saved by Jake who hugged his mother and whispered, "Easy, Mom."

Sean shook Sam's hand and asked, "How are you settling in? Is Misty Lake starting to feel like home?"

His eyes sparkled and it appeared he had just come in from the sun as his cheeks and arms were pink and covered with freckles that seemed to spread before her eyes. He stood about an inch taller than Jake and, she guessed, outweighed him by thirty pounds. If she had met him elsewhere she knew she would have found him intimidating and guessed he had used his size to his advantage during his years as sheriff. But now, seeing him smile and watching him turn to put an arm around his wife and squeeze her shoulders, she instantly liked him.

"I'm adjusting," she answered. "It's a different way of life than in Chicago but I like it. I'm starting to enjoy the lake, have even started swimming again, and my dog loves it here," she added and wondered where all that had come from, why she felt like she could tell him anything.

"I'm glad to hear that. We're pretty proud of our town, aren't we Jake?" Without waiting for an answer, he added, "If you need any help out there, you just let me know. The boys and I can take care of just about anything that needs taking care of. Isn't that right, Anna?" Again, before his wife could answer he turned to Jake and said, "Round up a couple of your brothers and get the volleyball net set up. People will be arriving soon, there's work to be done. Samantha, you make yourself at home and enjoy yourself today," he said with a wink as he shooed Jake out the door and into the backyard.

Left alone with a kitchen full of women, Sam grew instantly uncomfortable but Anna came to her rescue. "Ladies, this is Sam. Sam, this is everyone. You'll have a chance to get acquainted later but right now we've got food to get on the table. Sam, would you mind helping Karen with the fruit?"

Grateful for something to do, Sam headed for the sink. She washed, sliced, and plated fruit while Karen, keeping her voice below the level of the din, gave her the pertinent details on everyone in the room.

Before she knew it, Sam was in the McCabe's backyard with over a hundred other people. Cars pulled up, people walked from down the block, kids came bounding from all directions, and everywhere she looked there was food. She met more people than she would ever remember. After she let herself relax and told herself she didn't owe anyone anything more than she felt comfortable sharing, she enjoyed herself. Jake stayed with her as much as he could but he was often called away to help with something or to join in on a game of volleyball or horseshoes. She chatted with Kathleen and her husband, catching up on Kathleen's summer with her kids from Project Strong Start and learning about the houses that were going up for sale in town and around the lake. Stu introduced her to Molly who was feeling well enough to join the party. She ran into Lynn, met her husband and her twins, and was a nervous wreck after ten minutes of watching her chase after two toddlers who each wanted to do everything except what the other was doing. How Lynn could always seem to be in two places at once was truly a mystery.

Sam also met the rest of Jake's siblings and felt reasonably certain she had them all straight. In addition to Joe who was one year younger, there were the twins, Frank and Riley, who were three years younger and Shauna, who was seven years younger than Jake. They were a fun, noisy bunch and Sam felt welcomed by all of them. Shauna, in particular, went out of her way to make Sam feel at home. She chatted, telling Sam about graduating from the University of Minnesota in May with a double major in finance and art. She explained that while she was working at the bank right now, what she really wanted to do one day was open up her own antiques gallery. Sam was drawn in to the young woman's plans and dreams and wondered if she had ever been so full of hope for the future. Shauna was a bundle of energy and Sam didn't doubt she'd achieve her dream one day.

When Jake told her he wanted to introduce her to his great aunts saying they would never forgive him if they found out he had a girl there and they hadn't met her, Sam thought she was ready. Jake seemed almost apologetic, started trying to explain, then just told her she'd see for herself. Sam was a little confused but she had met so many people already, what difference could a couple more make?

Kate and Rose, the widowed sisters of Anna's mother, were sitting together under a big umbrella on the patio, sipping drinks and both talking at the same time, seeming to be on completely different topics. Sam heard one of the women talking about the turkey gravy their mother used to make while she swore the other was talking about bunions.

"Aunt Rose, Aunt Kate, I'd like you to meet Samantha Taylor," Jake interrupted.

"What's that, Jacob? You're looking for Seth Taylor? I think he died sixty years ago, didn't he, Rosie?"

"Oh, I think so. At least sixty years. I remember his funeral. It was raining like crazy as we walked from the church to the cemetery. Seems to me—"

"No, Aunt Kate, I said I want you to meet *Samantha* Taylor. She's a friend of mine, she just moved to Misty Lake."

"Oh, a friend of yours?" The woman looked Sam up and down and nodded her approval to Jake. "She's a pretty one, Jacob, don't you agree, Rosie?"

"Real pretty," Rose answered. "You like our boy, do you? He's a good boy, our Jacob. Did he tell you about the time when I was minding him and the neighbor dog bit him right on the behind? I had to take him to the emergency room, took twelve stitches to patch him up. I bet you still have a scar there, don't you, Jacob? Let me have a look." Rose leaned forward in her chair and, with her free hand, reached for Jake.

"Now, Aunt Rose, I'm sure Sam doesn't want to hear about that," Jake said as he quickly jumped back out of his aunt's reach.

Sam had to turn her head and stifle a laugh as Jake's blush rose up his neck and all the way to his ears.

Kate held up her empty glass and looked to Jake. "Be a dear and go get us refills. Do you need a refill, Rosie?"

Rose looked at the glass in her hand and said, "Well, I'll be darned, looks like I do!" Both the women started howling with laughter and held their glasses out for Jake who gave Sam a helpless look as he took them.

Sam murmured to Jake, "Do you really think you should get them another drink? What's in their glasses anyway?"

Turning his back to his aunts, Jake answered, "They drink Old Fashioneds, have as long as I can remember. We all learned years ago, though, that after their first ones, their drinks are strictly of the virgin variety. They never notice."

Sam sat down with the women as Jake went to refill their glasses. "So, Samantha, how long have you been in town and when did you meet our Jacob?"

"Almost four months now but I just met Jake recently."

"Do you think she knows Lois?" Rose asked Kate. Then, seeming to forget Sam was there, continued to her sister, "You missed Harvey Wallin's funeral on Tuesday."

"I told you I had a dental appointment I needed to keep. Was Lois there?"

"Of course she was there. She wouldn't miss a funeral."

"Up to the same old tricks?"

"You know Lois, she'll never change. She had to *sample* all the dishes before the family arrived, said she needed to make sure everything was okay to serve. I think she sampled Helga's macaroni and cheese about a half dozen times, that old bat. Then before the family was done eating she was wrapping up leftovers to take home."

"Did she bring her horrid green Jell-O again?"

"That's all she ever brings, that awful Jell-O that no one ever eats, then she takes home enough food to keep her fed for the rest of the week."

"What about Midge? Was she there?"

"She was, tried to get us all to feel sorry for her saying she has so much to deal with now that Wally's sick."

"Ha!" Kate barked. "Sick my foot. She likes to say *sick* thinking she'll get more sympathy that way, like the man has cancer or something. She's convinced he's crazy but she won't admit it. Did you hear what he did last week?"

"Dodging grenades behind the gas pumps over at the station? I heard. He's doing one hell of a job on Midge. He's got her believing he thinks he's back in Korea, running around all the time looking for his gun and shouting about rear attacks. I heard he squeezed into his uniform the other day and accused Midge of stealing his medals."

"She deserves everything he's dishing out. That mean old nag has been after him for almost sixty years, it's about time he figured out a way to shut her up." Then after a pause Kate added, "She cheats at cards, too."

"Everyone knows that, Kathryn."

The conversation rolled on with Kate continuing to talk about their card games and who was cheating and Rose talking about her singing group, even starting to sing to herself a couple of times. It was mesmerizing watching them, like some sort of bizarrely choreographed dance. Neither seemed to notice the other wasn't talking about the same thing, they both just carried on, occasionally even asking or answering a question. The topics changed, changed again, and still neither noticed the other was on a completely different subject.

When Jake returned with their drinks both women paused, took their glasses, and looked surprised to see Sam sitting next to them. "Now dear, what was it you were saying about moving to Misty Lake?" Rose asked.

"I…I was just saying how much I like it here," Sam smiled.

"That's good, that's good. Jacob, where are your manners? You show her around, introduce her to some people," Rose scolded.

"Yes, Aunt Rose, I will. Can I get you anything else?" But the sisters had already forgotten Jake and Sam and had resumed their conversation that now seemed to center around blood pressure medication and a sale on cat food.

Sam chatted, ate, and enjoyed herself. She was talked into a couple games of volleyball and helped her team to victory once she worked some of the rust off the techniques she had honed during a three-year stint on her junior high team. She didn't fare as well pitching horseshoes but had fun trying. A couple of times during the day Sam had caught sight of Karen, sipping water and looking a little green. When she asked her about it, Karen said the combination of the heat and the Mexican food she had eaten the night before seemed to be doing a number on her. Sam had tried to convince her to go inside where it was air-conditioned but Karen hadn't wanted to miss anything. Some of the older folks did head home earlier than they would have otherwise, giving up the battle with the high temperature and humidity.

Later that evening when everyone but Jake's family had left to watch fireworks in the park, Sam sat on the patio, sipping on lemonade and listening to the inside stories and jokes that all families seem to share. They all went out of their way to recall embarrassing stories about Jake and Sam found herself laughing so hard at times she had tears in her eyes. She heard about everything from split pants on the little league field to throwing up on his fifth grade teacher to taking the car out onto a frozen Misty Lake and, while trying to impress the girls in the back seat by doing donuts, knocked over the high school principal's fish house. Every time Jake tried to turn the conversation to something one of his siblings had done, it just served to remind someone of another Jake story.

"Okay, okay, enough! That's all ancient history," Jake pleaded. "And I seem to recall I wasn't the only one to get in trouble with the car. When Frank and Riley got their driver's licenses they both managed to get into accidents the first time they were allowed to take the car out by themselves. Remember, Dad?" Jake added when no one commented.

"Nice try, Jake," Riley said, shaking his head, "but that just doesn't compare with The History of Jake, now does it? I think everyone would rather hear about the time you tried to get Megan Perkins to sneak out in the middle of the night and her dad caught you outside her window. Nothing like the sheriff answering his door in the middle of the night to find his son, escorted by one of his deputies, on the doorstep."

Finally, Anna took pity on her oldest and announced it was time to head to the roof for a better view of the fireworks.

"The roof?" Sam asked Jake, slightly alarmed.

"It's a McCabe family tradition. There's a spot on

the garage roof we've been climbing up to for years. It gets us just high enough that we're above the tree line but not so high that Mom gets too worried."

Just as everyone started to get up Karen said softly, "Um, can you wait just a minute?" When Sam looked at her Karen was smiling but seemed nervous at the same time. She reached for Joe's hand and said, "I don't think I'll climb up on the roof this year."

"What's up, Karen? You're not suddenly afraid of heights, are you? I have a few Karen stories I could share, especially about the time you and some of your cheerleader friends tried to climb the water tower. You weren't afraid of heights that night!" Frank seemed ready to launch into a story but paused when he caught a look pass between Karen and Joe. Then, more concerned, he asked, "Seriously, what's up?"

"Well, we were waiting for the right time to tell everyone…we're going to have a baby!" Karen beamed and, in the way of all expectant mothers, rested a hand on her still-flat belly.

All at once, the group erupted. Shauna shrieked and did a little pirouette. Joe's brothers seemed to whoop in unison and engulf their brother, who looked a little dazed, with hugs and high fives. Anna was on her feet in a flash, her hand flying to her mouth as her eyes grew wide and she gave a little gasp. She made her way to Karen, wrapped her in a hug and fought for composure as the tears started to make their way down her cheeks. Sam could hear her stammering, seeming to struggle to get the words out, and guessed it was one of the few times the confident, in-control woman had been at a loss for words.

It was wonderful seeing the family so happy, so

united by joyous news. Sam felt a little pang thinking that over the last couple years the times her family had been so united were to grieve, not celebrate. It seemed like it had been a long time since her family was caught up in a celebration like the one playing out in front of her.

She quickly shook off the feeling, determined not to be responsible for hanging a dark cloud over the evening. She looked out over the group and noticed Sean was still seated, slightly outside of the hubbub. The porch light caught his eyes and Sam could see the glint of a tear. He seemed to still be in a state of shock, looking from one member of his family to another, staring, and, it appeared, mumbling to himself. When his eyes met Sam's he looked at her for a long moment then his face broke into a brilliant grin. "I'm going to be a Granddad," he said. Then, shaking his head as if still not quite believing it, he repeated louder, "I'm going to be a Granddad!"

Eventually, after things calmed down a bit, Sam made her way over to Karen to offer her congratulations. "I thought it was maybe a little more than the heat and some Mexican food. How are you feeling now?"

"Better. Overall I've been feeling pretty good. The heat today was a little tough, though. It seems like everyone's pretty happy with the news."

"That's an understatement. This is one ecstatic group, I'd say," Sam replied as she looked around her. The brothers were still huddled together, giving Joe a hard time about diapers and midnight feedings. Sean, who had disappeared a few minutes ago, reappeared with a bottle of Irish whiskey and a tray of glasses and began pouring drinks for everyone except the expectant mother who, instead, got a glass of ginger ale.

Once everyone had their glasses Sean held his up and said, "To my son and my daughter-in-law who today have made me realize again just how important family is." He put his arm around Anna and continued, "Now, if you'll allow an old Irishman a moment for an Irish blessing...

A newborn babe
Brings light to the house
Warmth to the hearth
And joy to the soul
For wealth is family
And family is wealth

To our grandchild, Sláinte!" Glasses clinked and there were more hugs and kisses all around.

13

Sam found her days were productive when she had all day to work but by Wednesday she was missing the kids and the energy they brought to her daily routine. She was making great progress on the china hutch and reminded herself she needed to get glass for the cabinet doors ordered. She was thinking something textured, nothing too complicated that it would block the view of the china and crystal displayed inside, but not just plain glass, either. She'd have to do some searching and see if she could find what she had in mind. It was something she was prone to do…picture something in her mind then drive herself mad trying to find just that thing. She'd done it with clothes, furniture, even a dog collar once. It used to drive Danny crazy when she'd try to keep him busy searching online for things he claimed didn't even exist. One of the dozens of tactics she had tried in order to keep him safe, she thought sadly.

The buzzing of her cellphone saved her from the all too familiar downward spiral when she let painful memories engulf her. Glancing at the readout she saw it was Karen. Sam was surprised but, she realized, pleased. After they exchanged greetings and some small talk, Karen got to the reason for her call.

"So, Sam, I was wondering if you're busy tomorrow and, if not, if you'd want to go shopping with me?"

Shopping? Sam wasn't much of a shopper, more of a buyer. Her girlfriends dragged her shopping when they could and she enjoyed the company, and the occasional shoe sale—she was a woman, after all—but spending hours just idly browsing had never really been her idea of a way to spend a day. "Well...I don't really have anything I have to do but there are a few things I've been trying to finish up before I get my camp kids back next week." She was stalling, trying desperately to come up with a good excuse not to go.

"Come on, you can take some time off. I need someone to help me shop for maternity clothes." She gave a little giggle. "Sometimes I still can't believe I'm really going to have a baby!"

"Oh, I don't know anything about maternity clothes, I'm afraid. I don't think I'd be any help." There. That was her out. What advice could she possibly offer on maternity clothes?

"You can give me your opinion. Please? I have the day off tomorrow. My sister is working crazy hours and my mom is out of town. I need a girl's help. I can't ask Joe, can you even imagine?"

"All right, I'll go with you. It'll be fun," she lied. "I

haven't done any shopping since I left Chicago, I suppose I could use a few things." How long could it really take, she thought. There couldn't be that many places in Misty Lake that even carried maternity clothes. Maybe they could shop for an hour or so then go to lunch. She could handle that.

"Wonderful! Thank you, Sam. I can't wait!"

"When should we meet? Maybe late morning, then I can take you to lunch? Where's the best spot for lunch in Misty Lake?" Sam asked, trying to match Karen's enthusiasm.

"Late morning? Misty Lake?" Karen repeated, sounding horrified. "Oh, no, no, sweetie. I'll pick you up at seven tomorrow morning. When one shops in Minnesota, one shops at the Mall of America."

The words sunk in and Sam felt slightly ill. She'd heard of the Mall of America, of course, but had successfully avoided it for years. Her girlfriends had tried more than once to convince her to join them on their girls' weekends to Minneapolis to shop and shop some more. They loved the place but to her it sounded like hell on earth. Four floors, hundreds of stores, and an amusement park? Oh God, she was starting to sweat.

When she remained silent Karen asked, "Sam, are you there?"

"What? Oh, yes, I'm here." Think, think, she commanded herself. Find a way out. An entire day of shopping? Impossible.

"So then I'll see you at seven?" Karen sounded positively thrilled at the thought.

She wasn't going to get out of it. She couldn't disappoint Karen. With a resigned sigh she said, "Sure, see you at seven," then hung up the phone and reached for the aspirin.

Several things happened Friday that had Jake more and more frustrated with Sam's case. Preliminary forensic results came back on the shirt and knife he had found in the woods at Sam's house and there was nothing helpful. The DNA left behind didn't match that of anyone in the database. Jake wasn't surprised but had been hopeful something might come of the testing. Assuming one of the kids from Project Strong Start was responsible, it was unlikely his DNA would be on file. The tests did show, however, that there was animal blood mixed in with human blood. Tests hadn't been done to determine the kind of animal but Jake was betting on raccoon.

He was going over the notes he had from his conversation with his father about the Andersons, the family Sam remembered owning the cabin next to her grandparents' place. The former sheriff vaguely remembered the family, said they came into town most Sundays for church, so he had been casually acquainted with them, and didn't recall there ever being any trouble at their place. Jake had checked back in the files and had not found any record of calls at their cabin. Sean McCabe remembered Roger Anderson and his wife, whose name he couldn't recall, as being friendly, down-to-earth sort of folks. He knew there had been kids, couldn't remember specifics.

Jake had made calls to the courthouse and had obtained information on the sale of the property from the Andersons to Sam's grandfather. The property had never been listed for sale so the parties involved must have maintained some contact over the years. Further checking into the Andersons led Jake to discover that both Roger and his wife Lucinda were deceased. The couple's three children all lived out of state. Everything he had uncovered seemed straightforward and he felt it was probably another dead end.

He glanced again at the report regarding the citation issued to a boat full of teenagers for reckless driving. Jake felt certain it was the kids responsible for causing Sam's harrowing tube ride. The kids weren't from Misty Lake, just in town for the day, and there didn't seem to be any connection to Sam.

Jake followed up again with Marc, Fred, and the rest of his team. No one had anything new to report. Neither Marc nor Fred had heard anything around town to indicate someone local might be responsible and the extra patrols around Sam's property hadn't resulted in anything.

He reread the emails he had gotten from Pete with files on the kids from Project Strong Start. There wasn't much to go on and Pete hadn't contacted him with any new information.

Since there hadn't been any more incidents and the investigation wasn't going anywhere, Jake had to tell himself he needed to treat this case as he would any other. He couldn't continue to devote extra resources if things remained stagnant. His investigations to date hadn't come up with much of anything for him to pursue and he knew it was his personal feelings that had him putting in extra time. He was looking over the notes he had on the kids from camp when his phone rang. Jake knew right away from the tone of Tom's voice that the news he was going to get from the camp director wasn't going to be good.

"Sheriff, I learned something today that I need to bring to your attention. Let me preface it by saying I'm dealing with the situation, trying to get more information, and will cooperate fully."

Jake felt his jaw clench. "What happened, Tom?"

"I found out one of our counselors has let Tyler Loomis take his car out at night on more than one occasion," Tom said in a monotone voice. "Apparently Tyler caught the counselor with some drugs, marijuana, I understand. Clearly any drug use is in strict violation of the rules of conduct here. Tyler made a deal with him not to say anything in return for the use of his car and the counselor helping him get away from camp at night."

Jake blew out a deep breath and struggled for calm. "Do you have dates? Obviously, I will be curious to see if any coincide with the vandalism at Sam Taylor's place."

"I don't have too many details yet. I've spoken with the counselor briefly. I haven't asked too many questions or fired him yet since I thought you'd want to talk to him."

"I definitely want to talk to him. And to Tyler, too. Wait a minute, isn't everyone gone this week, up to the Boundary Waters for a camping trip?"

"A few kids stayed behind for various reasons...health concerns, too many incidents of rule breaking at camp, and, in Tyler's case, I just wouldn't allow it. This was, of course, based on his previous record and before I knew about him leaving with a car. I kept a couple counselors behind, as well, to work with the kids who stayed."

"How did you find out about this?"

"One of the other counselors who stayed behind, Miranda, overheard a conversation between Tyler and the counselor in question. She came to me with the information right away." After a pause, Tom added, "Sheriff, I take full responsibility for this, it happened on my watch. I will deal with the situation working closely with you. I can't tell you how sorry I am. If it turns out Tyler or one of the other kids is responsible, I will cooperate fully in seeing that he or she is brought to justice."

"Do you have reason to believe other kids may have had access to the car and been away from camp at night?" Jake asked, fighting mightily to keep his temper in check. He knew his reaction was due in part to the fact that it was Sam who was the victim and he struggled to keep both his tone and his comments professional.

"Not specifically, just a hunch based on the counselor using *they* instead of *he* when I spoke with him earlier. Like I said, I didn't want to push too much and have him stop talking before you got here."

"Okay, Tom, thanks for calling me right away. Keep Tyler and this counselor separated. I don't want them talking to each other before I get there. I'm heading out now, I'll be there soon."

Jake had promised Sam he'd stop by and let Rigi out while she was gone shopping for the day. As angry as he was at the news he'd gotten from Tom, he found himself smiling as he remembered the call last night from Sam. Far from the excitement he might expect from most women on the eve of an all-day outing at the Mall of America, Sam had sounded downright terrified. When she'd said she was sure he'd be far too busy to let the dog out during the day so she'd better call Karen and cancel, he had laughed and assured her he'd have plenty of time. Originally, he'd thought he would use the time to look around her place a little more on his own, see if he noticed anything out of the ordinary without upsetting her. But now he had only thirty minutes to get his emotions in check before he met Marc at the camp to face Tom and the others. When Project Strong Start first set up their camp on the lake there were strict guidelines put in place to protect the town's residents. This was a clear violation and Jake knew he could close the place down immediately. While the dog ran in the yard chasing tennis balls, Jake considered his options.

The short conversation Jake and Marc had with Tom when they arrived at his office didn't provide any new information. Tom had kept Tyler and the counselor separated and hadn't spoken any more with either of them. The conversation with the counselor, whose name they learned was Blaine Hemmingway, was fairly short. Blaine was tall and thin and didn't look much older than most of the campers. He seemed scared of losing his job, of going to jail and, mostly, of his parents when they found out what happened. Apparently he stood to collect on a trust fund but had to keep himself employed and drug-free for two years. It wasn't looking good and he knew it.

Although he was cooperative, Blaine didn't know much more than what Tom had already told them. He was fairly certain Tyler had taken his car four times but couldn't remember exact dates. When given a calendar and pressed, he marked a few dates he thought sounded right and Jake checked them against the dates he knew there had been incidents at Sam's house. One matched, one was a day off so definitely a possible match.

Blaine also said he knew someone else went with Tyler at least a couple times but he didn't know the kid's name and couldn't provide a description, claiming it had been dark and the kid was wearing a baseball cap. Blaine had let the kids in and out of their cabin by temporarily disabling the security system then waiting for them and getting them back in the same way. As frustrating as it was, Jake hadn't really counted on getting a lot of information from Blaine, figuring Tyler, if they could get him to talk, would be the one to provide real answers.

As they made their way to the room in the main lodge where Tyler was being held, Jake and Marc stopped to pick up Tom so he could be present during the questioning. Based on what Jake knew of Tyler's past, he figured he had been through police questioning several times and didn't want to run the risk that he would claim later something was handled inappropriately. Tom was ready with Tyler's file in hand.

The three men were met with a sneer when they entered the room. Tyler muttered something under his breath and turned away.

"Tyler, I'm Sheriff McCabe, this is Deputy Crosby. We want to talk to you about taking Blaine Hemmingway's car and leaving the camp area." Tyler kept his back turned and didn't answer.

"We know you left the property at least four times. We want to know where you went and who went with you."

"I'm not telling you nothing," Tyler hissed.

"According to your file, you are still on probation.

Leaving the camp is a violation. You can talk to us here or we can take you into the station. Maybe a night in jail would change your mind."

"I've spent the night in jail before, doesn't scare me. And your hick jail is probably a hell of a lot better than the others I've seen."

"Where did you go when you left the camp, Tyler?" Marc asked when he noticed Jake's frustration mounting. "We've had some serious stuff going down in town and, unless you can convince us otherwise, we're looking at you as a prime suspect."

"What kind of serious shit?" Tyler looked up and both Jake and Marc caught the fleeting look of fear in his eyes before it quickly disappeared. "I didn't do nothing. Just drove around," he said, looking away again.

"Where'd you go?"

"I don't know, man, just drove."

"Did you stay around the lake? Go into town? Drive out of town?" Marc pressed.

"I told you, w...I just drove." Tyler's voice rose in anger as he glared at Marc.

"You started to say we. Who was with you?" Jake demanded.

Tyler looked at them, seeming to debate with himself on whether to answer.

"This can be as easy or as hard as you want to make it, Tyler. I can call your probation officer, talk to some guys I know on the Minneapolis force, let you spend the night in jail, and then see what sort of sentence you have left to serve in Minneapolis for breaking your probation. According to your file you're seventeen now, almost eighteen, you're looking at time in an adult facility.

Your cooperation could go a long way towards making things easier for you," Jake said, looking him in the eye.

Tyler was quiet for several minutes. Jake and Marc waited him out. Finally, "I told you all *I* did was drive around, maybe smoke a joint that dumbass counselor gave me when I caught him smoking and scared the shit out of him. It was that other kid who really wanted the car, said he had some stuff he needed to do, needed a way to get there. He dropped me off at this cabin not far away where there are some dudes always partying, left me for about an hour, maybe two, then came back and picked me up and we came back here."

"This other kid have a name?" Jake asked.

"Forget it, man, I ain't telling you nothing else." Tyler's eyes narrowed and he glared at Jake.

"Are you sure about that?"

"Seems like I can't remember nothing else, Sheriff," Tyler smirked.

"Okay, if that's the way you want it." Turning to the camp director Jake said, "Tom, we'll take Tyler with us. Since he has admitted to being away from camp and spending time at a cabin nearby, that puts him in the vicinity of the crime scene for at least one, possibly two, of the reported incidents. I will be in touch with his probation officer and have him contact you after he has worked things out with the Minneapolis police. Our investigation will continue, with or without Tyler's cooperation. If we find more evidence linking him to the crime scene and issue an arrest warrant you will most likely be called to testify."

When Marc began handcuffing Tyler the boy shouted, "Wait! Come on man, give me a minute. Maybe I can remember a name."

All three men waited as Tyler looked from one to the other, cursing under his breath. "Maybe it was Zach," he mumbled.

"Tom?" Jake looked to the director.

"Zach Fields?" Tom asked Tyler.

"Shit, I don't know his last name. The kid who's always wearing the baseball cap and following me around."

"That's Zach Fields, Sheriff," Tom confirmed. One of Sam's students, Jake knew from his earlier investigation.

"Do you know what Zach needed the car for?"

"I already told you, he dropped me off, disappeared for a while, then came back to get me. I don't know what he was doing."

"Nothing else you can tell us?"

"Nope."

Jake ran his hand through his hair and walked around the room. "Okay. You stay here for the time being. You can plan on seeing us again. Why don't you see if you can remember some more before then?"

Jake left the room followed by Marc and Tom and returned to Tom's office. "I don't believe much of what comes out of that kid's mouth but I get the feeling he's telling the truth about not knowing where Zach went," Tom said.

"Yeah, maybe. I want you to have someone watching Tyler at all times. When do the rest of the kids get back?"

"They're due back Sunday afternoon. One of the counselors checks in with me every evening. I'll talk to him about Zach, make sure he's keeping an eye on him and that he's not left alone."

Jake nodded. He knew Tom was doing his best to cooperate and was upset at the breach of security at the camp.

"What about Blaine Hemmingway?" Marc asked.

"Unless you want to talk to him again or file charges against him for possession of marijuana, I can have him out of here by this evening," Tom answered.

"It's going to be hard to prove any drug-related offenses after the fact. With this much notice I would assume he's gotten rid of any marijuana he still had and unless we'd find a substantial amount, the most we could charge him with is a misdemeanor. He'd get off with a nominal fine. Unless he has previous drug convictions?"

"No, no, definitely not. He couldn't have been hired here if that were the case. Maybe his parents knew of some drug use but he doesn't have a record."

"Okay. I would like to take a look at his car, though. If Zach or Tyler did, in fact, go to Sam's place we may find something in the car linking them to the crime."

"I'll go talk to him again, see if I can get an okay to search the car," Marc said.

"Sounds good. I'll wrap things up here with Tom then join you."

Later that afternoon, Marc and Jake sat in Jake's office going over the interview notes and the files on Tyler and Zach. The search of Blaine's car hadn't yielded much of value. There was a tool box in the trunk, nothing different than what might be found in thousands of other car trunks, but interesting in that the hammer was lying outside the box. Blaine claimed he didn't recall using the tools lately but said that before he came to camp, his brother sometimes used the car and it's possible the hammer had been out of the toolbox and he hadn't noticed it. Marc had bagged the hammer and kept it as possible evidence.

"Any ideas on where this party cabin Tyler referred to might be?" Jake asked Marc.

"There are a couple places on the lake that come to mind. Remember we had that noise complaint a few weeks ago out on Bay Street."

"Yeah, I was thinking that too. There wasn't anything illegal going on at the time, though, as I recall. Lots of drinking and loud music but everyone was of age."

"That time, yes. It might be worth checking out again. There's another place over on the other side of the lake I've heard some talk about. There haven't been any complaints, I've just heard some kids mention a place where there's been some partying. I've driven by a couple times, haven't seen anything but it's probably worth checking out."

"Good. Keep your ears open, if you hear talk about any place else, let me know. And take a drive by the other spots when you're on duty at night."

"Will do," Marc replied. Then, "What's your feeling on Zach? Do you think he's responsible?"

"There's a lot of reason to suspect him. The dates match up. If he really dropped off Tyler somewhere on the lake, he would have had plenty time to get to Sam's place and back. Sam has said his behavior in class is odd. She has never suggested she thinks he's responsible but I know she thinks he's up to something."

"What's the motive? Do you think it's personal

against Sam?"

"I can't come up with a logical motive other than he's angry at having to be at Project Strong Start and he's taking it out on whomever he can. To me, it doesn't seem like he knows Sam well enough to have anything against her personally."

Marc nodded his agreement. "So we check out some possible party locations on the lake, keep tabs on Tyler through Tom Lindahl, and wait for Zach to get back from the Boundary Waters so we can talk to him. Anything else right now?"

"No, Marc, I guess that's it for now," Jake answered, clearly wishing he could do more.

14

"So, how was the Mall of America?" Jake smiled over his glass at Sam. It was Saturday evening and Sam had agreed to dinner at Jake's apartment. He had been nervous, he realized, to see how she'd react to his apartment, to the dinner, to him. So far, so good.

Sam gave a small shudder. "Oh, God, Jake, that place. Have you seen it? Oh, of course you have, I think I'm the only person who hadn't. It's overwhelming. Did you know there are over five hundred stores? I think Karen went into most of them."

"Joe said she was really happy you went with her. You did a good thing, Sam."

"Oh, it wasn't really that bad once I got over the initial shock. Karen did have a good time, I think. I'm glad I went with her. She bought a pile of maternity clothes and even some baby clothes."

"I heard she wasn't the only one who bought baby

clothes," Jake winked.

"You heard that, did you? Well, I just couldn't resist, I had to buy something for the baby. Those tiny little outfits were just so adorable and I found these sweet little shoes, and a hat, it will be winter when the baby's born, after all." Sam grew quiet and Jake caught the wistful look in her eyes before she gave her head a little shake and smiled at him.

"Are you already planning your next trip to the Mall? There must be some stores and restaurants you missed."

"No. No! I need time to recover. A long time," Sam laughed. "It is an interesting place, though. Rollercoasters, an aquarium, a bowling alley, more restaurants than I've ever seen…it's really quite something. I guess I can see why my friends kept making the drive here from Chicago." She raised a brow and asked Jake, "What about you? Do you make frequent trips?"

He held up his hands and said, "Definitely not. A few years ago I ended up there just a couple days before Christmas trying to find a certain kind of candle my mom wanted. I still have nightmares. Screaming kids, crabby parents, sales people with smiles plastered on their faces but with eyes shooting daggers at everyone who asked a question. That reminds me, I have to get Shauna to do a favor for me again. It was her idea to go that day. Our deal is she's in my debt for life."

Sam laughed, picturing Jake following the whirling dervish Shauna through the jam-packed mall. But she guessed he would do just about anything for his mom, his sister, or any other member of his family. She looked around his apartment at the framed family photos displayed prominently on the tabletops and walls and thought again how fortunate he was to be surrounded by a big family so full of love. His entire apartment held traces of family. She had already spotted a crocheted afghan thrown over the back of the couch, an embroidered kitchen towel hanging on the oven door, and a homemade apple pie on the counter. Sam was willing to bet a lot on someone other than Jake being responsible for all of them.

His apartment surprised her. Instead of the mismatched furniture, sports magazines, and giant TV she had expected, she found his home to be cozy and warm with beautiful leather furniture, a few tasteful art prints, and a large shelf full of a wide variety of books. Well, and a giant TV. The lasagna he had in the oven smelled heavenly and it looked as though he had done everything he could to make her feel welcome from the flowers on the table to the music he had playing. She was touched.

He also had avoided the subject that she knew they'd have to discuss sooner or later. When he had called to tell her he had some new information on her case she hadn't wanted to hear it over the phone. He had assured her it was nothing that couldn't wait so she had opted to wait until tonight to hear it in person. She didn't want it to spoil the evening but knew she couldn't keep avoiding the topic.

"I suppose you should probably tell me what you learned about my case."

Jake studied her and hated the mixture of fear and apprehension he saw in her eyes. She had looked so happy just a moment ago. "I had a call from Tom Lindahl, the director of Project Strong Start," he began.

Sam's expression went from wary to frightened to

angry as Jake relayed what he had learned from Tom as well as from Blaine and Tyler. When Jake paused she was quiet for a moment, looking at him and unconsciously tapping her fingers on the table. When she spoke she had to fight for control.

"You're blaming the kids again even though you don't really have much to go on," she accused. "I get it that taking a car and leaving the camp is a big deal, obviously it's against the rules and these kids knowingly did something wrong, but it doesn't sound like you have any evidence that they were anywhere near my house."

"No physical evidence, no. But, like I said, Tyler admitted to driving around the lake. He also claims another boy dropped him off at a party and then left by himself with the car. Based on the time frame, the other boy couldn't have gone too far so you have to agree the possibility exists that one or both of them could have been at your place."

"Fine, it's possible. But why? I don't know Tyler. What reason would he have for damaging my property?"

Jake hesitated. He hadn't told her that the other kid involved was Zach but knew he had to. "You're right. I don't have a good reason for Tyler damaging your property. But he gave us the name of the boy who went with him. It was Zach."

Sam was on her feet in a flash. "Zach? My Zach? From my class? Don't do this, Jake, don't blame him just because I mentioned I thought he was acting a little strange the other day! I told you then I couldn't believe he'd do something like that and I still can't. I don't believe any of them could." She was shouting and blinking back tears.

"I'm not blaming him, Sam, I just wanted you to know what we learned. I'll need to talk to Zach when he gets back, see what he has to say about where he went with the car. At this point we don't have any other leads. You can't expect me to ignore this."

Sam took a few deep breaths and stared out the window at the sun just beginning to set. "I'm sorry, Jake. It just seems kids like Zach, like all of them, are always so easily blamed whenever anything bad happens. Make a couple mistakes and you're branded for life, you know?"

"I do know. It's easy to do and I've been guilty of it myself. But in my job we learn to play the odds, so to speak. Someone who has been in trouble in the past is, unfortunately, going to be a more likely suspect than someone who hasn't. But, that doesn't mean I'm ready to arrest Zach. I just want to talk to him, see what he has to say."

She nodded and went to Jake. "Just promise me you'll give him a chance. Please, give them all a chance," she said sadly and put her head on his shoulder as his arms went around her.

15

Sam hit the brakes harder than she intended and sent Rigi bumping into the dashboard. "Sorry, girl," she said, rubbing the dog's head. She had made an early morning trip into town for sandpaper and stain and was more than a little surprised to find a car in her driveway when she returned. "Who do you suppose is here?" she asked Rigi when she didn't see anyone around.

Sam didn't recognize the car and thought maybe it was someone looking for Sam's Woodworking. As she climbed out of her car she noticed the Illinois license plate just a moment before she heard her name and saw Susan running across the yard, her reddish gold hair flying behind her.

Her cousin crashed into her and wrapped her in a bear hug. "Surprise!" she laughed and hugged Sam again.

"Susan! What are you doing here? Why didn't you call? I would have been waiting for you."

"We wanted to surprise you. It's okay, isn't it?" Susan asked pulling back, her big emerald eyes looking questioningly at Sam.

"Of course it's okay! I'm so glad you're here. Wait...we? Who else is here?" Sam asked and looked excitedly across the yard to the house just as her younger cousin, Kyle, came around the corner.

"Sam!" he called, and lifted his hand in a wave. Sam swore he looked even taller than when she had last seen him but figured at twenty-five he must have finally stopped growing. He was easily 6'-4" and his broad shoulders and all-over muscular build had helped make him a standout during his college football days.

"When did you get here? And more importantly, how long can you stay?" Sam asked.

"We've only been here about ten minutes," Kyle said as he gave Sam a hug. "We've just been looking around a little. This is quite a place."

Sam looked from Kyle to Susan, worried they were going to resent the fact their grandfather had left almost everything to her. "It is quite something. I was shocked when I saw it the first time. You saw the pictures I sent, right?" Her eyes darted from Kyle to Susan, nervously trying to judge their reactions.

"It's fantastic!" Susan exclaimed. "I love it and I haven't even seen the inside. It all looks so different here than I remember."

"It really does," Kyle agreed. "There used to be a cabin over there," he said pointing in the direction of the old Anderson cabin.

"The cabin's gone. I guess Granddad bought the property and had the old cabin torn down. There's a lot I still don't understand. But, come on! Let me show you around."

Sam gave them the tour, answering what questions she could and later, over coffee and muffins, showed them the letter. "I guess I'm still having a hard time not being kind of mad at him," Sam admitted. "I wish he had told me—us—about it while he was still alive. We could have all enjoyed it, maybe Danny would have even…" She grew silent and her grief was evident in her expression.

Susan put a hand over Sam's. "I wish he had, too. But he had his reasons and we have to accept that. I think it just would have been too hard for him, too many memories. I'm sure it wasn't a decision he came to easily and I'm sure he didn't mean to hurt anyone by it."

"Suze is right, Sam. He did his best and enjoyed his life but I know, deep down, the pain was always there. There were many times at Christmas, a graduation, whenever, where I'd catch him with this far-off look, sort of removed from all the chaos around him, and I could tell in his heart he was someplace else, imagining what could have been."

"I know, I keep telling myself those things. I guess I just need to start believing them. So you guys aren't upset about this place? That he left it to me?" Sam asked tentatively. "You know you're always welcome here," she added.

"Upset? Really, Sam? Of course we're not upset. Right, Kyle?" Susan said looking at her brother who nodded his agreement. "I'm glad he left it to you. Besides, this way we can come visit whenever we want and leave all the work to you."

"It's a deal. I'm so glad you're both here. Tell me

what's going on at home...I mean, in Chicago. I guess this is home now, isn't it?"

Susan got a twinkle in her eye and started bouncing in her chair. "Well, we've been waiting to tell you something."

"What?"

"Let's see...Jason's doing well, working his butt off for that law firm but he claims he loves it. Whatever. I couldn't stand it but I guess that's his thing. Mom and Dad are happy and busy. Dad hints around about retiring sometimes but I know he's not ready. He's afraid to turn the business over to Brad, I think. Not that he thinks Brad can't handle it but I think he's afraid he won't know what to do with himself. Mom's still working at the flower shop and volunteering at church all the time."

"Okay...that's all good. Is that what you were waiting to tell me? Seems like I probably could have guessed most of it."

"Oh, just tell her, Suze," Kyle prodded.

Sam looked from one to the other. They seemed happy but it was odd how they were avoiding telling her whatever it was they wanted to tell her.

Finally Susan, looking like she was ready to burst, shrieked, "Brad and Mia are going to have a baby!"

The words came out so fast it sounded like one long word and it took Sam a moment to process the meaning. "They...but...how? Really?"

"Isn't it fantastic? They are so excited. They just told us, they wanted to wait until she was at least three months along. It's a miracle, Sam, it really is."

Sam knew they had been trying for years and had been told by more than one doctor their chances of conceiving were very, very low. They had prayed for a baby, the whole family had prayed. "Everything's okay? Mia and the baby are doing well?"

"Yes, everything is going just as it should. The doctor told them there's no reason to worry, that it's a normal pregnancy. The fact that their chance of conceiving was so low doesn't in any way affect the pregnancy itself."

"Oh, I just can't believe it. I'm so happy for them. When is the baby due?"

"Early January."

"Huh. Same as Jake's brother and his wife. I'd imagine Uncle Ben and Aunt Caroline are thrilled," Sam said, knowing how it had broken their hearts when their son and daughter-in-law had given them the news that it appeared they would never have children.

"Mom and Dad are over the moon. We only found out a few days ago and Mom has already started shopping for baby clothes."

Sam looked at Kyle who had remained quiet during the baby talk. He looked uncomfortable. "What's up, Kyle? Don't like all the baby talk?" Sam teased.

"It's fine, I'm happy for them, but do we really need to talk about all the...the *details*?" He fidgeted in his seat.

Just then Susan interrupted. "Wait a minute. Who's Jake?"

"Oh, he's the sheriff here in Misty Lake," Sam replied, trying to be vague.

"Why do you know the sheriff?" Susan demanded. "And how do you know his brother and his wife are having a baby?"

Sam sighed. "There have been a couple things...a

little trouble here. Jake came to check things out. I got to know him."

"What kind of trouble?" Kyle asked.

"What do you mean, 'know him?'" Susan asked at the same time.

"It's kind of a long story. You know what? I'm going to call Brad and Mia. Why don't you guys unpack, make yourselves comfortable, and I'll tell you everything after I talk to them?"

"Good idea. You got any beer, Sam? If we're going to be talking babies and sheriffs all afternoon, I'm going to need one," Kyle said, looking miserable.

Feeling sorry for him, Sam pointed to the fridge.

Later that evening, Sam and Kyle sat on the deck watching the sun set over the lake while Susan showered. "I'm glad we came, Sam. It's really good to see you."

It had been a good day spent talking, swimming, and goofing off almost like they had done when they were kids. Sam was happy, happier than she had been in a long time. "I'm glad, too. I've missed all of you so much. But, I'm starting to think I did the right thing by coming here. Putting some distance between myself and Chicago has helped. I can't say things are perfect but I think they're better than they would have been had I stayed in Chicago. Too many memories." She paused a minute then added, "That's how Granddad felt, isn't it?"

Kyle nodded. "I think so. You know, I'm proud of you. You've done an amazing job here with the house, your business, and with a group of kids from what I've been hearing."

"I think they've helped me more than I've helped

them. Spending time with them, trying to get them to believe they have possibilities in their futures…it's been good."

Kyle studied her. She had a desperate look in her eyes. "I know you, Sam. I have no doubt you're helping them. But please do me a favor? Try to remember that, in the end, the choices they make are their choices. You can teach, guide, encourage, and support but their lives and their decisions are ultimately their own. If one of them makes a mistake, it's not your fault." When he saw her shoulders shake on a sob, he went to her and held her tight.

That's how Jake found them, Sam and a man he didn't recognize wrapped in an embrace on her deck. The jealousy that racked him from head to toe came as a surprise. Had he ever felt something so strong and so fast before? He didn't think so. He had come to give her a report on his conversation with Zach. Apparently he should have called.

Kyle caught sight of Jake first and stepped in front of Sam to face the man making his way towards the house. "Can I help you?" he said, his voice none too friendly.

Sam, startled for a moment, peeked from behind Kyle to see Jake square his shoulders and look Kyle in the eye. Kyle, meeting the challenge, seemed to get taller before her eyes as he attempted to move Sam further behind him. Determined to diffuse the tension, she put a hand on Kyle's arm and stepped forward to quickly make introductions.

"Hi, Jake. This is my cousin, Kyle Taylor. Kyle, Jake McCabe, Misty Lake's sheriff."

Jake felt the vice around his heart loosen and

stepped forward with his hand extended. "Kyle, good to meet you. Sam has talked a lot about her cousins. Was this a surprise visit?" he asked, looking from Kyle to Sam.

"It was. We figured Sam must be getting homesick about now and Susan and I were both able to block off some vacation time. The fact that it's been close to a hundred degrees in Chicago may have played a part in our decision."

Sam wrapped an arm around his waist and hugged. "Well, whatever the reason, I'm glad you're here."

Susan came out through the sliding glass door with a questioning look on her face. Sam made more introductions and Susan's eyes grew wide when she learned the man on the deck was Jake. As she tilted her head and studied him, Sam quickly suggested everyone have a seat. She threw a warning look at Susan who was standing behind Jake grinning crazily and giving two thumbs up.

"Did you talk to Zach?" Sam asked Jake, figuring that was the reason for his visit.

"I did, but we can discuss it later," he answered, looking around to gauge Sam's cousins' reactions and wondering how much Sam had told them.

"You can say whatever it is you have to say in front of them. I've already told them what's been going on." Susan was still grinning like an idiot and Sam needed to get her alone for a minute. "Why don't Susan and I go grab some drinks and snacks? We'll be right back," she said as she grabbed Susan's arm and pulled her from her chair.

"You think you can take it down a notch?" Sam asked when she had dragged Susan into the kitchen.

"But he's so cute!" Susan laughed. "You didn't tell me how cute he is."

"Oh, for crying out loud. Don't embarrass me."

"Embarrass you? Would I do that?"

"Yes."

"Well, dear cousin, it seems as though you might need a little help in the romance department. As long as I'm here, I may as well do what I can."

"Susan," Sam pleaded.

"Oh, don't worry. That gorgeous sheriff of yours won't know what hit him."

Outside, Jake and Kyle found a lot to talk about as they discovered both had played college football, both came from big, meddling families, and both cared deeply about Sam.

"Is it more bad news you have to give her tonight?" Kyle asked, hating the thought of her getting upset again.

"Actually, there's not a lot of news. I didn't learn much of anything from the conversation I had today. The kid I talked with was anything but cooperative."

"One of Sam's students?" When Jake looked unsure of how much to tell him, Kyle said, "She told us you suspect one or more of the kids from this camp on the lake might be responsible for the stuff going on around here."

"It was one of her students, a boy named Zach. I know she's not going to like even talking about it, she's ready to defend those kids until the end. It's a little unsettling, actually. She gets so upset and worries so much about them I'm afraid it's not good for her. I understand caring about them and wanting to help, but it seems like there's more to it with Sam."

Kyle was quiet, debating what to tell Jake. If Sam hadn't told him, maybe it wasn't his place to do so but he felt like Jake should know what he was dealing with and thought it might even help in the investigation if he knew where Sam was coming from.

"Has Sam ever talked to you about Danny?" Kyle began.

"Her brother? Yes, she's talked about him several times. I can tell they were close and that losing him was almost more than Sam could bear."

"She's never told you how he died?"

Jake was suddenly on edge, afraid of what he was going to hear from Kyle. Should he have pressed Sam harder for details? Was there something he needed to know in order to help her? He looked at Kyle and shook his head no.

Kyle took a deep breath, glanced in the house to be sure Sam and Susan weren't on their way out, and began. "Danny was a drug addict. It's not easy for me to say the words. We all tried, for a long time, to deny it and we all tried, for a very long time, to help him. Sam more than anyone."

It wasn't what he had expected to hear but it explained so much. Of course Sam would try to help the kids from Project Strong Start. She was trying to do for them what she had been unable to do for her brother.

Kyle continued. "He went through treatment programs. He'd be better for a while then relapse. Sam tried so hard, tried to get him to work in the shop with her, tried to get him interested in school. She even got Rigi hoping that having a puppy to care for would help him. I think Danny tried too, but he just couldn't kick it."

"I've seen what drugs can do to kids, to anyone. We may be a small town but we aren't immune to the problem. Addiction is ugly, there's no other way to describe it."

"Danny had his share of run-ins with the police. Sam and our grandfather had to bail him out on more than one occasion. There were times when the police showed up at their door looking for Danny. It was hard for Sam to realize they were doing what they had to do and not just blaming Danny based on his past."

Jake washed a hand over his face. He wished Sam had told him, he would have tried to be more sensitive, more understanding. He had never intended to hurt her.

"The night Danny died he was at a party with some guys who were nothing but trouble. He had promised Sam he wasn't hanging out with them anymore but apparently that was a lie. The police showed up, there were drugs everywhere. Danny panicked, I guess. He jumped into a car that wasn't his and took off. The police followed. Danny was in no condition to be driving. He headed to the highway, hit the median, and flipped the car. He was killed instantly."

Kyle's face was stony as he stared into the night. Jake could tell it wasn't an easy story for him to share. So much tragedy in one family. Jake realized, not for the first time, just how lucky he was.

Before they had a chance to discuss anything more, Sam and Susan returned loaded down with drinks and snacks. Susan was grinning from ear to ear while Sam eyed her warily.

The four talked and joked and it was Jake's turn to

hear old stories about Sam. Eventually the conversation turned to Jake's interview with Zach. He hadn't really said much of anything, Jake told them. He denied any involvement, said the only times he'd been any where near Sam's place were during class.

"I'm inclined to believe him," Jake said, "Marc had the same feeling. But, we agree he's hiding something. I tried to explain to him that if he's innocent, telling us what he was up to when he left with the car would be in his best interest. He wouldn't budge."

"What do you want me to do tomorrow when he comes back to class?" Sam asked. "Talk to him about what happened? Ignore the situation?" She seemed tense, as if she had been afraid of what she'd hear about Zach.

"Don't bring it up. I'll handle everything with Zach. If he says anything about our interview just let him talk. It's possible he'll tell you more than he was willing to tell us. But I don't want you in the middle of anything, Sam. If you start to feel uncomfortable or as if you're in any sort of danger, please call me right away."

"I'm not going to be afraid or feel like I'm in danger with those kids, Jake," she said, clearly exasperated.

"Okay. Good." Jake let the subject drop, not wanting to do any more to upset Sam. A short time later he said his goodbyes and headed home knowing a great deal more about Sam than when he had arrived.

He sat and planned, his anger and hatred close to the surface. It was frustrating when he was unable to watch her, to know what she was doing. He would have to make his move soon before the cop figured things out. He wrapped his hand tightly around a knife he had been holding, his eyes becoming nothing more than slits as he plotted. She would pay, in more ways than one, he told himself as he violently swung his arm downward, driving the blade deep into the scarred wood.

16

The week was going by quickly with Sam enjoying the mornings with her students and the afternoons and evenings with her cousins. The kids seemed refreshed after their week away. Jimmy was full of camping stories he was just bursting to share, something that didn't surprise Sam. What did, however, was how often the other kids chimed in with their own comments. That never would have happened a few weeks ago.

The atmosphere was a little different without Katie but Sam had already heard from her and her happiness was apparent even via email. She had her dad, her brothers, and her beloved cat together again and it sounded as though everything was going well. Sam was pleased she had followed through on her promise to keep in touch.

Zach was still quiet, usually speaking only when spoken to, and he hadn't mentioned anything about his visit with Jake and Marc. Sam was happy to avoid the topic.

So on Thursday morning when Sam heard the door to the shop open and turned to see a young man with red hair mostly hidden under a dirty cap, a face with freckles and scars competing for space, and wearing stained, ripped jeans, she was startled and caught completely off guard. When Jimmy looked up and gave a muffled yell, Sam quickly put two and two together and determined the man barging into her shop was Jimmy's older brother, Blade.

Sam's first thought was to protect Jimmy who had jumped off his stool and moved away from the door. Sam made her way toward the man, willing her knees not to shake.

"Is there something I can help you with?" she asked, sounding much calmer than she felt.

Blade's eyes darted around the room and finally back to Sam. "Just looking for my brother," he snarled.

Blade was wearing a leather jacket even though the temperature had to be in the eighties. When he reached inside the pocket, Sam spread out her arms in an attempt to shield the kids.

Blade laughed cruelly. "What do ya think, lady, I'm gonna shoot? I told ya, I just want to talk to my brother."

"I'm afraid you can't do that right now. If you want to talk to your brother, you're going to have to go to the office at Project Strong Start and try to arrange things with someone there. Right now, I'd like you to leave."

Sam knew her voice was beginning to waver. She was trying to figure out how to get to her phone without Blade realizing what she was doing. She couldn't see a way to manage it. All of a sudden, she realized the rest of the kids in class had left their seats and were standing beside her.

Jackson was the first to speak, his voice low and menacing. "The lady asked you to leave. I think you'd better do it."

Davis, for as much as he liked to antagonize Jimmy, was clearly ready to protect him. "Yeah, man, get lost. Jimmy doesn't want to talk to you."

Mario was inching closer to Blade and Sam started to panic. Blade was going to hurt one of them.

"Sit back down, everyone. Everything is fine," Sam looked from one to the other, pleading with her eyes for them to back away. When her eyes met Zach's she caught a quick flash of fury in them before he quickly reached his hand into his pocket and turned to Blade.

"Miss Taylor said get out so get the hell out," he hissed. Sam froze, certain Zach must have pulled a knife, and was terrified of what was going to happen, but before Blade had a chance to react, a large arm reached out from behind and grabbed him, pinning him against the wall.

Sam didn't know where Kyle had come from but her relief was so great, she collapsed onto the nearest stool. She was on her feet again in a moment, though, remembering Zach and afraid he would still be going at Blade with a knife. When she looked and realized it wasn't a knife but a cell phone he had pulled from his pocket, she allowed herself to fall back onto the stool.

Marc was the first to arrive, having been closer he beat Jake by a few minutes. Kyle still had Blade restrained in the shop while Sam had taken the kids outside. Marc quickly handcuffed Blade and Kyle joined Sam and the kids. While Marc stayed with Blade, Jake got the rundown on what had happened, asking questions of the kids as well as Sam.

"We'll take him in and question him at the station. Are you sure you and the kids are all right? I can call an ambulance, have everyone checked out," Jake said.

"I don't think that's necessary. He never touched anyone, except Kyle, and it was Kyle who did most of the touching. But he's fine. I think he wishes Blade would have fought back a little harder so he could have knocked him around some."

"How about the kids? How's Jimmy?"

Sam looked over to the yard where Jimmy sat in the grass with the rest of the kids and Susan, who had joined them. "He's scared, really scared. When Blade walked in the shop he went white and almost ran to the other side of the room."

"I can have someone come out and talk to him, we have people on call to help in situations like these."

"I already called Project Strong Start and talked to Tom Lindahl. He's on his way with a van to pick up the kids himself. He knows some of the details and said he'll have someone ready to work with Jimmy. Jimmy's been quiet, hasn't really said much of anything since his brother showed up."

A few minutes later Tom arrived and after a short conversation with Sam and Jake, loaded the kids in the van and headed back to camp.

"I need to get him to the station," Jake said, indicating Blade who was handcuffed in the back of Marc's patrol car. "Are you going to be okay?"

"Of course, don't worry. Besides, Susan and Kyle

are here, I won't be alone."

"Okay. I'll call you later this afternoon. If you need anything or think of anything you want to add to your statement, just call." He moved closer and kissed her, holding on for an extra hug before he headed to his car and drove off following Marc.

Sam watched until they were out of sight then turned and made her way to the front porch where Kyle and Susan were waiting.

"Doing okay, cuz?" Kyle asked, his eyes betraying him and showing much more concern than his voice.

"I'm fine. I'm just glad you got there when you did." She gave a little shudder thinking about what could have happened. "If he had hurt one of those kids…"

"Or you!" Susan chimed in. "He could have hurt you, too."

"Well, he didn't and now, hopefully, he'll find himself back in jail and Jimmy won't have to worry about him for a long time. Jake said he had a gun in his jacket. I guess it wasn't loaded but since he's on probation that should still be enough to put him away for a while." Her knuckles turned white as she gripped the porch railing.

"Do you think the kids will be back tomorrow?" Susan asked. "I heard the camp director mentioning special group sessions tomorrow to talk about what happened."

"Actually, they never come on Fridays, it's just Monday through Thursday. I assume they will be back on Monday, though. I'll check in with the director tomorrow and see how things are going. I sure hope they come back," Sam said, clearly worried.

Later that afternoon, once Sam had finally convinced Susan and Kyle she was fine, they left for their planned outing into Misty Lake to get some groceries and to look around a little more. Sam wanted some time in the shop, she hadn't put many hours in on the china hutch since her cousins had arrived.

When she heard a car door slam her heart gave a quick start before she heard a voice call out loudly, "Sam? It's Sean McCabe."

Sam opened the door that her cousins had insisted she lock to find Jake's father standing in her driveway, smiling. "I hope I didn't startle you. Jake told me you had a scare out here today."

"Mr. McCabe, how nice to see you. Jake told you about that, did he?" Sam had an image of Jake calling his dad and giving him a report on what went on earlier and the two of them deciding it would be good for the former sheriff to stop by, make sure things were okay. It was sweet.

"Oh, well, once a cop, always a cop, I guess," he blushed. "I like to stay on top of what's going on around here. Everything okay?" he asked, becoming more serious.

"Everything is fine. I'll admit it was frightening for a while this morning but things are back to normal," she answered, smiling and doing her best to convince him.

"I'm glad. From what I hear, that kid is nothing but trouble. I hope they can lock him up for a while."

"Me too. Would you like to come in, have a cup of coffee, take a look around? I hear there's been quite a lot of curiosity surrounding my house."

"I don't want to trouble you, Sam. I actually came to discuss some business with you."

"Oh?"

"Well, Anna and I are going to be celebrating our thirty-fifth wedding anniversary this fall and I'd like to get her something special."

"Congratulations! Come inside and let's talk," Sam said, leading him to the shop. "Do you have something in mind or are we going to brainstorm?"

"I've been thinking about that, she's hinted around a few times about…" As they entered the shop, Sean stopped in his tracks and stared.

"Mr. McCabe?" Sam looked at him questioningly.

"That's it. How did you know? Oh, I guess you couldn't have known but it's exactly what I was picturing." He was looking at the hutch as if it were the answer he had long been seeking.

"This? The china cabinet? You were thinking something like this for Mrs. McCabe?"

"Well, yes. It's just what I was thinking. Oh, but you must be making it for someone else, of course. Maybe we can come up with something similar?"

Sam thought for a moment then smiled. "Do you know what, Mr. McCabe? I think I was making it for you."

"What do you mean, making it for me? We've never talked about anything like this."

Sam's voice took on a far away tone. "It's something I've been thinking about building for years. My grandfather used to talk about building a special cabinet for my grandmother but he never had the chance. It was always in the back of my mind and lately it's become something I just needed to do. The process has been therapeutic, if that makes sense," she said as she ran her hand over the smooth wood, a motion that always served to soothe her.

"But surely you want to keep it for yourself. It obviously has a very special meaning to you."

"No…" then firmer, "No. I really don't need to keep it, I just needed to build it. If you think it's something Mrs. McCabe would like then it's yours. I can do the rest of the work to your specifications." Sam suddenly felt as if a huge weight had been lifted and she was beaming at Sean.

"Are you sure, Sam?" Sean looked again at the cabinet. "Anna would love it. I love it. If you're certain that you want to part with it, I certainly want to buy it."

"I'm certain. Let's talk details."

"Only if you start calling me Sean," he warned as he settled onto a stool next to Sam and began planning the finishing touches on Anna's anniversary gift.

17

On Saturday evening Sam found herself once again surrounded by a group of McCabes. Before Sean had left her shop he had talked her into joining the family for a dinner to celebrate the news of their future grandchild. Sam had argued it should be just family but Sean was adamant. She had been there when the news was first announced, she had gone shopping with Karen, and she was creating a gift for Anna that was sure to make him a hero. She was practically part of the family, he had insisted. When she explained her cousins would still be visiting, Sean had insisted they come along, too.

Susan had been excited about the opportunity to meet Jake's family and even more excited about Sam and Jake having another chance to spend time together. Kyle hadn't offered much of an opinion, having learned long ago it was much easier to just do whatever the women involved told him to do.

Like Sam's previous visit, the dinner with the McCabes was a noisy, fun-filled affair. Jake and his siblings tried to outdo one another in the story-telling department, resulting in lots of laughs and some embarrassed grimaces. When it came time to clear the table and wash the dishes, Sam insisted on helping. Anna, claiming the kitchen was too small for many helpers, assigned the rest various tasks.

Once it was quiet in the kitchen Anna asked, "Are you doing okay after the incident on Thursday? Jake told us about it. You must have been terrified."

"It was pretty scary for a while but it was over quickly, thanks to Kyle. I don't like to think about how things might have ended if he hadn't shown up when he did."

"I'm sorry it happened, Sam, and I'm sorry it seems you've had more than your share of trouble since you got here. That's not how things usually are in Misty Lake. It's normally a pretty quiet place, and a safe place."

"I'm sure that's the case and I'm sure any problems I've had are over. Jake doesn't think Jimmy's brother was responsible for any of the other things that have happened but since things have calmed down in that department, I'm betting it's all over. I can't spend all my time looking over my shoulder."

"No, you can't. That's no way to live, I agree, but you have to be cautious at the same time." Then, before Sam could respond, Anna said "And speaking of Jake…"

Were they speaking of Jake? Sam wondered. She sensed Anna was getting to the real reason it was just the two of them in the kitchen.

"I've heard the two of you have been spending more time together."

Small towns, Sam thought. Of course Jake's mother had heard about every time they'd been together. "We've seen each other a few times," Sam began tentatively.

"Well, I just want you to know I'm pleased. Jake is a good boy and he's been on his own for far too long."

"Now, Mrs. McCabe...Anna," she corrected herself at Anna's raised eyebrows. "We're really just friends. We've had dinner a couple of times but most of our time together has been the result of the trouble I've seemed to attract since I got to Misty Lake."

"Hmmm," was Jake's mother's only response.

Sam rushed to explain before Anna got the wrong idea. "Your son is very nice, Anna, but it's nothing serious. We met because he's the sheriff and he's unfortunately had to come out to my place on a few occasions. It's just business. Yes, we've had dinner, but like I said, it's mostly just been to discuss the case and Jake's progress. It's not like we've had a lot of dates or like we've met each other's families...well, I guess I've met you and Jake has met my cousins but, really, that just sort of happened, it's not like we planned it. It's just business," she repeated.

Sam realized she was rambling and was out of breath. When she looked up Anna was smiling with a knowing look on her face. She came to Sam, put a hand on her arm and calmly said, "You're in love with my son."

"What? No. In love? Definitely not. I mean, it's not that he's not a great guy but that's just not how it is. I'm sorry if I've given you the wrong impression, I certainly didn't mean to, but in love? No. No."

"It's okay to be a little frightened, Sam. Believe me, I understand."

"Understand what?" Sam asked weakly.

"Being afraid to love someone who puts himself in danger every day, day after day."

Sam looked at Anna and tried to force herself to calm down. Was she in love with Jake? Was she afraid? Did Jake's mother really see it before she could even admit it to herself?

"Sit down, Sam," Anna said as she led Sam to the kitchen table. "Tell me what you're feeling."

"Like I said, it's nothing, really," Sam began before Anna interrupted.

"Sam, you can talk to me. You can ask me questions and I'll do my best to answer. I'm not trying to take the place of your mother but I am a mother, maybe talking to me will help," she said kindly.

Sam dropped her head and nodded. "I lost my mom a long time ago but I still miss her, still wish I could talk to her, ask her advice."

"I lost my mother a long time ago, too. The hurting and the wishing never really go away. Now, I have my mother's sisters, Kate and Rose, and I love them both dearly, but somehow it's just not quite the same."

Sam looked up to see a grin on Anna's face and both women laughed at the same time.

When the laughter died down and after Anna had chased away two of her sons who had heard the laughter from the kitchen she said to Sam, "Now, talk to me."

"I'm not sure I know where to start."

"You're scared. Do you want to talk about that?"

"Okay. How did you do it? How do you do it? How can you watch them go out the door every day and not be scared?"

"Oh, I never said I wasn't scared. That would be a lie. There've been times when I've been terrified. More so with Jake, I think, than with Sean, but terrified nonetheless."

"Why more with Jake?" Sam asked, curious.

"I love my Sean with all my heart, I have since the day I met him, and losing him would be unbearable, but Sean was already a police officer when I met him. It was part of who he was and I came to love him as a police officer. That's not saying I was crazy about him putting himself in harm's way, but there was something about seeing him in that uniform." She wiggled her eyebrows and laughed. "The longer we were together the more I learned to trust him and have confidence in his ability and his determination to stay safe."

"Now, when Jake said he wanted to follow in his father's footsteps? I hit the ceiling. When you have children your focus becomes your children, taking care of them, teaching them, keeping them safe. It doesn't matter if that child is an infant or a high school senior. When you hear they are knowingly choosing to do something that's potentially dangerous, instinct kicks in and you try to protect. I fought Jake for weeks, months actually, before he and his father convinced me I had to let him do what he wanted to do."

"How did they finally convince you?"

"Let me tell you, when Jake sets his mind to something it's not easy to change it. He bombarded me with facts and statistics trying to convince me he could choose many other more dangerous professions. Did you know a police officer is not even in the top ten of most dangerous jobs? It falls somewhere behind loggers, fishermen, farmers, and garbage haulers."

"I didn't know that," Sam mumbled.

"In the end it wasn't the statistics or the colored charts and graphs he presented me but the fact that it was what he really wanted. If he could keep up the badgering and the speeches for that long, I knew he would never really be happy without at least giving it a try. I'll admit, I was hoping he would change his mind but…" Anna shrugged. "And don't think I didn't make him swear all sorts of promises to me."

"So how do you handle the dangers that go with the job? How do you get through your day not knowing what their day will bring?"

"Early on, I spent many, many days worrying. It got worse after Jake was born. Thinking about the possibility of being widowed with a baby was paralyzing. One day Sean sat me down and told me if I wanted, he would quit. Just like that. He said I was more important than a job and if it was too difficult for me, he would leave his job. A job I knew he loved."

"He said that?"

"He did and I knew he meant it. Right then and there I decided if he loved me enough to quit then I loved him enough not to let him. I prayed a lot, I still do. I also started focusing on the fact that it was far, far more likely nothing bad would happen than that something would. Why not dwell on the statistics that practically guaranteed he'd be home for dinner? And why not focus on how proud I was that he worked so hard to keep the town, and those who lived in it, safe?"

"That makes sense, I suppose. I guess I'm just so afraid of losing another person I care about, it's hard to let myself care too much."

The sadness in Sam's eyes almost broke Anna's heart. Gently she said, "But what's the alternative, dear? Shutting yourself off, not letting yourself love, is no way to go through life. As hard as it is, you have to look to the future and not to the past. I have to believe it's what your family would have wanted for you."

"I know. Logically, I know. I recently found a letter my grandfather wrote for me before he died. He said a lot of the same things you just said, but it's so difficult. Sometimes I think things are better, I'm happy, having fun, and then, bam. Something triggers a memory or I start feeling sorry for myself and it's as if I'm reliving it all again. I almost feel as if I'm really back at the hospital hearing the news that my parents and grandmother are dead. Or I'm getting the news about Danny or my grandfather. I can't imagine what would happen to me if I ever have to face something like that again."

"I think you're stronger than you believe, Sam. Look what you've done here in Misty Lake. You picked up and moved to a strange place, started a business, you're working with a group of kids who are going to be much better for the experience, and you're making my son happy. I think that's pretty amazing."

"I don't know…"

"You can't let fear control your life. You don't want to look back one day and find only what ifs instead of a lifetime of beautiful memories."

Sam looked at Anna and slowly nodded. She let out a ragged breath. "You're right and I'll try. I can't promise it will happen over night, but I promise I'll work on it."

"Good. Remember I'm here if you want to talk. Anytime. Now, let's finish these dishes and join the party."

Susan grabbed a chair, deciding to help Riley return the extra chairs to the basement, the job assigned him by his mother. As she followed him down the stairs she couldn't help but notice the long, lean legs, trim waist, and broad shoulders. His wavy brown hair had auburn highlights. She had friends who paid hundreds of dollars every month in an attempt to achieve what Riley probably never gave a thought.

"The chairs go right in here," Riley said, leading her down a hallway to a storage room. The pictures on the wall caught Susan's attention and she stopped to look more closely.

"These are fantastic."

Riley came back and picked up the chair Susan had been carrying. "Frank took them, he's our photographer."

"The photos are great but I meant what's in the photos. Before and after, I assume." The hallway was lined with framed side-by-side photos, interior and exterior shots of what looked to be several different houses. First was a picture of a room, a porch, even a staircase all in various states of neglect. Following was a picture taken from the same angle but looking dramatically different. The kitchen in one photo had been gutted and rebuilt with stunning cabinets, granite countertops, and a beautiful wood floor. The old, worn staircase had become nothing short of a work of art. The faded, tattered carpet was gone, replaced with gleaming wood stairs set off by gorgeous railings and newel posts. The transformations were incredible.

"Does he take photographs for people when they are remodeling?" Susan asked. "Or take advertising photos?"

"Well, yes, he does take advertising photos but these are pictures he took of work I've done," Riley answered as he headed down the hall with the chair.

"You did this? All of this?"

"You don't have to sound so shocked."

"I didn't mean it like that, it's just that the work is amazing. You are obviously quite talented, Riley McCabe."

"It's what I love, being good at it is a bonus."

"Do you flip houses?"

"I haven't yet but I would like to. Right now I'm doing remodels, building decks, finishing basements, that sort of thing."

"Wonderful," Susan said sincerely. "You choose your jobs, set your hours, don't have a boss breathing down your neck." Susan sighed. "Wonderful," she said again.

"I think it's pretty wonderful but there are bills to pay. I can't always afford to be too picky about jobs and oftentimes my hours are longer than they'd ever be working at something else. Then there are the homeowners. I may not have a boss breathing down my neck but have you ever tried to work when a mom decides it will be okay for her kids to 'watch' while she runs to the store? Or when a retired architect scrutinizes your every move and tells you daily what you're doing wrong? Or when a bored housewife changes her mind *six times* on where she wants outlets in the new designer kitchen she's probably never going to use for anything but mixing margaritas? I could go on."

Susan laughed. "Okay, I guess it's not perfect but if you're happy, at least most of the time, then I'd say you're pretty lucky."

"What do you do that you think my job is so wonderful?"

"Oh, hospitality stuff, hotel management. Nothing exciting, trust me."

"Sounds interesting to me. I would imagine you could tell lots of stories."

"There's really not much to tell," Susan answered quickly.

Obviously, she didn't want to discuss her job so Riley let the subject drop. "I suppose we should head back up."

"Right. So what do you think about becoming an uncle?"

"You know, I'm pretty excited about it. The idea of a little guy running around here sounds kind of cool. And thinking about Joe trying to handle him after I've spent the day getting him all wound up with candy and roughhousing? Priceless."

"It could be a girl, you know."

"That works. I'm sure I can find a way to get a girl wound up, too."

Susan studied him. I bet you can, she thought. I bet you can.

18

Sunday afternoon Sam was sitting on the dock with Susan and Kyle willing the time to pass slowly. They had gone to church that morning at Susan's insistence with her cousin telling her it was time for her to go back. Susan had been right. Sam felt good, at peace. And if she was going to follow through on the promise she had made to Anna, church was a good place to start. Seeing the McCabe family all seated together in what Sam assumed was their regular pew had been a comforting sight. And watching Susan watch Riley McCabe had been interesting, to say the least.

Sam had spoken briefly with Kathleen Melby after mass. The realtor was even more bubbly than usual since an old house on the lake was finally going on the market and she had the listing. She had explained the location, telling Sam it wasn't far from her house, but Sam wasn't familiar with the property. Kathleen had hinted she might stop by on her way to take pictures of the property.

Now, though, Sam was dreading the fact that her cousins would be leaving after lunch. The house was going to seem so empty and she wasn't sure how she was going to fill the void.

"I guess I better head in and get packed," Kyle said pulling his feet from the water and standing up. "Suze, I'll leave you to talk to Sam." He gave Susan an odd look, Sam noticed, as he headed for the house.

"What was that all about?" Sam asked.

"I've been wanting to talk to you about something. Tell you something, I guess."

"What is it? You know you can tell me anything," Sam said, growing worried.

She looked nervously at Sam. "I quit my job. My last day was right before we left to come here."

"You quit The Billingsley? Why? I thought you were happy there."

"I was, for a while, but not lately. You know Stephen Billingsley took over the management of the hotel from his father last year?" When Sam nodded, she continued. "He's insufferable. He's always asking me out, hinting that I could be in line for a promotion if I agree."

"Susan, that's sexual harassment. You don't have to put up with that and you definitely shouldn't have to quit because of it."

"I know. Believe me, I considered talking to someone about it but, in the end, I figured, why? I hadn't enjoyed working there for a long time and I really didn't want to fight to stay. Stephen is such a pompous ass, it was really quite enjoyable slamming my resignation letter on his desk." She was grinning at the memory.

"Okay, if that's what you wanted. Do you have something else lined up?"

At this, Susan looked uncomfortable. "Not exactly. Well, it's not really not exactly. It's just no. And don't bother lecturing me because Mom and Dad have already done plenty of that."

"I wouldn't lecture you, Suze. I'm just concerned, I guess. What are you going to do?"

Now she looked even more uncomfortable and was quiet for what seemed like a long time. "I was sort of thinking about staying in Misty Lake for a while."

"In Misty Lake? Really? That's…that's wonderful!"

"Do you really think so?"

"Of course, I'd love to have you here."

"Oh, no, I don't mean I expect to stay here. I'll look for a place, for a job. I'm tired of Chicago, I need a change of scenery. I have some money, I can afford to rent a place."

Susan had always been a little rash. She had switched colleges twice before graduating, had once bought a car then sold it and bought another within a month, and had broken up and reconciled with boyfriends more often than Sam could possibly remember. Now, Sam worried she hadn't given this decision enough thought.

"Susan, don't be ridiculous. Of course you'll stay here. If you're sure Misty Lake is really what you want. It's a much different way of life than Chicago."

"I know and that's what I love about it. I don't know that I'll stay forever, but right now I need to try something different."

"Do Uncle Ben and Aunt Caroline know your

plans?"

"I told them before I left. They're not crazy about the idea but they'll get used to it. I'm going to call them and ask them to ship some of my things I packed up before I left. The hardest part is the fact that Brad and Mia are going to have a baby. I almost changed my mind when they told us the news but I really think this is the right thing to do."

"Okay, then it's decided. Welcome to Misty Lake, roomie."

As they made their way back to the house Susan asked, "Since I'm going to be a Minnesotan, how about a trip to the Mall of America?"

Later that afternoon, as Sam and Susan were playing in the yard with Rigi, Kathleen arrived as she had hinted she might. Sam was surprised to see her in jeans and looking almost casual. As she got closer Sam noted the jeans were designer and neatly pressed, the blouse a pretty, filmy silk, and the tennis shoes Gucci. Gold dripped from her ears, wrists, and around her neck, as usual. Even when she attempted casual she was dressed to the nines. Sam quickly corralled Rigi before the dog could slobber her hello all over Kathleen's five hundred dollar shoes.

"Hi, Sam. Hi, Susan. What a beautiful day! You must be loving the fact you're living at the lake this summer with as hot as it's been. Have you gotten yourself a boat yet? That seems to be the first thing everyone does when they move here. If you haven't and you're interested, I know someone who could help you out, just let me know."

Sam had gotten used to the rapid fire pace at

which Kathleen spoke so just smiled and answered, "Okay."

After talking a few more minutes about the weather, the latest news from town, and quizzing Susan on her plans, Kathleen grew more serious.

"Sam, are you doing all right? I mean, really all right after everything that happened here last week?"

"I'm fine, Kathleen. Thank you for asking."

"I want to offer a proposition. I spoke with Tom Lindahl and told him I could take a couple of your kids if you don't think you want to continue with the classes."

"Oh, that's—" Sam started but Kathleen kept talking.

"I can only imagine what a scare you had last week. Tom and I agree it's perfectly understandable if you'd like to end your involvement with the camp, at least for the time being. Now, I can't take all five of your students, but I can talk to some of the other volunteers and it won't be any problem to place them with someone else. I'll work it all out, you don't need to worry about a thing."

When she finally stopped for a breath Sam said, "Kathleen, I appreciate the offer but everything is fine. I'm fine. I want to continue working with the kids. I love the time I spend with them and there's just no reason to stop."

"Sam, no one will think any less of you if you want to step back. What happened would be enough for anyone to make that decision."

"Kathleen, I don't want to step back." Sam was starting to get frustrated and took a breath, trying to keep her temper from flaring. "I want to work with these kids. I am going to finish out the summer and, if Project Strong

Start will have me, I will volunteer again next summer. I haven't for a minute considered quitting and I'm not about to consider it now. I really do appreciate you and Tom trying to help but nothing is going to change. I am going to do all I can to help these kids."

Kathleen looked to Susan who had stayed quiet up to this point. Susan just gave a shrug and said, "I think her mind's made up."

Turning back to Sam, Kathleen said, "Well, okay, if you're sure. Just remember the offer is still on the table. If you change your mind you only have to call."

"I'll do that."

Kathleen paused a beat. "Well then, I'd better get going. I'm heading down the road to check out that property I was telling you about. It's an old farmhouse, the only one left around the lake. It hasn't been inhabited for years. The family that owns it sold most of the property but kept the house and a few acres. Now, it's been handed down to a great granddaughter who lives in Texas and just wants to be rid of the place. I have to get inside, take a look around, but I'm betting whoever buys it will want to tear it down and rebuild. It has to be in terrible condition."

"Thanks for stopping by, Kathleen, I really do appreciate your offer to help," Sam said sincerely, hoping to soften her earlier comments.

Kathleen smiled, gave a little wave, and started heading for her car. All of a sudden Susan bounded after her. "Would you mind if I ride along? I'd like to see more of the area and Sam's heading to work in the shop. I need something to do."

"Of course I wouldn't mind. I'll give you a tour of the lake, it will be fun." And hopefully she could ferret out a little information about Sam. Sam's latest reaction had Kathleen more worried than ever.

"Do you mind, Sam? I can stick around if you don't want to be alone."

"Not at all, take your time. I've got plenty of work to do. I took a little too much time off this past week. And I'm not afraid to be here alone."

He watched the two women drive off and knew that meant she was alone. Maybe now was his chance. No cop or dumb jock to save her this time. He could get into her shop, he'd done it before. She'd never have time to call for help. Then, once he'd taught her a lesson, everything he deserved would be his.

He started to climb out of the culvert where he had been hiding, well out of sight. Suddenly, the dog started barking and racing back and forth along the driveway, never taking her eyes off of him. He threw himself back down onto the damp ground just as the woman came out of the shop to quiet the dog.

"Rigi! That's enough! Sam looked around, didn't see anything, and was just ready to walk across the road to take a closer look when she saw two deer, a doe with a fawn closely behind, zip quickly back into the trees.

"Okay, girl. Everything is fine, you silly thing," she said, rubbing Rigi's ears. "It's just deer, and I think they're cute, so be nice. Besides, you're going to have to get used to sharing the area with them. They were here first, you know."

He watched as she petted the dog for a minute then headed back into her workshop leaving the dog outside. He'd never get close now, he knew. Well, there'd be another chance. His hands trembled slightly as he clicked the safety back on the gun and stuck it deep into his pocket.

19

"I need to buy a car," Susan announced over breakfast.

"I told you, you can use mine."

"I know, but that's not a long term answer. I need my own car."

Sam studied her cousin and worried that she was making another rash decision. "Why don't you just keep using mine until you're sure you want to stay in Misty Lake," Sam answered carefully, not wanting to upset Susan.

"Sam, would you stop worrying about me? I told you, I gave this decision plenty of thought. I didn't just up and quit my job and decide to move here, it was something I was tossing around for a long time."

"Okay, okay, I'm sure you gave it a lot of thought. But do you really think you want to buy a car so soon? What did you do with the car you had in Chicago?"

"I sold it right before Kyle and I left so I have that

money to use to buy something here," she said with a bright smile. "Do you mind if I take your car this afternoon and go look around, see what's for sale at the car lot in town?"

"No, of course not. I'll just be working. I have a couple jobs I need to get started."

"Great. I'm going to do some laundry this morning, thought I'd take Rigi for a run, then I'll head into Misty Lake later."

"Sounds good," Sam replied. "I was thinking, it's Friday, do you want to go out tonight? See what the nightlife is like in Misty Lake? I still haven't been in town on a weekend night, it's probably time."

"Um, I don't know. Let's see how the day goes. I might be a while looking at cars." She seemed reluctant, frowning a little at the idea.

Strange, Sam thought. Usually that conversation went the other way with Susan badgering Sam to get out of the house. "Okay, let me know later."

"Will do," Susan answered, her smile back in place.

Several hours later Susan walked into the sheriff's office with a purposeful spring in her step. After being directed to Jake's office, she knocked lightly on the door that was slightly ajar and peeked inside. Jake was seated behind his desk with Riley across from him. Both men looked up as Susan entered.

"Hi!" She said brightly. "I hope I'm not interrupting."

"Come in, Susan," Jake said getting up to pull another chair up to his desk. "What brings you here? Is everything okay?"

"Oh, everything is fine, I didn't mean to worry you," she answered, noting the concern in Jake's eyes. Perfect, she thought.

Jake let out the breath he didn't realize he'd been holding since seeing Susan at his door. "Riley's just here bugging those of us who actually work for a living so, no, you're not interrupting anything."

Susan looked at Riley, leaning back casually in his chair, his long legs stretched out and crossed at the ankles. He was looking her up and down, his eyebrows raised. A little arrogant, she decided.

"Day off?" she asked sweetly, looking at Riley. Without waiting for a reply, she turned to Jake. "I'm actually here for some advice, if you have a minute."

"Sure."

"I need to buy a car. What do you know about the people who run the car lot in town? Honest? Am I going to get a fair deal?"

"Yes, I think you will. One of Riley's best buddies runs the place." Then, looking at his brother, "You're not doing anything, why don't you take her over there, talk to Kurt, and get her a good deal?"

Riley scowled and practically burned a hole in Jake with his eyes. "I might have to get back over to the jobsite if that inspector ever gets his act together," he mumbled.

"You said he was at least a day behind schedule. I'm sure you can find time to help Susan."

Susan watched the exchange between the two and bit her lip to keep from laughing. Riley looked from Jake to Susan and back again before spitting out, "Fine, sure, I have time."

"Well, thank you very much, Mr. McCabe. I'm sure your time is valuable, I'll try not to take up too much of it," she said sweetly.

When Jake smothered a laugh, she turned to him. "As for you, Sheriff McCabe, I guess I'll be needing a favor of you, too. Since I'm sure with such excellent assistance I won't have any trouble finding a car, and since I obviously can't drive two cars, Sam's car will need to be driven back out to the lake." She handed Jake the keys. "She mentioned this morning that she wants to go out tonight so how about if I tell her you'll be there around seven? You can pick her up, take her to dinner, show her the nightlife in Misty Lake. Then later, she can drop you at your place and drive herself home."

She turned a radiant smile on the brothers who both looked a little shell-shocked. Jake was the first to recover.

"I think I can manage that," he said, quickly warming to the idea of a night out with Sam, even if it hadn't been his idea.

"Perfect." Then, turning to Riley, "Shall we, Mr. McCabe?"

Riley slowly got to his feet, glaring at his brother as he did so. Susan stood at the door waiting, her bright green eyes sparkling with laughter.

"Well, then, let's go. And for God's sake, call me Riley," he grumbled.

"So was this your idea or Susan's?" Sam asked as Jake maneuvered her car down the driveway.

"Well…"

Sam laughed. "Don't worry, I know how Susan

works. She wouldn't admit it to me but I figured she had something to do with this."

"It's not like I didn't want to do it," Jake protested. "I probably would have thought of it myself, eventually. Maybe," he added, realizing the conversation wasn't going at all as he had intended. "It was a really busy week."

"I said don't worry," Sam reassured him and laid a hand on his arm. "Tell me about Friday nights in Misty Lake."

Jake glanced at her to make sure she didn't seem upset. When he saw her smiling, looking happy and relaxed, he relaxed, too.

"It's busier in the summer than in the winter although we get a fair number of people snowmobiling and ice fishing. We've got a few places worth checking out. The Hideout has a live band just about every weekend, some of them are pretty good. It draws those looking for a little more action. Mick's has been Mick's forever, I think. It's a small bar usually filled with locals who all know each other. If you want a fancy drink, it's not your place. You'll get a beer or a whiskey, some peanuts, a game of darts or pool, not much else. Sally runs For Heaven's Steak, hands down the best place for a nice dinner. But, if it's pizza you're looking for, you're in luck because I haven't found better than what you'll get at The Brick."

"Wow, that's quite an advertisement for your town, Sheriff."

"I guess when you live someplace your entire life it's easy to advertise."

"So what's our plan for tonight?"

"I thought I'd leave that up to you. What are you

in the mood for?"

"The pizza sounds tempting, although you have to remember I'm from Chicago. We take our pizza seriously."

"I promise you won't be disappointed."

She wasn't. The pizza was delicious. They argued briefly over the merits of thin crust versus deep dish with Sam defending her city's famous deep-dish pies but, in the end, admitting she actually preferred thin crust. "You have to promise not to tell," she said, swearing Jake to secrecy.

Later, they stopped by The Hideout for a drink. The band was good and the place was crowded. Jake seemed to know most everyone so there was a steady stream of people stopping by to say hello. There were several curious glances and some outright staring which Sam found entertaining. Apparently she was the object of much speculation, because of the house on the lake as well as for the fact she was out with Jake McCabe.

Jake's brother Frank stopped by with his date, a pretty blonde he introduced as Cynthia, a medical student. "I heard your cousin gave Riley a run for his money today," he said to Sam.

"I didn't get too many details out of Susan but you're probably right. She has a way of getting people to do what she wants. How mad was he?" Sam asked, cringing.

"A lot less than he made out to be, I think. He went on and on about her endless questions about the cars, needing to test drive a dozen before making up her mind, and how she talked Kurt down so low on the price he looked a little dazed when it was all said and done. Riley acted annoyed but I think he was impressed."

"That sounds like Susan. You can tell Riley,

though, she really was grateful for his help whether she admitted it to him, or not."

"So she's really staying in Misty Lake instead of going back to Chicago? Does she know what winter is like here?" Frank joked.

"I guess she'll find out. I guess we'll both find out."

Jake and Sam walked down the street hand in hand. It was a warm, humid night and the far-off rumblings suggested a storm was on its way.

"It's been quite a summer with all the heat and humidity. I really can't remember one this bad," Jake said.

"I'm glad I'm here to experience one for the record books."

"I'm glad you're here, too," Jake said, stopping and turning Sam toward him. He leaned down and kissed her.

Sam felt light-headed as she closed her eyes and melted into Jake. Desire warred with reason. She ran her hands up his back and into his hair, pressing closer, and taking the kiss deeper.

Jake held Sam tighter, an involuntary groan starting somewhere in his throat escaped when she ran her hands over him. "Come home with me, Sam," he breathed.

Sam turned her head and rested it on his shoulder, suddenly very much aware they were in the middle of Main Street. Her heart was pounding with Jake's matching hers beat for beat.

"I can't, Jake. I'm sorry. I...I'm just not ready." She stepped back slightly, looking him in the eyes. "I'm sorry for…for making you think differently. I don't know what to say. I don't want to hurt you and it's not that I don't want to, I just can't. I know that doesn't make any sense but can you try to understand?"

She seemed desperate, Jake thought, and on the verge of tears. He reigned in his desire and held her, kissing the top of her head. "I understand, Sam. I really do. You have to know how much I want you but not until you're sure."

"Oh, Jake." She buried her face in his shoulder and wondered when, or if, she'd ever feel normal again.

They started walking again, the booming thunder growing louder. "I'm driving you home," Jake said. "The storm's getting closer, I don't want you out by yourself."

"Don't be silly. I can drive myself home. Besides, if you drive my car then you'll be stuck out there without a car."

"I'll call Marc and have him swing by and pick me up. He's on duty tonight and he should be out patrolling around the lake about now. Don't argue, Sam," he said firmly as she started to do just that.

They hadn't discussed Jake's investigation all evening but Sam brought up the subject on the drive home. "What's your feeling on my case? Nothing has happened for a while, do you think it's all over?"

Jake debated with himself on how to answer. He didn't want to scare her but he didn't want her to become complacent, either. "Honestly, I don't think it's over. I wish I did but it seems too easy. I'm inclined to believe Jimmy's brother didn't have anything to do with the vandalism, he just happened to show up in the middle of everything."

Sam wanted to believe the opposite, that Blade was responsible, and that it was all over. "Well then, who?"

"I don't know. We've broken up a few parties around the lake recently. We showed Tyler's picture around, got a few people to admit to seeing him there a couple of times. If he was there and if Zach wasn't, we still don't have a good explanation for where Zach went."

"He didn't give you anything when you talked to him?"

"He hardly said a word. About all we got out of him was that he admitted to leaving with Tyler and that he had something he needed to do. He swore he wasn't anywhere near your property but he wouldn't tell us any more than that. He's a tough kid. I get the feeling he needs help, wants, in a way, to ask for it, but won't."

"I wish he'd ask," Sam said sadly.

"I wish I could feel completely confident that there was no way for Zach, or any of them, to get away from the camp undetected. There haven't been any problems in the past that I'm aware of but I think that if one of them wants it badly enough, he, or she, will find a way to get around the security measures."

Sam didn't respond, just stared into the dark, lost in her thoughts.

"How did the week go with all of them? How is Jimmy doing?" Jake asked after a few minutes.

"Things were pretty normal. Jimmy was quieter than usual the first part of the week but he seems to be himself again."

"Only a few more weeks and they'll all be heading home." Jake glanced at Sam to judge her reaction.

"I know," she sighed. "In some ways it seems like

the summer has gone by so quickly. Even with the problems, it's been wonderful. I hope they've gotten at least half as much out of the program as I've gotten working with them."

"I think you can count on it."

"If you believe that then how can you continue to think one of them is behind everything?" Sam tried to keep her voice casual but knew the frustration she felt was coming through.

"I need to look at all the possibilities, Sam. Zach's story is suspect and he's not doing anything to help his cause. You can't deny it makes him look guilty."

"We've been over this so many times. Just because they have problems in their past doesn't mean these kids are bad kids or that they're going to be in trouble for the rest of their lives. They just need help, need people to believe in them."

Jake debated but decided it was only fair to let Sam know what Kyle had told him. "Like Danny?" he asked gently.

Sam whipped her head around to look at Jake with wide eyes. "What about Danny?"

"Kyle told me about him, about how he died. I'm so sorry, Sam."

"I didn't know he told you," Sam whispered. "I should have told you a long time ago."

"You didn't owe me any explanations."

"No, but it wasn't really fair of me to get so upset with you and never try to explain." She paused a moment then added, "Can you understand, even a little, why I want to help these kids? Why I need to believe in them?"

"Of course I can. I want to see them succeed, too,

but I can't ignore the facts."

"I know, and I can't stop believing."

"And you shouldn't. You're good for them, Sam," he said, taking her hand and lifting it to his lips.

20

It was amazing what a couple weeks of calm, ordinary days could do for a person, Sam thought as she made her way to the shop. She and Susan had settled into a routine sharing household duties, finding time to have fun together, and knowing when to stay out of the other's way. Susan had taken a part-time job at It's a Lake Thing, the home décor and gift shop in town. When Sam had questioned her on why she hadn't looked for something more along the lines of what she had been doing in Chicago, Susan had shrugged saying for now, she just wanted something fun. Sam had swallowed her opinions and let it go.

Classes with her students couldn't be going better. The kids were completing their projects and gaining confidence in their abilities by the day. A couple, who had already finished, were working on picture frames and learning how to use a mitre box. Sam was proud of them all.

She and Jake were dating. The thought still made her a little giddy and she felt like a teenager as she skipped through the yard with Rigi at her heels. They had gone to a movie, had dinner at For Heaven's Steak with Joe and Karen, took in a Misty Lake Renegades baseball game, spent a Saturday shopping for groceries and making their own dinner, and even attended an informal class reunion with some of Jake's high school friends. Things a real couple did.

Perhaps best of all, though, was the fact that there hadn't been a hint of trouble for over three weeks. Sam had forgotten ordinary could feel so good.

She made her way into the shop with a spring in her step, determined to get a couple hours of work done before the kids arrived. When she spotted the Renegades cap on the hook inside the door she tenderly picked it up. Jake had bought it for her at the game, along with a huge bucket of popcorn and a sticky poof of pink cotton candy. He had been so sweet when he dropped the cap on her head telling her he didn't want her to burn her nose. He'd tugged a little on her ponytail then kissed the nose he had professed concern over. If she had had any doubt left that she was in love with him, that simple gesture had erased it. Smiling, Sam pulled the cap on and got to work.

She stood back a little and watched Jackson work. His concentration was intense as he measured for the placement of hinges on his nearly-completed jewelry box. It was truly a work of art. Sam doubted she could have done better herself. True, she had guided and assisted but he had done the work and the modifications to the original design were all his. She had been giving him as much space as possible for weeks but couldn't help herself today.

"Jackson, I have to tell you, I am so impressed with your work. This jewelry box is as well made as anything you'd find in an expensive store. You should be very proud."

"Thanks, Ms. Taylor. I guess it turned out pretty well, didn't it?"

"That's an understatement. It's fantastic."

Embarrassed by the praise, he dropped his head and mumbled a reply.

"I was talking to Mr. Lindahl the other day," Sam continued. "I asked him a little about your school. He said woodworking classes are offered." She let the thought hang.

"Yeah, I guess."

"Do you think you might give it a try at school? I know you'd do well."

Now he looked up at her. "Maybe. I talked to one of the counselors at camp the other day—we all had to—about school. I guess there are a couple classes I need to re-take in order to graduate. I don't know if I can fit a wood shop class in my schedule."

He seemed ashamed by the admission and Sam couldn't help but think that if they had had the same conversation at the beginning of the summer, his attitude would have most likely been one of defiance, instead. It was humbling to think she may have made an impact on him and she fought to keep her voice steady as she answered him.

"I had to re-take a class in high school. It was an English class. I didn't like the teacher and didn't like the assignments. I couldn't understand why I needed to pretend I was a piece of fruit and write a poem about my feelings."

Jackson gave her a doubtful look. "It's the truth," Sam said, tracing a cross over her heart. It was ridiculous," she said, laughing. "I had to go to summer school and write poems that year instead of taking driver's ed."

Jackson chuckled and Sam's heart melted. It was the first time she'd heard him laugh.

"Hopefully, if you want, you can fit in a woodworking class. If I can remember that far back, it seems senior year tends to have some room for electives. If I can help in any way, just let me know," she added.

Jackson nodded and bent over his jewelry box once more.

When Sam stood up she noticed Zach was watching and listening intently. He seemed troubled but quickly looked away when he caught her looking his way.

Hmmm, Sam wondered. Could she get through to two of them in the same day? She made her way over to Zach's spot and studied his hunched shoulders and bent head. Something was definitely wrong, he had been even more withdrawn than usual and this wasn't the first time she had noticed him looking at her as if he wanted to ask her something.

"How're things going today, Zach?" She tried to sound as casual as possible.

"Fine," he mumbled without looking up.

"It looks like you're just about finished. You've done a good job."

"Thanks."

"Do you need any help with the finishing work?

With…anything?"

He hesitated and glanced up at her then quickly around the room before putting his head back down. "No."

Feeling helpless, Sam sighed. "Okay, but all you have to do is ask if you need anything, Zach." She waited a moment. When he didn't respond she moved on, desperately wishing he would ask for help.

Sam showered quickly after the kids left and was rushing to get her hair and makeup done when Susan stuck her head in the bathroom.

"Going out?"

"I'm meeting Jake for lunch."

"Another date? What's that, about ten in the past two weeks?"

"Maybe."

"Wow, I just moved in and now you're going to go and get married and kick me out," Susan whined.

"No one said anything about marriage. It's just lunch. I mean, really, married? I don't think so." Sam was shaking her head.

"Hey, calm down. I was just kidding," Susan grinned. "I…" she studied Sam in the mirror. "OH MY GOD! You're in love with him!"

Sam whirled around. "What? No. It's just…" She put her hands over her eyes and peeked at Susan. "How did you know?" she squeaked.

Susan grabbed her and hugged her tight. "I guessed from the first time you talked about him. Then when I saw you two together I was even more certain. I've just been waiting for you to catch up!"

"It's kind of scary," Sam admitted. "What if he doesn't feel the same way?"

"He's crazy about you, Sam."

"I know he cares about me, we have fun together, and I know he'd like to take our relationship to the next level, so to speak, but love? I don't know."

"I've seen the way he looks at you. I don't think you have anything to worry about."

"But how do I know? And am I supposed to tell him? Or do I wait for him to tell me first? I don't know how this works."

Sam was pulling her hands through her hair and looking utterly distraught. Susan took pity on her cousin. "Oh, sweetie," she said, hugging her and rubbing her back. "Calm down. This is a good thing, a happy thing. Now, I can't claim to have a lot of experience in this particular area but if we can believe the movies and novels, you'll know. You'll just know."

Sam sat across from Jake and looked at him over her burger and fries. "They really tried to tell you it was oregano?" she asked, referring to the two teenagers Jake stopped to help earlier in the day.

"They did. They claimed their grandmother was Italian and cooked a lot. When I said it didn't look or smell like oregano they changed their story and admitted it was marijuana but said it was from Colorado so it was legal."

"Did they realize they were in Minnesota?"

Jake gave an eye roll. "They started talking over each other trying to come up with a plausible story. It was all I could do not to laugh. Possession of that much marijuana with intent to sell is a crime, of course, but at that point I was almost thinking their bigger crime was stupidity."

"So they told you to get the jack out of the trunk?"

"Yes," he said, having a hard time believing it himself. "When I stopped to see if I could help them with their flat and asked them if they had a jack, they told me to grab it from the already opened trunk. There were six bags of marijuana just lying there in plain sight."

"And they were just kids?" she asked, looking a little sad.

"Brothers, sixteen and seventeen. You know, though, the only thing they said that I really believed was that this was the first time they had done anything like this. They claimed they've never even smoked pot and I believed them. They seemed so naïve—clueless, really. I mean, they sent me to the trunk for the jack! These aren't hardened criminals by any stretch. They want to buy a fishing boat and said a friend told them that he had a way they could make some easy money."

"I hope they learned a lesson," Sam said. "Hopefully this will be enough to keep them away from the stuff."

"I have a feeling it will. And, if they didn't get enough of a scare riding in a police car and spending some time in jail, I'm pretty sure their father will take care of the rest. He was none too pleased when I called him. He even asked if it's okay if he lets them sit in jail for a little while before coming to get them. He's determined to teach them a lesson."

"Sounds like a good dad. I hope he gets through to them."

"He will," Jake said, putting a hand over hers. Then, determined to get a smile back on her face, he asked, "What do you think about this weekend? What do you feel like doing?"

"Well, since you asked," she said with a sly grin, "I'm thinking about buying a boat. Do you want to go boat shopping with me?"

"Really? I didn't know you were interested in having one."

"I've been here for months and have hardly been on the lake. I think it's time. Besides, a boat would be fun. Now, I'm not talking about anything like Joe has. I was actually thinking about a pontoon."

"That's definitely not like what Joe has."

"Do you think it's lame? My thought was I would use it to cruise around, Rigi could come with me. Maybe I'll even start fishing, who knows?"

"I think it sounds perfect. You know, I have a boat parked out behind Joe's place. I haven't put it in the water this summer since Joe has his new one. It's nothing as fast and fancy as his but it moves pretty well. If you'd like, I could move it over to your place, teach you how to drive it, and you could use it whenever you want."

"You could do that." She studied Jake. She didn't want to make it seem like she was going to consider his boat hers, didn't want to make it seem like they were sharing property. Although, he had suggested it, she thought. "That'd be good. I think I'd still like to look around a little at pontoons, though. It seems like it might be a little more relaxing floating around in a pontoon. Besides, they kind of remind me of the old raft we'd drag out into the lake and jump off when we were kids. I might have to invite all my cousins here for a game of King of the Pontoon."

She was beaming, her eyes twinkling, and Jake knew he'd move heaven and earth to help her find the pontoon of her dreams. "Then we'll look at pontoons this weekend."

Sam glanced at her watch. "I suppose you need to be getting back soon? I'll just finish these fries," she said, popping one in her mouth.

Jake grinned at her. "Enjoy your lunch?"

"Ha! I suppose you thought I'd order a salad or something girly. But you know what? I've been swimming almost every day, swimming hard, so I decided I deserved to splurge a little. Besides, this was delicious," she said, as she finished the very last french fry and licked a drop of ketchup from her thumb.

"I'm glad you enjoyed it. And you're right, I do need to get back."

Just then his radio crackled. "We have a domestic at 158 Spruce, reports of shots fired."

"10-4," Jake responded. "On my way." He turned to Sam give her a quick kiss and found her frozen, eyes wide and terrified. "Sam?"

She grabbed his arm and squeezed tight. "Oh God, Jake," she whispered, barely able to get the words out.

"Sam, it's okay. Everything will be okay." He hated leaving her, wanted with every ounce of his being to stay, but knew he had to go. "I'll call you soon, very soon. I promise." He put an arm around her, hugged her tight, threw some bills on the table, and darted out the door.

Sam sat and stared after him, unmoving. Shots

fired. The words replayed over and over in her head. He was going to get shot, he was going to die and leave her, too. Another cop would ring her doorbell, give her the news that someone else she loved was gone forever.

Her head was spinning with horrific images and she felt nauseated. Gripping the edge of the table, she told herself, No! She had to do something. She couldn't sit back and let it happen again. She wouldn't.

Stumbling to her feet and knocking over her chair, she reached for her purse and staggered out the door, oblivious to the stares of those around her. She was looking around wildly, trying desperately to remember where she'd parked her car when she felt hands reach out and take her by the shoulders.

"Samantha," a voice said, calmly, reassuringly.

Sam turned and tried to focus. Jake's father looked back at her, his kind blue eyes filled with understanding. "Oh, Sean! It's Jake, shots fired, he left, we need to do something." She was pulling on his arm, trying to drag him with her down the sidewalk.

"Samantha, please try to calm down," he said gently.

"But he's going to get hurt! What if he gets hurt?" Sam shouted frantically.

"He's going to be fine, he knows what he's doing." Sean started to slowly lead Sam down the street to a deserted bench. Once he had her seated he took her hands and said, "You need to trust in his ability. He's been in situations like this before, he can handle things."

"Every situation is different," she argued. "The dispatcher said 'domestic.' I know that's bad."

"You're right, domestic disputes can be bad,

emotions tend to run high and people become unpredictable. Like I said, though," he continued when Sam grew even paler, "Jake is experienced, careful, and, if I may brag a bit, well trained." He grinned hoping to get Sam to relax.

"What's going to happen? What will he do?" If she couldn't do anything to help, she needed to understand the situation, the dangers.

"First, he won't go alone, there will be at least one other officer there with him. They will wear vests, bulletproof vests, it's procedure. Then, they will do what they can to assess the situation, determine if anyone is injured, try to talk to those involved, reason with them." Sean continued to tick off steps in protocol as matter-of-factly as possible sensing Sam needed something real to concentrate on rather than imagining the worst.

"Is it scary?" she asked weakly.

"It can be." He wanted to be honest. "Most police work is routine, even mundane, but there are times when it's scary. Other jobs are like that, I would imagine."

"I guess." She had calmed some but her hands still shook slightly as she reached in her purse for her phone and held it tight, willing it to ring. "He said he'd call," she said softly.

"And he will. It may take some time to get everything wrapped up, but he will call, don't you doubt it."

They sat in silence for a while, Sam thinking over what Sean had told her and Sean waiting patiently. Eventually Sam asked, "How did you find me?"

"Jake called me. He told me about the situation, that he had to leave you when you were upset and frightened, and asked if I would check on you. I was nearby, it didn't take me long."

"He called you?" Sam was touched, deeply touched, and the tears that had been held at bay by fear started to flow.

"There, now," Sean said, leaning her head onto his shoulder and thinking Anna had been right, Sam was in love with their son.

They sat, Sam's tears slowing then eventually stopping. "I should probably head home." Now that she had herself somewhat under control, she started to feel foolish.

"Why don't you let me buy you a cup of coffee and we'll wait together."

Grateful for his understanding, Sam gave a quick nod and they made their way down the sidewalk to The Whole Bean. Once they had their coffee, they wandered to the park and found a picnic table in the shade. Sean kept up a running dialogue, regaling Sam with stories of Misty Lake's history and some of its more colorful residents.

They both jumped when Sam's phone chirped. She punched a button and quickly answered, "Jake?"

Sean watched the tension and fear melt away as Sam talked briefly with Jake. When she hung up she turned to him looking relieved but exhausted. "He's fine, he said everything was taken care of quickly and easily."

"See now, didn't I tell you?" Sean said kindly.

"Thank you, Sean. I'm not sure what I would have done if you hadn't come along."

"I'm learning that it's not easy to be the one left to do the waiting. The only advice I can give you is to trust in Jake's ability and know that he's going to do everything he can to keep himself, and those around him, safe. He's a good cop, Sam. Believe that."

21

Sam knew she had been pulling away, had been a little distant with Jake, but she couldn't seem to quite get back to the way things had been before. It wasn't that they weren't still seeing each other, talking and texting during the day, and having fun, they were, but she knew Jake noticed the change. She had talked to Susan for hours, listening to advice, agreeing with her cousin that she needed to move past it but still not quite able to unlock that part of her that had seized up when she had heard the call on his radio.

She had also talked with Anna, who had called after Sean reported back to her on his afternoon with Sam. She had helped Sam work through some of her feelings, had shared experiences of her own, and it had helped. Some.

Determined not to let herself fall back into a pit of despair, she put a smile on her face and gave Jake a big wave as he headed toward her dock with his boat. It wasn't as big as Joe's, she could tell, but it was bigger than she had expected after Jake had downplayed it. She loved the way the bright blue seats and trim looked skimming over the water. The captain didn't look bad either, she thought, as Jake eased the boat up to the dock, shirt off, bronzed skin glistening, and eyes hidden behind aviator sunglasses.

"Nice boat. I can't believe you haven't used it all summer. It seems a shame to keep in on land," Sam commented as she grabbed a rope and helped secure the boat.

"I guess it's been a busy summer. I've only been on the lake a few times with Joe. We'll have to make up for lost time."

They did just that. Once Jake, Sam, and Susan had loaded a cooler and the dog into the boat, they spent a beautiful afternoon on the water. It took Rigi a little while to get her sea legs with her stumbling from one seat to another, apparently trying to make sense out of the bumpy ride. After a while, though, she found a spot in the front of the boat where she could sit with her face in the wind, which she did until the waves eventually rocked her to sleep. They stopped for a quick visit with Joe and Karen, anchored the boat at the sand bar to cool off in the water, and Sam and Susan had their first fishing lesson.

"It's not the best time for fishing," Jake consoled the frustrated women, neither of whom had had so much as a nibble. "The middle of the day with so much traffic on the lake, no one is going to be catching anything right now. We'll try again another day, either early morning or in the evening."

"I don't know," Susan said skeptically. "It's not

really very exciting, is it? I mean all you do is sit here."

"It's fun when they're biting. Besides, a fish dinner makes any boredom worthwhile."

"I can't imagine how long it would take to catch enough to make a meal," Susan grumbled.

Jake began heading back to Sam's house while continuing to try to convince Susan to give fishing another chance. Sam gazed at the shoreline and picked out her house, pleased that she was becoming more familiar with the lake. Just as she was appreciating how pretty her house looked, she noticed the smoke.

"Oh, my God! Fire!" she shouted. It looked as if the smoke was coming from directly behind her house.

Jake and Susan jerked their heads to look where Sam was pointing. Jake punched the engine as he yelled to Sam, "Call 9-1-1!"

They raced to shore. Susan screamed, "Go!" to Sam and Jake as she grabbed hold of the dock, quickly tied up the boat, and secured Rigi's leash to a tree to keep her out of danger before chasing after them.

A fire was raging on the back of the lot, near the shop. As they got closer, they could see garbage cans engulfed and the fire spreading close to the corner of the shop. Jake sprinted for the garden hose and began doing what he could to contain the flames.

"Do you have gas or anything flammable in there?" Jake yelled to Sam.

"There's some paint thinner, a small propane tank," Sam answered, trying to force her brain to work.

Damn, Jake thought. Even a small amount would speed up the fire if the flames reached it. "Move the cars back!" he shouted.

Sam tore back to the house for keys, throwing a set to Susan as she ran back. As she scrambled to get the cars out of the way, Sam prayed for the fire trucks to arrive. She ran back towards Jake, feeling helpless. She watched in horror as the flames inched closer to her shop. Even through the clouds of smoke she could see the far corner and one wall already blackened. There were flames spreading into the field, as well, and coming close to the tree line. Jake was furiously spraying but the garden hose was no match for the quickly advancing fire.

Finally, she heard the far-off wail of sirens. Hurry, hurry, she silently pleaded. In moments, a truck pulled up followed closely by a second. She stood huddled with Susan watching as the fire fighters hurried and, with incredible precision, quickly began waging battle with the flames. She saw one of them spot Jake and yell, "No one inside?"

Jake shouted, "No, all clear," as he backed off and let the fire fighters take over.

It was surreal, Sam thought, watching them scramble to save her shop, her house. Later she would realize it was all over fairly quickly but, at that moment, time seemed to slow down and Sam felt as if she stood for hours watching and waiting.

Once the fire was out she answered questions and watched as Jake and the fire chief combed her yard for clues. It was easily determined that the fire had started in the garbage cans and had been intentionally set. The smell of gasoline was prevalent. She assessed the damage to her shop and was grateful to find that, aside from charred siding and some minor water damage inside, things were more or less intact.

Eventually Sam and Susan headed inside with Rigi, there being nothing more for them to do outside. Sam opened a bottle of wine and the cousins, tired, scared, and angry, stared at each other as they sipped.

Eventually, Susan spoke. "What the hell is going on, Sam?"

"I wish I knew. I really believed it was all over but obviously not. This is a whole new level of evil," she snarled.

"You sound pissed off," Susan said, admiration in her voice.

"You know what? I am. This has gone on long enough. I'm going to look into installing security cameras, alarms, whatever I need in order to put a stop to this. I'll talk to Jake, see what he recommends. This is my property and I'm sick and tired of someone thinking they can do whatever they want."

Susan smiled. "That's my girl."

Later, Jake joined them and they talked, trying to come up with possible suspects, a motive. Sam asked him questions about security measures, what she could do, what he thought she should do.

"Why don't I give you the number for the security company I mentioned a while back? I've worked with them, the owner, Mitch, is a good guy. He knows what he's doing and he'll be honest with you, telling you what you need and what you don't need."

Jake felt in his pockets for his cell phone and realized he didn't have it. "It must still be on the boat, I didn't even notice it wasn't in my pocket with everything that's been going on. I'll be right back," he said as he headed out to retrieve his phone.

When he returned, Sam knew immediately something was wrong. His face was grim as he listened to voicemail. "What is it?" she asked as soon as he disconnected.

He ran his hand through his hair and sighed deeply. "I had messages from Tom Lindahl and from the office. Zach is missing."

Sam was on her feet. "Missing? What do you mean, missing? How can he be missing?"

"The kids had free time, most were swimming, playing volleyball in the water. When they came in for dinner, Zach wasn't there. The only explanation Tom had was that he just swam away from the camp and climbed out of the water somewhere else."

"How can he be sure? What if he had trouble in the water? He could have drowned." Sam's voice was rising, her fear palpable.

"I'm going to call the office and call Tom. I'll get more details but based on the message I had from the office, it sounds as though they've searched the lake, even sent a diver down. Let me see what I can find out," he said as he walked outside angrily punching numbers.

"This just gets worse and worse," Sam said. "They're going to want to blame him for the fire." She sounded crushed.

"It's not that much of a stretch." Susan held up a hand to stop Sam when she immediately opened her mouth to argue. "I know, you don't want to believe it. I don't either. All I'm saying is you can't ignore the facts. He was away from camp when some of the other stuff happened here. Now, he's missing today when there's a fire. He's been very reluctant to talk, to tell his side of the story, from what I hear. And, you said yourself you think he's hiding something."

"I know," Sam admitted. "I just don't want to have this fight with Jake again. He's going to suspect him, I'm going to defend him. We've been round and round with this too many times."

"Try to stay calm for now. Let's wait and see what Jake has to say," Susan suggested.

It didn't take long to realize the news wasn't going to be good. When Jake came back inside he was muttering to himself and making notes on his pad.

"Here's what I know. Zach was reported missing around four-thirty. He had been in the lake with most of the other kids. They all got out at four o'clock to head back to their cabins to clean up before dinner. When his cabin counselor checked everyone in, Zach wasn't there. The camp ran its own search for about thirty minutes before calling 9-1-1. A team is out there now, they've searched the water and are continuing to search the area but there hasn't been any sign of him."

"Does Tom have any idea at all where he thinks he could have gone?"

"No. Fred has been working to get a record of his calls and texts to see if that tells us anything. A description has gone out to all the agencies in the area. There are a lot of people looking for him. We'll find him. I'll see to it."

"Because you think he started the fire," Sam said accusingly.

"Because I don't know who set the fire," he said hotly. Then, more gently, "Listen, Sam, I don't want to argue with you. I'm not accusing him of anything. Right now, I just need to find him. And I need to figure out who is responsible for everything going on here. We're going to be spread pretty thin. I need to go, I should have been in the office already. I called my dad, he's on his way here to stay with you."

"Jake, we don't need a babysitter."

"It's not up for debate. Someone is looking to hurt you and until it's over, I'm not leaving you alone at night. Sorry, Susan, you don't quite cut it as a bodyguard," he said to Sam's cousin who was still sitting at the table watching the volley between Sam and Jake.

"I can't believe you told your dad to come out here. He must think I'm completely helpless!"

"Come on, Sam, you know that's not true. He's a former cop, the former sheriff. He would have had my hide when—because it would be when, not if—he found out I left you here alone. He understands I need everyone on my staff working on the missing persons case and working on what has become an arson and vandalism case. Unfortunately, my team isn't big enough to post someone here right now."

Knowing it was an argument she wasn't going to win, Sam relented. "Fine," she said, walking to him and wrapping her arms around him. "Go. Find Zach. We'll be okay. I promise I'll behave for the babysitter," she teased and gave him a quick kiss.

"Thank you," Jake said, relief evident in his voice. Just please stay inside, keep the dog tied up so she doesn't wander. I'll check in with you when I can." He gave a wave to Susan and as headlights shone through the window and he spotted his father's car, headed out to meet him.

22

Sean McCabe stayed Saturday night, Jake Sunday night. Riley stopped by during the day on Sunday and spent most of the afternoon there under the guise of checking out the damage to Sam's shop and giving her an idea of what would be needed to repair the exterior. Sam knew Jake had told him to come over so she and Susan wouldn't be alone. Nothing more happened at Sam's and there was no sign of Zach.

His cell phone records showed calls and texts to one number almost exclusively. The number belonged to a teenaged girl from Minneapolis. Jake had asked the Minneapolis police to go to the address listed on the account but they had found the house empty. After talking with neighbors, they had learned the family that lived there was on vacation, apparently staying with family out of state. They were working to use cell phone records for the other family members to try to locate them but so far hadn't had any luck. Since the girl Zach had been communicating with wasn't the missing person, the phone company needed a search warrant to provide detailed information and that would take until Monday morning. Tensions were running high and by Monday the few words that were being spoken in Sam's house were sharp ones.

Sam hadn't gotten any work done on Sunday, finding that even her shop couldn't provide a distraction, so she was looking forward to the arrival of the camp van. She had been worried Project Strong Start wouldn't let the kids come back after all that had gone on, but Jake had called Tom and had assured him he would have extra patrols around Sam's house. Jake had also explained his belief that the person after Sam wouldn't approach when there were so many people around. Everything to this point had indicated someone afraid of being seen, working under cover of darkness or when there was clearly no one home. Sam had been grateful for Jake's help and had called Tom herself to thank him and to discuss further safety measures for the kids.

She was worried about how the kids' moods would be affected by Zach's absence and guessed they'd have questions she couldn't answer. Finally, Stu pulled in her driveway. She saw the concern on his face and saw him take in the charred siding before he spoke.

"Sam, how are you doing?"

"I'm okay, Stu. It wasn't the best weekend I've ever had but I'm okay." Turning to the kids who were also all staring at the fire damage she said, "Hi, guys. Head inside, I'll be right there."

"I feel just awful about everything you've had to deal with. You don't deserve this," he said sadly.

"Thank you. I hope it's over soon but I'm more concerned about Zach. I wish he'd show up. I just can't help but worry something terrible has happened to him."

"You don't think he's responsible for this?" Stu asked gently, pointing toward the shop.

Sam let out an exasperated breath. "No, I really don't. I know something was going on with him but never had any indication he was angry or resentful, that he had any kind of problem with me. I can't come up with a reasonable explanation for him doing something like this."

"Then I'm sure you're right about him." Stu looked around then asked, "Are you alone here today?"

"Yes, Susan is working, but there's nothing to worry about. Nothing has ever happened during the day and when I've been nearby."

"Well, that may be but I think I'll just wait right here for the kids. I'll call over to the camp and let them know I'll drive the van back once they're done."

Sam opened her mouth to argue then decided to just accept the offer to help. "Thank you, Stu. Go inside, help yourself to coffee or whatever you'd like."

"No, I'll just stay put," he said firmly.

With her emotions so close to the surface, Sam could barely mumble her thanks and give Stu a quick hug before she had to turn and rush into the shop so he didn't see the tears that were threatening.

She stepped quickly into the adjacent room in order to have a moment to compose herself before facing the kids. The last thing she wanted was for them to see her on the verge of tears. They needed strength and confidence right now, she knew. Her plans were thwarted, however, when she stepped into the workroom to find the kids all seated, projects and tools set neatly in front of them, and all quietly waiting for her instruction.

She was overwhelmed by their gesture. Most mornings she had to almost shout over the racket to get their attention and then spend several minutes telling them to do the same things she told them to do every morning before she had the sort of cooperation she was seeing right now. She blinked furiously to keep the tears at bay and took a few deep breaths before daring to speak.

Rather than ignore everything that had happened since she had last seen them and wait to see what kind of questions they asked, as had been her original plan, she decided they deserved whatever explanation she could give them.

"You guys are awesome," she began. "Thank you for getting everything ready and organized so quickly. As you noticed, there was some more trouble here over the weekend. Someone started a fire outside on Saturday evening. Luckily, we noticed it soon and were able to call the fire department."

"Who did it?" Jimmy demanded.

"I don't know. The police are working on it and I'm sure it won't be long until they find the person who's responsible."

"Did anyone get hurt?" Mario asked.

"No, everyone is fine. No one was inside here when the fire started. The fire department got here quickly so there wasn't even that much damage." Sam wanted to downplay the incident, didn't want them to worry.

"Do the police think it was Zach? He's missing, you know."

"I know, Jimmy, but no, they don't think it was

Zach. They're just worried about finding him to make sure he's okay."

Jackson looked skeptical. "He was acting really weird. He could have done this."

"Why do you say that? Did he tell you something before he disappeared?" Sam prayed Jackson knew something that might help find him.

"Nah, he never said anything but he was even weirder than usual. He was jumpy, wasn't paying attention to anything or doing anything except texting. It was really strange when he went swimming, he'd never done that before."

He must have had it planned, Sam decided. It made her feel better, in a way, made it seem likely he was trying to get away. She hadn't been able to shake the fear that he had drowned even though Jake had told her the water rescue team had done a thorough search of the lake.

"Well, I don't think he did it. I think maybe something has been bothering him but I'm sure he didn't do this."

When they all stayed quiet she said, "Should we get started? This is our last week, I want to make sure you all finish everything."

As they worked, Sam walked around and talked to each of them individually. There were a few more questions, some more concern expressed about Zach. She did her best to answer and reassure.

Stu was reluctant to leave her alone when the class was over. "I'll drop them off quickly then come back for a while. I don't have any plans this afternoon."

"Please don't worry, Stu. Riley McCabe should be here soon. He's picking up some materials to repair the outside of the shop and will be here this afternoon to do the work."

He didn't like it but agreed. "Okay, but you be sure to get inside and wait for him there. I don't want you outside by yourself. Please be careful, Sam," he added with a solemn look on his face.

"Promise," Sam answered with a smile.

When they drove off, she ducked into the shop to straighten up and get Rigi before keeping her promise and heading for the house.

He watched the van leave and knew she was alone. He knew the schedule well so had only waited a few minutes, hidden behind a large oak tree and well out of sight. Once he was sure the van was gone and wasn't coming back, he darted across the clearing to the shop where he had seen her go.

The door creaked slightly as he pushed it open and he heard her gasp as she whirled around to face him.

Sam heard the door and her heart thudded wildly in her chest. Not knowing what to do, she grabbed a hammer from the bench and spun around. "Zach!" she said, shocked to see him standing in front of her.

Competing thoughts raced through her mind. He couldn't be here to try to hurt her, couldn't be the one responsible for all of the hatred played out on her property. But then why was he here? He looked scared, almost crazed, as they stared at one another. He took a step toward her and she couldn't help herself, she jumped back.

She saw the hurt creep into his eyes and immediately regretted her action. Still uncertain but determined to give him a chance, she carefully replaced the hammer and asked, "Zach, are you okay? Where have you been?"

"I need help. I had to wait until the van was gone or I know you would have sent me back to camp but I can't go back now. Please, will you help me?"

The words came out quickly and he was nervously shifting from one foot to the other almost as if he were getting ready to run. Trying to calm the both of them Sam answered, "I'll try to help. What's wrong?"

"It's Chelsea. My girlfriend. She's…" he looked around, seemingly unable or unwilling to look Sam in the eye. "She's having a baby. Now. She's alone. I don't know what to do."

Once the words were out, his shoulders seemed to slump and he stared at the floor. "Oh, God, Zach, where is she? I can call for an ambulance."

"No! She's scared, doesn't want to go to the hospital, she's afraid they'll call her parents. I didn't know who else to ask."

"Her parents don't know where she is? Do they know she's pregnant?"

"They kicked her out when she told them," Zach said angrily.

Sam wanted to help, was struggling to make sense out of the story. "So, she lives around here?"

"No, no," Zach said, clearly getting frustrated. "She came up here because I was here at Project Strong Start. She found an old cabin, she's been staying there."

Things were starting to fall into place. Zach must have been leaving camp to see her, to try to help her. The girl must be terrified, alone and a baby coming. Deciding quickly, Sam said, "Okay, Zach. Let me go grab my keys. Get in the car, I'll be right back."

Running for the house with Rigi, Sam tried to think. She knew nothing about delivering a baby, the very thought terrified her. On the drive, she would try to convince Zach to let her call the police, to get some help. He'd have to agree, the two of them couldn't possibly give Chelsea the help she'd need. She got Rigi into the house, grabbed her purse and keys, double-checked that her cell phone was still in her pocket, and wracked her brain. What else? Should she grab some bottled water, blankets, a basic first aid kit? She had no idea what she'd find when she got to the cabin. Making a quick decision to take a few things with her, she turned and dashed for the kitchen, almost tripping over Rigi who, sensing her distress, was circling her feet.

She never saw him, just ran headlong into him. His arm came around her neck and he put a hand over her mouth. She couldn't see his face, just heard a rough voice. "Quiet! Not a sound or you'll leave me no choice but to use this." He waved a gun in front of her face. Every muscle in her body tensed. She struggled wildly to free herself until he put the gun up against her head and shouted, "Stop!"

Sam froze. Her heart pounded and her breath came in ragged gasps. She couldn't get her mind to focus. She needed to get to Zach, to get to Chelsea. Who was in her house? Oh, God! Had he hurt Zach? she wondered. No, she reasoned, there hadn't been time, she had just left Zach. But maybe he had someone with him? Maybe someone else had Zach? Oh, please, let Zach be okay, she prayed.

"Are you listening?" he demanded. Sam realized he had been talking and she had no idea what he had said. She nodded her head, trying to turn away from his stale, boozy breath.

"Good. You listen carefully. I'm going to take my hand away and you're not going to make a sound. Got it?"

She nodded again. Slowly he lowered his hand and Sam gulped in air feeling as though she had been underwater. He loosened his grip enough for her to move away slightly and turn around. She didn't recognize the man. He was dirty, disheveled, and had a messy, overgrown beard.

As if reading her mind he said, "You don't remember me, do you?"

"I'm sorry, I don't," Sam whispered.

"My dad let all you spoiled brats use our beach, our boat. He used to think it was so fun when all of you were here. 'Go play, Richard,' he'd tell me. As if I wanted to play with you and your cousins. You always thought you were better than me. Do you think I didn't know you were laughing at me? Now, you don't even remember me."

Richard Anderson, Sam thought to herself. One of the neighbor kids they sometimes played with when they spent time at the lake. He had had a brother and a sister, she remembered. His father would sometimes take them for tube rides behind his boat, let them fish off his dock. He had been a nice man, friendly with her grandfather. She couldn't recall any tension between them and Richard, she only remembered having fun, occasionally all getting together to play night games.

When she didn't reply, Richard continued. "Now you think you're something special, living in this fancy house, letting your mutt run around on my property."

Sam had forgotten Rigi was in the house until Richard mentioned her. She glanced at the dog and saw her standing stock-still, hackles raised, and a low growl emanating from her throat. Richard was ignoring her. Stay back, Rigi, she silently pleaded.

Richard continued his rant. "I suppose you and your crook of a grandfather thought it was pretty funny stealing the property from my dad. That was supposed to go to me, you know! I deserved it. I wasted all my summers here when I would have much rather been home with my friends, people who actually cared about me. But you had to take it all away from me, didn't you? Didn't you?" he shouted when Sam didn't respond.

"I didn't know anything about this place." Sam choked the words out as Richard's hand went around her throat.

"DON'T LIE TO ME!" he yelled. "Everyone thinks they can lie to me, take what's mine and I'll just let it all happen. Well, you're all wrong. You're going to pay."

It was obvious he was unstable, most likely drunk as well, and Sam was terrified. She didn't know how to deal with him, didn't know what to expect from him. Riley should be arriving within the hour. Would he be able to help? Did she have that much time?

Before she could figure out how to respond to Richard, she caught sight of Rigi out of the corner of her eye. Upset by the yelling and knowing Sam was in danger, the dog lunged. Her jaw clamped around Richard's arm. He screamed in pain as he swung the arm holding the gun and kicked his leg.

Sam watched, horrified, as his booted foot caught

Rigi in the midsection and the gun connected with her head. The dog's limp body slid across the wood floor, crashing into the wall where she remained, motionless.

"Nooo," Sam wailed. She lashed out at Richard, desperate to get to her dog.

In a rage, Richard swung blindly at Sam, catching her on the side of the head. Stars danced in front of her eyes as she staggered, only staying on her feet because Richard still maintained his grip around her neck with his other hand.

"Sit!" he bellowed as he pushed Sam toward a chair. He kept the gun pointed in her direction with a shaky hand as he looked at the bloody wound Rigi had left on his forearm. He grabbed a dishtowel and wrapped it around his arm, swearing as he did so. Then he reached into his jacket pocket, pulled out a bottle, and drank deeply.

Sam fell into the chair, blinking and trying to clear the fog. She gingerly touched her head and felt a very tender bump already forming. When she gave a little moan, Richard seemed to remember she was there and snarled at her, "Shut up and let me think." He found another dishtowel and tied Sam's hands behind her back and to the chair.

23

Zach waited impatiently, tapping his fingers on the dashboard of Sam's car as he stared at the house willing her to hurry. After five minutes he couldn't sit any longer and ran for the house. The front door was still standing open and he was just about to step inside and call out when he heard a man's voice say cruelly, "Shut up and let me think."

Zach stopped in his tracks, knowing something wasn't right. He quietly stepped back out of sight and listened. When he didn't immediately hear anything more he dropped to his hands and knees and crawled along the deck until he was under a large window. Very slowly he inched up until he could just peek over the edge of the window. He saw Sam being roughly tied to a chair then the man point a gun at her head and laugh.

Silently, Zach dropped back down to the deck. Moving slowly, trying not to make any noise, he moved further down the deck to the side of the house where he knew he'd be out of sight as long as the man stayed with Sam in the kitchen. When he got to the yard he ran as fast as he could for the trees. Once he was deep enough into the woods that he was certain he was out of sight, he fell to the ground and tried to catch his breath.

He had to get back to Chelsea, he'd been gone too long already, but he couldn't leave without trying to help. He still had Sheriff McCabe's card in his wallet. He looked at it, deliberating. He was afraid if the sheriff found him here it would give him more reason to think he'd been the one responsible for the vandalism. He'd arrest him or, at the least, send him back to camp. If he told him about Chelsea, the sheriff would want to send an ambulance. Knowing he had to make a quick decision in order to help both Chelsea and Ms. Taylor, he dialed the sheriff's cell phone.

"Sheriff McCabe." The sheriff's voice crackled in Zach's ear, the reception cutting in and out.

"Sheriff McCabe, this is Zach Fields," Zach said as he moved back closer to the house hoping for a better signal.

"Who…not clear…"

Zach tried again. "Sheriff, it's Zach Fields from Project Strong Start. I'm at Ms. Taylor's house."

Jake had been on hold waiting to speak with an officer in Minneapolis familiar with Zach's history hoping to get some idea of where he may have gone when his cell phone buzzed. Not recognizing the number but seeing the Twin Cities area code, he had answered. Now, he was struggling to make out what the person on the other end of the line was saying. The connection was terrible but

Jake was sure the caller identified himself as Zach Fields and Jake was relieved to hear from the boy and to know he was okay.

"Zach, where are you?" Jake tried again.

The connection improved and he was fairly certain he heard Zach say he was at Sam's house. Jake was on his feet and out the door, yelling to his assistant to get backup out to Sam's. Jake couldn't make sense out of the call. Was Zach calling to brag after hurting Sam? Was he giving the police some kind of warning?

"Zach, tell me what's going on," Jake said in a steady voice.

"Some guy's got Ms. Taylor. He has a gun," the boy said slowly, obviously also frustrated with the poor connection.

This time Jake heard him clearly. Zach was calling to try to help Sam, not hurt her. "Okay, Zach, listen to me." When Zach was silent Jake said again, "Zach, are you listening?"

"Yes, yes," the boy whispered.

"Do you know who the man is?"

"No, I've never seen him before."

"Did he see you?"

"No, I don't think so."

"Where does he have Sam...Ms. Taylor?"

"They're in the house, in the kitchen. I think he tied her to a chair. He has a gun."

Jake didn't understand Zach's involvement or why he was calling, but there wasn't time for too many questions. He needed to keep the boy safe and get to Sam.

"Okay, Zach, I want you to stay back, don't let him see you. I'm on my way, I'll be there in a few minutes.

I'm going to leave my car down the road a ways, I don't want him to see or hear the car. You have to stay out of sight, don't try to come to me. Do you understand?"

"Yes."

"Can you see the house from where you are?"

"Yeah, most of it."

"Stay back, but if you can, watch the house. Let me know if you see anyone come out."

"Okay."

"Stay on the line, Zach. I need to radio in so I'm going to set my phone down for a minute but I'm not hanging up."

Zach could hear him talking, explaining the situation, and telling the others to come in quiet. He couldn't see movement anywhere around the house or the yard. Zach was getting more worried about Chelsea by the minute. He had to get back to her, had to bring help. He realized the sheriff was talking to him again.

"Zach? Are you still there?"

"Yes."

"I'm almost there, I'm going to park my car in a minute. When I do, I have to hang up. You need to stay where you are and let me take care of things. Stay out of sight," Jake repeated, hoping the boy would listen.

Zach listened but knew he couldn't do what Sheriff McCabe asked. He needed to get to him, to tell him about Chelsea, and to get her some help. He disconnected the call without answering and began to move through the woods towards the road.

The phone went dead. Frustrated that he hadn't gotten a response, he could only hope the call had dropped due to the spotty service and that it hadn't been Zach's decision to hang up on him. He radioed quickly to Marc to see how far out he was then quietly exited his car and started making his way towards Sam's house.

Jake saw Zach before Zach saw Jake. The boy hadn't listened. Jake watched as Zach scrambled down the road, crouched and looking over his shoulder. Jake got closer then called to Zach.

Zach's head spun around, his eyes darting back and forth until he spotted Jake. Jake held up a hand indicating Zach should stay where he was and closed the distance between the two.

"I told you to stay put," Jake said. "What are you doing here?"

"I need help," Zach began. "I ran away from camp because—"

Jake interrupted. "Zach, we have to talk about this later. I need to see what's going on in the house. Stay here," he ordered.

As Jake started moving, Zach reached out and grabbed his arm. "No!" he said forcefully. "You need to listen. I have to get help to my girlfriend. She's having a baby. Right now."

Jake saw the fear and desperation in the boy's eyes. Struggling for calm he asked, "Where is she? Isn't there anyone with her?"

"She's in a cabin not far away but she's alone. She needs help right now!"

"All I can do right now is call it in, try to get an ambulance to her. Do you have an address?"

"No, I don't know the address. I just know how to get there."

"Zach, I can't leave here. Wait for Marc—Deputy

Crosby—he should be here any minute. If you can give him directions to the cabin he can call for help."

"But—" Zach argued.

"Zach, I'm sorry. I can't do anything else right now. Please, stay here and wait." With that, Jake took off at a run.

Richard had been pacing, muttering under his breath about getting back what was his, but making little sense. Sam was frightened. Her arms ached from being pulled and tied tightly behind the chair. Rigi still hadn't moved and Sam was sick with worry. Her cell phone had vibrated a few times with incoming calls. Thankfully Richard hadn't noticed. Sam prayed that whoever was trying to call would realize something was wrong when she didn't answer.

Suddenly, Richard slammed a fist on the table in front of Sam. "This is what's going to happen. You're going to come with me. I have a friend in St. Paul who is a lawyer. He's going to draw up some papers giving my land back to me. You're going to sign them. Then you're going to add in a little bonus for all my pain and suffering. Fifty thousand dollars should do the trick."

He was calculating in his head as he again tipped the bottle to his lips. He'd get a tidy sum when he sold the property. That would take some time but the fifty thousand would work to hold off the thugs demanding money now. But, maybe if he went to the track, made a few sure bets, that fifty thousand would turn into a lot more.

Sam looked at him, waiting for him to say or do something. He made his demand then seemed to withdraw into his own thoughts. She became more and more convinced he was unstable. What he was suggesting was insane. He'd never get away with it. She'd only have to claim she signed the papers under duress. Nothing he forced her to sign would ever hold up in court. Did he really believe it would work? she wondered. Or, did he plan to kill her once the papers were signed, thinking if she wasn't there to argue he'd get away with everything?

"Get your purse, your identification, whatever bank papers you need to withdraw money. We're going to get out of here before anyone shows up." He pulled a knife from his pocket and started to hack away at the towel binding her to the chair. He swung the knife carelessly and Sam was all but certain he would cut her.

Somehow he managed to free her after a couple minutes then pulled her roughly to her feet. Her arms tingled and she flexed her fingers trying to get feeling back. Holding tightly to one arm and keeping the gun pointed at her, Richard pushed her and demanded she get her things.

Jake saw the man shove Sam forward and yell at her to get her purse then watched as he staggered slightly following Sam through the kitchen. He was injured or impaired in some way, Jake figured. It could be an advantage if his reflexes were dulled, but he knew it could also be an incredible disadvantage if the man was under the influence and had a distorted view of his abilities and of the situation.

Stepping slowly and carefully into the kitchen, Jake leveled his gun at the man. "Police! Freeze!" he said forcefully but calmly.

Richard spun around at the words, waving his gun out in front of him. He lost his grip on Sam as he stumbled and fell heavily into the table.

Sam's relief at hearing Jake's voice was incredible. She looked to see Jake standing still, feet slightly apart, and his gun pointed at Richard. When she felt Richard's hand slip from her arm she twisted quickly to put some distance between them. She was just about out of reach when Richard tripped and fell against the table, pinning her between the table and the wall. In a move she wouldn't have thought him capable of making, Richard's hand darted out and grabbed Sam's ankle causing her to crash to the floor.

He was next to her in a flash, wrapping an arm around her neck and pressing the gun to her temple. His hands were unsteady, his breathing shallow and rapid.

"Drop the gun," Jake demanded. "Let her go."

"Oh, I don't think so," Richard answered. "You're going to drop *your* gun and let us leave."

"I'll let you leave once you let her go."

Sam watched Jake, sure and steady, his eyes never leaving Richard's.

"No can do, Sheriff. She needs to come with me." His words slurred and he swayed slightly.

Jake saw the nearly empty bottle on the table, watched the man struggle to focus, and knew the risk of him acting irrationally or doing something unintentionally was great. Jake took a step forward and said again, "Drop the gun. Don't do something you'll regret."

"I won't regret anything when I have back what's mine!" Richard shouted.

"So far you haven't hurt anyone. Don't turn this into something more serious. Let her go, we'll talk, and we'll get things figured out." Jake was keeping his voice soft and steady hoping to calm the man, to get him to see reason.

"No. She's coming with me. Now, out of my way."

Richard was struggling to his feet, keeping his grip on Sam and the gun pointed at her. As Sam was pulled up, she caught sight of Rigi stirring in the corner. Stay down, she silently begged.

Richard was up, taking a couple shuffling steps toward the door when the dog got to her feet and let out a loud, menacing bark. The shock was enough to cause Richard to turn to the sound and it was all the opening Jake needed. He was on top of Richard and had the gun out of his hand before Richard knew what happened.

Sam scrambled out of the way and towards the dog. As she wrapped her arms around Rigi, the dog licked her face and whined. "Oh, sweetie," Sam soothed, petting her and trying to keep her calm.

Jake had Richard handcuffed and was already leading him out of the house. Marc and Fred had arrived and met Jake on the lawn.

"Read him his rights and get him out of here," Jake said, handing Richard over to his deputies. He was just ready to turn back to the house to check on Sam when he heard his name.

"Jake! What's wrong? What happened?" It was Karen, with Joe trying to hold her back, running across the yard. "Is Sam okay? I was trying to call her, she didn't answer." Karen was nearly hysterical.

"I think she's fine, I'm just going back in to check on her. Come on," he said, deciding that having a nurse with him was a good idea.

They found Sam still on the floor holding the dog. She was crying and when she saw them begged, "Please help me get her up. She's hurt, I need to get her to a vet."

"What about you, Sam, are you okay?" Jake asked as he rushed to her side. He saw a bruise on her cheek already turning purple and watched as she unconsciously lifted her hand to her head.

"I'm fine, don't worry about me. Please just help me with Rigi, I don't want to hurt her more moving her."

"Just let me take a quick look, Sam," Karen said crouching down beside Sam. She checked the bump on her head, looked at her cheek, and noticed blood on her arm. "There's blood, Sam, are you cut?"

"What? No, I don't think so. I think it's from him. Rigi bit him and he was bleeding."

"The bump on her head is going to hurt, she's going to have a headache, but I don't see any signs of concussion." Karen directed her comments to Jake when Sam ignored them all, continuing to stroke the dog.

"Let me get the dog," Joe said, leaning over and gently lifting Rigi, carefully cradling her as she fidgeted uncomfortably. "Karen and I can take her to the vet. You finish up whatever you need to do here and you can meet us. I know Dr. Fischer, he'll take good care of her."

"I need to go with her," Sam argued.

"Let Joe take her," Jake said gently. "Let's figure out what happened here. Maybe you can also tell me about Zach."

"Oh, God, I forgot about Zach. He needs help, Jake, I was going to go with him but then that…that man showed up. Where is Zach? Is he okay?"

"Joe, take the dog. Karen, can you stay?" Not sure

what was going on, Joe and Karen agreed.

After Sam had quickly gathered Rigi's current immunization records, Joe left with the dog. Jake, Sam, and Karen hurried back outside where they found Zach arguing and pleading with Fred.

"I need to see Ms. Taylor," they heard him shout.

"You'll have to wait here, son. They will be out soon," Fred answered.

As soon as Zach caught sight of them he ran to them. "Sheriff, Ms. Taylor, you said you'd help. We have to go, she's been alone too long." He was desperate, bouncing impatiently and waving his arms.

"I'm sorry, Boss, I can't make heads nor tails out of what he's saying," Fred apologized. "He doesn't want to give me much to go on."

"Thanks, Fred, I'll talk to him." Then, to Zach, "Calm down, Zach, we'll do everything we can. Now, where is your girlfriend?"

"It's not far. I don't know the names of the roads but I can tell you how to get there."

"Have you talked to her? Is she doing okay?"

"She's not answering the phone. I've got to get back there!"

"Okay, give us just a minute. We'll be quick," he added seeing the frustration on Zach's face. "Wait by the car."

Zach looked like he wanted to argue but went to the car to wait.

"Do you know more than I do about what's going on?" Jake asked Sam.

"He showed up here right after the camp van left. He said his girlfriend is pregnant, apparently she's in labor, and she's alone somewhere in a cabin. That's where he had been going when he left camp and why he ran away. He said her parents kicked her out when they learned of the baby. It sounds like she's on her own except for Zach."

"Why didn't he call for an ambulance?"

"He said his girlfriend doesn't want to go to the hospital. She's afraid they will contact her parents. Is that how it works, Karen? Would they call her parents?"

"It depends on her age, the circumstances. Oftentimes girls change their minds at the last minute when they're faced with the delivery. They get scared, end up wanting their parents there."

"Karen, would you be willing to go with him, see what's going on? I don't want to call an ambulance before someone can talk with her and see how she's doing."

"I'll go, no problem."

"I'm going to send Fred and Tim with you, I'm not letting you go alone. Zach's just going to have to accept that. Call me as soon as you get there and assess the situation."

"Let me talk to him first, Jake?" Sam asked. When Jake nodded she hurried to Zach.

"What happened in there?" Karen asked after Sam left.

"Some guy demanding Sam give him back what's his. I didn't get too many details but I figure it was one of the old neighbors who had the property next door. He feels cheated, I guess, blames Sam."

"When I called Sam and she didn't answer, I knew something was wrong. Joe called Riley, he said he was running behind schedule, some delay at the lumberyard, so we figured she was here alone. Thank God you got here when you did."

"Zach was the one who called me. He saw the guy in there with a gun pointed at Sam and had the sense, the nerve, to call me even though he had a lot of his own issues to deal with. We owe him a lot. See what you can do to help his girlfriend. Try to talk her into going to the hospital if there's still time."

"I will."

Sam was on her way back so Karen hurried to the patrol car to join Zach and the deputies.

As the cars pulled away and it was just the two of them, the enormity of what had happened hit Sam. "I think I need to sit down."

They went inside, Jake got Sam some water, some ice and aspirin for the bump on her head and they sat, side by side, on the sofa. Although he had a lot of questions and would eventually need a statement, Jake was quiet, waiting until Sam was ready to talk.

"I'm glad you got here when you did, he really scared me. He seemed crazy, half of what he said didn't make any sense."

"Zach called me on my cell phone, he's the one who told me what was going on. He's a brave kid."

Sam nodded. "I hope Karen can help his girlfriend, I hope she can get them to a hospital. Zach was so scared, I can't imagine how the girl must be feeling."

"Karen will take good care of them."

"I need to get to the vet to check on Rigi. Do you think she's going to be okay?"

"She'll be fine. Joe will call as soon as Doc Fischer checks her out."

"Do you think he would have tried to killed me?

His plan never would have worked, he would have realized that eventually. He would have realized, too, that he couldn't let me go. I kept thinking he was going to kill me." Her voice was barely more than a whisper.

Jake closed his eyes wanting to block the memory. That had been his biggest fear, too. Seeing a gun pointed at her had been the single most terrifying moment of his life. Now, hearing the fear in her voice, all he wanted to do was take it away. He slowly stroked her hair.

"I don't think he would have had the guts. Whatever bravado was fueling his actions would have worn off quickly when the booze ran out."

Sam was quiet, suddenly exhausted. Her head hurt. She wanted to curl up next to Jake and try to stop the images that were racing through her mind, to convince herself that everything was finally over. She knew, though, she needed to get to the vet, needed to check on Zach and Chelsea, and needed to call Susan before she heard from someone else. She pushed herself up and to her feet as her phone buzzed.

"Joe, how's Rigi?"

"She's going to be fine. Dr. Fischer checked her out, she's got a couple fractured ribs and a cut on her head that needs a few stitches but she's going to be just fine."

Relief washed over Sam as she thanked Joe. She was smiling as she gave Jake the report. "I need to go see her. Joe said she'll be sleeping for a while yet and that the doctor wants to keep her overnight but I want to see her. Do you think you can take me? Or do you need to take care of things here?"

"Things here can wait. I'll need to complete a report and I'll need a statement from you but it can wait.

Let's go see that dog of yours. I think I owe her a thank you. Maybe a medal."

"I told you she'd rise to the occasion when she needed to," Sam said proudly.

24

It had been three weeks. Rigi was healing nicely, the biggest challenge being trying to keep her quiet and resting. People had been stopping by almost daily, checking on her, spending time with her. Stu and Molly had been by with Molly returning the favor and bringing a delicious chicken dinner for Sam and Susan. Kathleen stopped by more than once, checking on Sam but also spending time talking with Susan. Sam hadn't asked too many questions but she was curious as to what the two of them were up to. Jake's family seemed to have worked out a schedule as one of them stopped by every day with offers to help with yard work, cook dinner, or run errands.

Her final session with the kids from Project Strong Start had been a bittersweet day. Sam was so, so proud of the progress they had all made over the summer and was anxious for them to head home and back to school with new-found confidence. Saying goodbye, though, had been hard. She had shed a few tears and, even though the boys tried not to show it, there had been some emotion on their part, as well.

Zach hadn't been back to class but Sam had visited the hospital and had met his beautiful, healthy son, Thomas. Karen had managed to talk them into going to the hospital, not too difficult as Chelsea had been frantic by the time they'd arrived. Once the baby was born, Chelsea had reconsidered and contacted her parents. They had come to the hospital and had taken their daughter and grandson home. Zach had worked out an arrangement to leave Project Strong Start a few days early, wanting to be close to Chelsea and the baby. During Tom Lindahl's talks with Zach before he left, he had learned that the shoplifting had been things Chelsea had needed or wanted when she learned she was pregnant. Zach, in his misguided way, had been trying to help. Sam knew they were facing a difficult road but hoped the young couple would make the right choices for their son's sake.

Sam found getting back to a normal routine was more difficult than she had expected. It had taken a couple of weeks until she felt safe in her house, when an unusual sound didn't make her heart stop. Sleep hadn't come easy the first few days, as she seemed unable to close her eyes. Rationally, she knew the danger was past, Richard Anderson was in jail and was no longer a threat, but the scare he had given her didn't quickly fade.

Jake had spoken with Richard's sister, Paula, and had learned of Richard's history of alcohol abuse and gambling problems. He had been very angry with their parents when the lake property was sold to Sam's grandfather. Both Paula and their brother, Bill, lived out of state and hadn't been interested in the cabin so Richard had assumed it would be his. Paula had explained that their parents refused to turn it over to Richard knowing he'd immediately sell and gamble away the profit. Neither Paula nor Bill had heard from Richard in several years, not since the last time he had come asking for money and they had both refused. Some more investigating had led Jake to a trail of gambling debts and some very impatient loan sharks. Apparently trying to get the land back from Sam had been Richard's plan for paying off his debts. He also had a police record with a couple of arrests for disorderly conduct and an attempted robbery charge that had eventually been dropped.

Once Susan had calmed down and come to terms with the fact she hadn't been there when Richard had shown up, she had been a tremendous help. She always seemed to know when Sam needed to talk and when she needed to be left alone. They had spent many late nights talking about the past, about losing Danny, about their grandfather's decision on the lake property, and about the recent attacks on Sam's property and on Sam herself. Sam was finally coming to terms with the tragedy in her past and, for the first time, really felt ready to move forward. By Labor Day Sam was ready to host a party at her house to thank everyone who had helped her through the summer.

While it wasn't quite the size of the McCabe's Fourth of July picnic, Sam's yard was crawling with people laughing and having fun celebrating the end of the summer. Joe brought his boat over and both he and Jake were pulling skiers and tubers around the lake. Sam looked across her yard and realized how thankful she was to her grandfather for bringing her to Misty Lake. She loved the life she was making for herself. She was surrounded by people who cared about her, her business was growing, and she had made a difference in the lives of some kids who had needed someone to care. And there was Jake. She watched him playing Frisbee with Frank and Shauna and her heart was filled with love. With the chaos of the last few weeks their time together had been limited but she hoped that would change soon. She was ready to talk to him about her feelings, about their future, and take her chances that he felt the same way.

Sam made her way to the deck to check on Stu and Molly who were sitting in the shade with Jake's great aunts. Molly looked a little dazed as she tried to keep up with the conversation between Kate and Rose. The current topics seemed to be the new choir director at church and Rose's recent trip to the hair salon.

"How's it going here, Stu," Sam whispered.

Stu shook his head in reply. "I learned long ago to just agree with whatever those two say. As long as you nod and say, 'Isn't that the truth' once in a while, you're fine. Molly tries too hard. She'll have a headache tonight, mark my words."

Sam squeezed his hand and smiled at him. "You're the best, Stu. Thank you. For everything."

"Oh, go on." Stu said and blushed bright pink.

Sam caught sight of Kathleen and Susan huddled together by the lake. Telling herself it was time to be nosy, Sam headed their way.

"What's so interesting that you two have your heads together all the time?"

Kathleen seemed a little uncomfortable as she looked at Susan waiting for her to answer. Sam was even more curious. She couldn't imagine what they were trying to keep from her.

"Suze, what's going on?"

"Oh, okay, Sam. I guess it's time I told you." She looked at Kathleen who gave a little nod before she continued. "Remember that old farm house on the lake I looked at a few weeks ago with Kathleen? I'm going to buy it."

"I'll just leave you two to talk," Kathleen said, making a quick exit.

Of all the things Sam had thought it might be, that certainly wasn't one of them. "You're buying an old farm house? Um, why?"

"I've given this a lot of thought, I've done research, I've been talking to Kathleen about it, and I'm going to turn it into a bed and breakfast."

"A bed and breakfast?" Sam didn't know what to say. She wanted to pepper Susan with questions…How was she going to afford the property, the repairs, everything that would be needed to get the place up and running? But, she held her tongue.

"I know you're worried it's too much, but think about it. I've worked in hotel management for years, I even have a degree, and this is just the sort of thing I've wanted to do forever. I want my own place, someplace where I can make the decisions, set the rules. There's nothing else like it on the lake or anywhere nearby. I can make it work, I know I can."

She seemed so excited Sam couldn't help but be excited for her. The practicalities were still nagging at her, though, and she had to ask. "Isn't it expensive? I know the place isn't much but it's still lakefront property, it can't be cheap. And what about all the repairs and rebuilding that will be needed? Can you really afford all of that?"

"I made an offer, it looks as though the owner is going to accept it. She really wants to be rid of the property and was happy to get an offer so quickly. I have some money from Granddad and have some savings. I've talked a little with the bank about a loan to get the place in shape. We're still working on that but I know it will all fall into place." Ever the optimist, Susan was beaming.

Sam considered and made a quick decision. "I want to invest. I believe in you and I want to help you realize your dream."

"No, Sam, I'm not taking your money," Susan said with finality.

"I said it's an investment. You'll run the place, make the decisions. I'll be a silent—a very silent—partner."

Susan looked torn. Sam reached out and hugged her. "Come on, Susan, accept my offer."

"Oh…okay!" Susan gave a happy shriek and a little twirl. "I can hardly believe it. This is going to be so amazing, I can't wait to get started!"

"Have you checked out contractors, given any thought to who will do the work?" Sam asked as they headed back to the party.

"Oh, I have. He may not know it yet, but I know who's going to do the work," she said slyly as she fixed her eyes on Riley McCabe.

Later that evening, after Jake had docked the boat for the night, he and Sam finally had a chance to talk. "Let's take a walk," Jake suggested.

"I have all these people here, I can't just leave," Sam protested.

"Look around, everyone is having a good time. They won't miss us."

Glancing over her yard, Sam figured he was probably right. "Okay. Where are we going?"

"Let's just walk."

They were quiet for a while as they wandered, hand in hand. "It's been quite a summer," Jake began.

"Yes, that's one way of putting it."

"There was a time when I thought you'd leave."

"There was a time when I thought I'd leave, too," Sam said honestly.

"I'm glad you didn't."

"So am I."

Jake stopped and sat down on an old log, patting it to invite Sam to sit beside him.

"Are you all right, really all right, after everything that happened? I know it's been rough."

"It was rough, for a while, but yes, I'm all right." She was, and it felt good, she realized.

He pulled her closer and kissed the top of her head, a gesture Sam had come to love. "I've been wanting to talk to you," he began.

Sam couldn't miss the nervousness in his voice and worried about what she was going to hear. "I've been wanting to talk to you, too."

"Please, let me go first." He had to say what he needed to say. It had taken him a long time to work up the nerve, he couldn't stop now. "Sam, I know you don't like my job, you worry, you think it's dangerous, but it's what I want to do. I hope you can understand that."

"Okay," Sam said, unsure of where he was going.

"It is a dangerous job but actually there are a lot of things I could be doing that are more dangerous. Did you know being a pilot, a fisherman, a logger, or a farmer is more dangerous than being a cop?"

"Actually, I did."

Jake's forehead creased and he looked sideways at Sam but continued. "I know you were scared when I took that domestic call and I can't promise there won't be others like it in the future, because there will be, but I want you to know that I'm careful and I'm good at my job."

"I know you're good at your job, I've seen you in action. Do you know that when you walked into my kitchen when Richard was holding me at gunpoint I stopped being scared? At that moment I knew I'd be okay. You were so calm, so professional, so sure of what you were doing, I didn't have to be afraid any longer. I never doubted for a minute that you'd take care of things."

"Really?" He sounded pleased but not quite convinced.

"It's true, Jake. I was so proud of you and so confident that you knew just how to handle the situation. I can't promise I'll never worry, but I might worry a little less."

"I love you, Sam."

The words caught her by surprise and she couldn't answer. He loved her, too? She had never known could feel the way she felt right then, as if everything she had ever wanted had suddenly been given to her. A warmth spread through her body and she wanted to hold on to the feeling forever.

"Sam?" He watched her freeze and his world

stopped moving as he waited and hoped for a response from her.

"Oh, Jake." She threw her arms around him and buried her face in his shoulder.

Still a little unsure of what her reaction meant, he continued. "Sam, I love you more than I thought I could ever love anyone. You make me laugh, you make me think, you make me want to experience everything life has to offer with you, because of you. Marry me, Sam. We belong together."

She slowly pulled back wondering if she was imagining things. Then she saw the ring resting in his palm. "Oh, Jake," she said again as tears started rolling down her cheeks. "Yes! Yes, I will marry you! I love you, Jake, I love you so much."

Then she was in his arms and the kiss was like nothing she had ever felt. From the top of her head to the tips of her toes, she was alive. Her life, her future, her everything was here, right here, with Jake. Suddenly she was laughing, throwing her head back and laughing with the tears still wet on her face.

They spent some time talking, planning, and enjoying everything about the moment. Sam could hardly take her eyes off the ring that caught the fading sunlight and sparkled...and looked like it was right where it was meant to be.

Finally Jake said, "I suppose we have to head back."

"I suppose. I kind of wish everyone would leave."

"I can have them out of here in five minutes, just say the word."

Sam smiled. "I can't be rude."

"Do you want to tell them? I have to warn you, my mom might turn herself inside out when she hears the news."

Sam considered. "Not yet," she decided. "I want tonight to be just you and me."

She reluctantly tucked the ring in her pocket, rose up on her toes to kiss Jake, then took his hand in hers as they slowly made their way back to the party and toward their future.

Turn the page for a preview of the next book in the Misty Lake series

The Inn at Misty Lake

By Margaret Standafer

1

Susan blew the hair out of her eyes, wiped the sweat from her forehead, and wondered, not for the first time, if she was in over her head. She looked around at the mess surrounding her and almost gave in to despair. Almost. Instead, she allowed herself five minutes to sit in front of the fan and gulp a bottle of water before turning the music up a little louder and getting back to work.

She could have the rest of the kitchen floor torn out by evening, she told herself, then swore as her hand slipped off the crowbar she was using to pull up faded yellow linoleum and landed a nice uppercut on her jaw. She rubbed her chin, moved her jaw back and forth a couple times, and as the sting subsided, had to laugh at herself. She'd learned a lot in the few weeks she'd been in the 'remodeling business' but she thanked God daily she didn't have to make a living at it. It was hot, dirty work. But, all the sweat would be worth it when she turned the old farmhouse into the best bed and breakfast in Northern Minnesota.

To think that only a few months ago she'd still been working at the Billingsley Hotel in Chicago and putting up with the pompous and utterly worthless Stephen Billingsley. Once he took over the day-to-day operations from his father, Susan had known she needed to get out. He had asked her out repeatedly and, when she refused, made her life at work miserable. Besides, she was tired of Chicago, tired of the Billingsley, and tired of working for someone else.

She knew her parents, her brothers, her friends—everyone, really—thought she was crazy. Her cousin Sam hadn't said much and had even invested in Susan's dream, but Susan knew she had her doubts, as well. She'd show them, she promised herself. She already had so many ideas she had started writing them down…in a notebook she kept well hidden in her dresser at Sam's place. She wasn't ready to share everything just yet. She needed to work on her friends and family gradually, let them warm to the general idea of a bed and breakfast before she sprung too many details on them.

As she attacked the floor with renewed vigor, she silently prayed that the heat would give way to cooler, October-like temperatures soon. So far, the blazingly hot summer they had endured was holding tough, apparently unwilling to let go, and forcing most of the upper Midwest to sweat through the early days of autumn. Certainly not the weather she would choose for the work she was doing. The heat seemed to surround her, sapping her energy and making the job all the more difficult. Not to mention the fact that the high temperatures served to intensify the odors that the one hundred and fifty-year-old house sitting vacant for forty years had developed. Susan sneezed as dust billowed when a section of floor splintered under the force of the crowbar then wrinkled her nose against the smell. She had swept and shoveled and done everything she could to clean out the mess left behind by animals that had sought refuge in the house over the years. It wasn't as bad as it had been but the smell was still unpleasant. Riley had assured her pulling up the old flooring would help, another reason she couldn't wait to have the job behind her.

Riley McCabe. She didn't know whether to smile or curse when she thought of him. When she first met him, it had been his work that had grabbed her attention. A series of framed photos proudly displayed at his parents' house and showcasing before and after pictures of remodeling and restoration work he'd done had intrigued Susan. Even through photos, the quality of his work and the care and conscientiousness he put into it was apparent. She had peppered him with questions to learn about his business and, in the process, found the man to be interesting, thoughtful, and funny. And, at times, infuriating.

When she'd approached him about working for her he'd been hesitant. She'd walked him through the place, given him an overview of her ideas, and his advice had been to tear it down. The front porch was crumbling, the roof was almost beyond repair, the plumbing, wiring, and heating systems were long outdated, and it was filthy. Susan, however, had pointed out the hardwood floors hidden beneath ragged carpets, the beautiful floor-to-ceiling windows and the huge, cozy-looking fireplace in the parlor, and the intriguing brick wall behind the rusted cabinets in the kitchen. Knowing Riley had been itching to flip a house after years working as a contractor doing additions and remodels, Susan had pressed. She had used the fact that taking the job would mean he'd have steady employment to her advantage. He needed work and she needed someone she could trust to do it right. While restoring an old farmhouse might not have been exactly what he'd had in mind, in the end, he hadn't been able to refuse the challenge…or the guarantee of months of work. And if Jake, Riley's older brother and Sam's fiancé, had added his two cents and had helped convince Riley to take the job as she suspected, fine by her. Riley wasn't due to officially start for a couple more weeks but he had been stopping by to lend a hand and give advice when he could.

It was funny how a visit to Misty Lake to see Sam and the house she had inherited from their grandfather had turned into a life-changing adventure. A little bit at loose ends after having quit her job just before the trip to Minnesota, Susan wasn't sure where life was going to take her next when Kathleen Melby, the local realtor who had helped Sam out with the paperwork on her house, had mentioned an old farmhouse going up for sale on the lake. From there, things had started to fall into place. Susan had already decided she wasn't going back to Chicago, the house was listed at a reasonable price, opening a bed and breakfast would finally give her the chance to be her own boss, and hiring Riley McCabe to do the work would give her a chance to get to know him better. Win-win.

She headed outside to the dumpster with yet another load of old linoleum just as Riley's truck pulled into her driveway. "Well, speak of the devil."

"Talking to yourself again, Red? You really should see someone about that, seems like it's getting to be a problem," Riley answered as he slammed the door of his truck closed.

"Figure of speech, McCabe," she snarled as she looked at her watch. "I didn't expect you this early."

"The inspector was actually on time and, since he can't ever find fault with my work, it was a quick visit." He looked her up and down, taking in the sweaty, stained t-shirt, the reddish gold hair that, he'd learned, tended to curl when she sweat, and the shockingly green eyes that were right now narrowed to slits and glaring at him. She was stunning. Not that he'd ever admit it.

"Are you here to help or to waste my time?"

"Easy. What's gotten into you today? You're even more unpleasant than usual."

Susan blew out a breath and mumbled, "Sorry. I'm hot, sweaty, and tired and that damn kitchen floor is going to be the death of me."

Riley noticed the nicks and cuts on her arms and, if he wasn't mistaken, a bruise forming on her chin. He'd have to ask her about that later when she was in a better mood. Feeling sorry for her as he knew very well how miserable tearing out an old floor could be, he grabbed his tool box, threw an arm around her shoulder, and said, "Let's see if I can't take care of it before it does you in."

Two hours later the last of the ugly yellow linoleum was gone and Susan and Riley were sitting on the dusty kitchen floor savoring the ice-cold beer Riley had miraculously produced from the cooler he had stashed in his truck. Susan had stopped snapping at him about an hour before, Riley figuring she was simply too tired to put in the effort. Right now, as she leaned against the wall, eyes closed and the cold can held to her neck, he was betting she was close to falling asleep sitting up.

"I think we should call it a day. The floor is out, that's a big step. You look exhausted and, besides, it's going to get dark soon."

Susan chose to ignore most of what he said and

didn't bother opening her eyes. "That reminds me, when is the electrician going to be here? Have you heard back from him? I'm going to need to be able to work here after dark and obviously the days are getting shorter. I need some working lights run into the different rooms."

Riley just shook his head. He wasn't sure if he'd ever met a more stubborn woman. "Actually, I did hear back," he began slowly, "there'll be an electrician here tomorrow."

Susan's eyes flew open and she was on her feet. "What? Tomorrow? Are you serious? Why didn't you tell me earlier? I thought it was going to be a couple of weeks, at least."

"I called in a favor. You're welcome," he added when she just stared at him.

"Oh, Riley, that's wonderful! Thank you. Really…thank you. I can't believe you were able to arrange it."

"No problem, I'm anxious to get things going here, too. Which reminds me of a little more news."

She waited, shifting from one foot to the other and her eyes dancing, all tiredness seemingly forgotten. When he pulled a notepad from his pocket and made a couple notes, picked up the empty beer cans and tossed them in a garbage pail and still didn't say anything, she threw her hands in the air and shrieked, "What?"

Grinning and paging casually through his notepad he began ticking off on his fingers, "Well, like I said, the electrician will be here tomorrow, looks like the plumber will be here on Monday, the roofing crew by the middle of next week…oh, and I can start full-time on Thursday."

He almost pulled out his phone to capture the

moment. It was the first time he had seen her at a loss for words. Her eyes were wide, her mouth opened, then closed again as she turned away, taking a deep breath and running her hand through her hair. After a minute she turned back to face him.

"It's really happening," she said softly, looking a little dazed. "I mean, I knew it was happening, it's about the only thing I've thought of for the past two months, but this just makes it so real."

"It's really happening. You're not going to change your mind, are you?"

"No, of course not," she brushed the idea aside then wrinkled her forehead. "All the permits are ready? Is there anything else that needs to be done right now?"

"I have the permits. I stopped and picked up everything on the way over here. You're ready to go."

She blew out a deep breath then slowly smiled. "Oh, Riley." She walked to him and hugged him. "Thank you for everything. Thank you for making everything happen so quickly. I know you thought I was nuts when I said I wanted to try to get some of the big stuff done before winter and I know I've driven you crazy already and you haven't even officially started working here but you still made all this happen. I appreciate it."

Riley was surprised. He'd never seen this side of her. Teasing, irritable, bossy, and determined he'd seen plenty of, but appreciative? Humbled? No. That he hadn't seen. He supposed she showed it to others but never to him. He found he kind of liked it. And, he found he enjoyed the feeling of her in his arms.

"You're welcome," he mumbled, his words getting lost in the hair that seemed to be surrounding him and flooding his senses. It was both a relief and a curse when she moved away and began twirling around the kitchen. He had been about to reach for that hair, to finally feel the fiery golden waves between his fingers, but he quickly realized that would have been a mistake. A little more flustered than he cared to admit, Riley watched as Susan moved around the kitchen, then into the dining room and parlor, all the while talking and imagining the finished product. He couldn't help but smile at her enthusiasm, her dreams, and visions. The simple hug had been a thank you, nothing more, and he was glad he hadn't made a fool of himself.

She was excited, and a little scared. The doubts that had been there all along but she had done her best to smother, once again reared and she wondered if it wasn't all a big mistake. This was a huge undertaking, expensive, time-consuming, and with no guarantee of success. She stared out the window at the lake, picturing in her mind the way it would look when everything was done, with people enjoying the beach, the canoes and paddleboats she planned to have available, relaxing in the garden with lemonade in the summer or in front of the fire with hot cocoa in the winter. Or, maybe gearing up for the night's events. Which reminded her…, "Um, Riley," she began, heading back to the kitchen.

He was still leaning against the wall, looking at her with a funny expression as if he couldn't quite figure something out. She ignored it and continued. "I was thinking…the old barn out back?"

Riley immediately grew wary and narrowed his eyes at her. "What about the old barn. I thought we agreed it was coming down. Or, maybe we'd turn it into a garage for guests." He didn't like the look in her eyes and was afraid to hear what sort of a hare-brained scheme she had cooked up.

"Well, yes, we did talk about that but don't you think it would make more sense to really use the space? I think turning it into an event center would be much more logical, and better for business. Just think, I could host wedding receptions, family reunions, all kinds of parties, even girls' weekends. The space could be reconfigured to suit just about any sort of gathering. We'd just need to run plumbing out there, probably do some work on the electrical, put in a bar—oh, I already have something in mind for that—maybe section off a couple smaller rooms, not really a big deal."

"Not really a big deal? Are you kidding? Do you know how much additional work you're talking about?" His voice was rising as his mind raced with the practicalities.

"Calm down, calm down. It doesn't all have to be done at once. I just thought since the electrician and plumber would be here soon, it would only make sense to have them do the work in the barn at the same time."

She was smiling, immensely proud of herself, and it had Riley wondering what in the hell he had gotten himself into. He had done some difficult jobs over the years, some painstakingly tedious ones, some, in his opinion, downright ridiculous ones, but this one might fall in a category all its own. He eyed her, tapping his fingers on his thigh as he took a deep breath.

Susan nervously waited for his reaction. She hadn't planned on springing this on him so soon but when he told her the schedule for the subcontractors, it really couldn't wait. She had figured he wouldn't like it but she was confident she could convince him. It was her place, after all, she had the final say. But, she knew she needed him on board. If he refused to tackle the extra work she'd have to look for another contractor and that was something she didn't want to think about.

Finally, Riley gave a huge sigh, shaking his head and looking towards the ceiling. "Fine, let's go walk through and you can tell me what you're thinking. We'll have to draw up more plans, see what kind of additional permits we need."

She threw her arms around his neck again, jumping up and down while she did so. "Thank you, thank you, thank you! You'll see. It's going to be amazing. I have so many ideas."

They headed to the barn with Susan barely able to contain her excitement. "Just so you know," Riley warned, "if I think your ideas are stupid or impractical, I'm going to tell you."

"Sure, sure, then you'll tell me how to fix it so it's not stupid or impractical," she said with a grin.

Riley didn't know whether to be annoyed or impressed by the fact that her ideas were neither stupid nor impractical. He made a few suggestions, a few changes, but mostly just for form's sake. He found himself swept up in her vision and felt as if he could see the finished event center as clearly as she could. They talked, argued, negotiated, and finally agreed on some of the details. When it got dark enough that the small lantern they'd carried with them to the barn didn't do much more than create some shadows, Riley knew it was time to call it a night.

"All right, that's enough for tonight. I'll draw some of this up, run it by you in a day or two, and I'll talk to the electrician and the plumber about the additional work. Right now, I need a shower and something to eat. And you need some sleep." He couldn't see the dark circles around her eyes in the dusty, gray light of the barn but he knew they were there.

As they left the barn, Susan thought ahead to the next day and started to worry. "What do I need to tell the electrician tomorrow? I'm not sure I understand all the blueprints well enough to explain what I want. What if he has questions I can't answer?" She was biting her lip and twisting her hair.

"Don't worry, an electrician knows how to read blueprints and I'm only a phone call away."

"Okay. What if we haven't thought of everything? What if I want to change something or add something later?"

"Relax, Red. The subs aren't going to finish everything at once. There's some work they need to do initially then they'll be back later on as the work progresses." Riley climbed into his truck and started the engine. "Everything will be fine. I'll try to stop by some time during the day to check on things."

"Thanks, that would make me feel better."

"Okay then, see you tomorrow." He gave a little wave as he started to back out, then stuck his head out the window and added, "Oh, by the way, electrician's name is Cindy." With a devilish wink, he revved the engine and sped off.

Margaret Standafer lives and writes in the Minneapolis area with the support of her amazing husband and children and in spite of the lack of support from her ever-demanding, but lovable, Golden Retriever. It is her sincere hope that you enjoy her work.

To learn more about Margaret and her books, please visit
www.margaretstandafer.com

Made in the USA
Middletown, DE
10 November 2017